TALKING TO

Herself

Printed in the United States of America.
First Edition Printing, 2020

Published by Melissa Powell Gay, LLC
Graphic Design by Inkwell Book Co.

ISBN print 978-1-7350582-0-7
ISBN ebook 978-1-7350582-1-4

www.MelissaPowellGay.com
www.InkwellBookCompany.com

TALKING TO

Herself

MELISSA POWELL GAY

Books by Melissa Powell Gay

·

Mt Pleasant Series:
When Are You Leaving
Every Now and Then

·

Parkland Tales: Stories for 3 a.m. Readings

·

Talking to Herself

"

Time is a network of rivers flowing on their infinite courses, never stopping and sometimes bending into one another.

"

Desmond Kurts
twenty-first-century philosopher

Prologue

Dimming house lights hushed the audience. The host and her guest approached matching chairs on center stage and stood by them.

"Welcome to Boston's Free Will Forum series, where the mindful seek answers. I'm your host Dr. Deepa Hernandez." After the audience's applause, she boomed out, "In these times of extended life expectancy, what defines us as human? If our bodies are saturated with microscopic mechanical components, are we still natural beings?"

She extended her arm toward her guest and continued with her opening remarks, "Tonight, we have with us Dr. Roberto Stancil." The pair nodded in acknowledgment as the crowd gave the guest a standing ovation. Once the applause faded away and the audience settled back into their seats, she motioned for him to sit with her.

"Dr. Stancil's accomplishments are many and far reaching. Most recently, he's returned from the Armstrong Research Center on the moon. While he's not at liberty to discuss the Armstrong project, we've asked Dr. Stancil here tonight to share with us his amazing insights from his development of organic nanochip plasma, or biochip plasma as most call it. His work in the field of medical treatment delivery systems earned him a Nobel Prize. Biochip plasma has ushered in the age of human interconnection to common devices and support systems through machine-to-machine communication technologies. Thanks to his teams, we are as connected to the global collective memory as our refrigerators or our vehicles. We're all becoming cyborgs, just like in the movies."

Polite laughter, mixed with nervous murmurs, rippled through the crowd.

Dr. Hernandez continued, "We find ourselves in an evolved state. No longer are we *just* organic matter. All of us in this very auditorium in some way have benefited from Dr. Stancil's discoveries. However, with this panacea of healing enlightenment comes new challenges, challenges that weren't considered as we rushed to eradicate cancer and inequitable gene mutations. With pure intentions we've opened Pandora's box. Now, we must deal with the consequences."

Dr. Hernandez paused. The audience sat in absolute stillness.

"From minute electromechanical devices the size of a speck at the end of a mite's nose, trillions and trillions of data bits, which make up the biochip plasma, use artificial intelligence to enable a healthy human cell to rejuvenate itself. Restoring the brain, the heart, the liver, entire body systems. And creamier skin and firmer abs."

She looked up from her notes and winked at the audience.

"In other words," she continued, "we've drunk from the Fountain of Youth. But what are the repercussions? What are the practical and moral implications of people choosing to live beyond their natural capacity, essentially living forever?"

She faced her guest and said, "Let's begin with this question, Dr. Stancil. How do you, as a person of science, reconcile the 'natural versus mechanical' conundrum? Some call this path of 'nouveau organic' irresponsible, perhaps immoral."

Tenting his fingertips in front of his lips, Dr. Stancil relaxed in his chair, conveying to the audience that he had all the answers.

"As humans," he said in his calm manner recognized the world over, "we are but the sum of our unique memories. Once our memories' hosts, our physical bodies, become sustainable, we, in essence our memories, can exist forever. And some research is showing promise that a person—or sustainable host—could have the capacity to *revisit past* experiences. However, to answer your question, I cannot, as a scientist, place judgment on who should become sustainable and who should not. That is for us as a collective species to decide."

"Of course. On revisiting past experiences, you're referencing the amazing claims of Dr. Desmond Kurts and his fascinating theories on bending time?"

"Of course," Dr. Stancil said.

"Revisiting past experiences? Some, like Dr. Kurts, say that's a euphemism for time travel."

Shifting in his seat, the scientist harrumphed. "Well, ah, Professor Einstein might have something to say about that. If we're here to discuss the relativity of time—"

A man from the third row stood and shouted, "What you're doing is disrupting the natural order of life. Your principles are corrupt and despicable. Have you no conscience, sir?"

"Ah, Mr. Darnley, we meet again." Squinting from the glaring stage lights, the doctor scanned the audience for the familiar heckler.

Two security guards approached the man and escorted him from the auditorium.

Chapter One

G azing out the window of a hover trolley, Amara Vivian Graves spied the glitzy marquee hologram over the Ashe Boulevard Cultural Center. The philosopher and self-professed time expert Dr. Desmond Kurts was slated to speak on New Year's Eve, only four weeks away. Like the rest of the world, her howntown of Richmond, Virginia planned to ring in 2050 in a spectacular way. Streaming news reports overlapped one another with stories about Dr. Kurts and his theory of "the bending of time." He claimed he'd traveled to the year 1999. The entire country seemed enraptured by his accounts of life before the exploitations of virtual reality, artificial intelligence, and eternal living.

If only it were true, Amara thought.

Leaning her head on the window, she entertained the fantasy. If only she *could* go back to this exact day, two years ago. The day she stood at the front door of the home they shared and watched John Willis-Reyes Darnley walk out of her life for a second time.

The trolley stopped. Her locator, clipped to her shirt, vibrated. It needn't remind her that Oakwood 12 was her stop. Her sixty-nine year old brain wasn't that eroded. According to her wellness coach, Dr. Candace Stone, Amara's short-term memory exceeded the expectations of a person half her age.

Amara sighed. She was having one of her days, off-kilter and clumsy.

The last two Decembers had tormented Amara with memories of past Christmases. Being British, on his father's side, her husband John loved celebrating the Victorian-themed winter holidays. He insisted they decorate a tree even though most of the country had given up on the tradition. While they were still of school age, their children were bribed with candy to read aloud from John's paper edition of *A Christmas Carol*. After the children had gone out on their own, she'd listen to John read the story of a misanthrope haunted by mini-ice age ghosts. With an island of gray tuft atop his balding head, he looked very much the part of Ebenezer. Christmas was John's thing.

The rain picked up as she jogged the short block to her Oakwood Street apartment located in the old Upper Fan District. Tears mixing with rain flooded her contact lenses. At her front door, she blinked hard once and commanded out loud, "Open door."

A blurred message streamed across the optic screen on her right eye, "Unable to access. Please try again." Her security options were set on the highest sensitivity mode. When she started using the lenses, John had insisted she set the bio reactions at a high level. "I want you to be safe from identity pirates." In the golden years of their marriage he'd become the doting husband.

The contact's screen flashed yellow, then displayed the old terms of service.

She calmed herself and tried again, "Open door."

The lock clicked and the door slid open.

Rosie, ever faithful, greeted her in the small foyer.

"Rosie, I've had a day. When did I get these access lenses?"

The service humanoid robot, or bot, announced, "Four years. Nine months. Expiration date is January. One. Two thousand. Forty-eight."

"Oops." She'd allowed her subscription to lapse almost an entire year. She tossed her jacket over Rosie's arm.

John had wheeled Rosie through the front door of their old house on Grace Street one day shortly after his retirement from practicing law. She was all they could afford. One of the first home service models, the Don Key 484 looked and acted, sort of, like a human. Except, Rosie's server capacity couldn't handle the food preparation app in Amara's new apartment. The whole-home controller refused to connect with Rosie, citing breach of security protocol. But Rosie was a whiz at scouring the toilet and shower. She loaded and unloaded the dishwasher, vacuumed and mopped, and did the laundry.

Rosie dusted.

Rosie's AI learning system didn't have the capacity to understand that John had died so she set two places at the table and ordered for two from Happy Garden Eats every Wednesday. For this reason, Amara refused to trade her for a newer model. Someone, even if it was just an outdated robot with a bent antenna, had to keep the remembrance of John Darnley alive.

The transparent monitor suspended from the ceiling flashed as it lowered. Megs Daugherty's yellow aura flooded the room. She leaned forward in a chair in her all-white living room. "Well?"

Amara struggled with her rubber boots.

"What did the director say? Do you get to keep your position?"

Amara managed the volunteer program at Hope Home, a residence for people in transition. Their guests were never referred to as homeless but residents. She'd been asked to stay after her shift.

The director wanted to "have a word."

One of the volunteers dropped off his second-hand robot, Brad, as a working proxy most days. Brad tried to override Amara on everything. One day, after a tiresome argument with him about scheduling the director for front desk duty two weekends in a row, she'd had enough. She ordered Brad to the corner of her office and shut him off. Brad's silence filled her day with such positive energy that in subsequent days, she'd sent him straight to his corner. When Brad's production hours dwindled, his owner complained to the director.

"I've been suspended until after New Year's," Amara said. "The director reminded me that tampering with another person's bot is a criminal offense."

"The arrogance. What about people claiming legacy credits for work performed by an AI?"

"It's not illegal as long as the person owns the bot, Megs."

"Well, it should be."

"I don't think they're going to invite me back after my suspension."

"What'll you do for legacy credits?" Megs asked. Legacy credits had replaced social security income. Able-bodied retirees gained supplemental credits in their state legacy account by working for state and non-profit organizations.

"Something will come up."

"I can get you on at the center." Retired from a career in real estate management, Megs now herded visitors at the Ashe Boulevard Cultural Center for her supplemental legacy credits. "We need volunteers to help with the time capsule celebration."

Amara plopped in the middle of her sofa. "I'll think about it."

"Don't take too long. The slots are going fast."

"What would I be doing?"

"Helping people with their artifacts. Each person, or family, bids on a time capsule, it's about the size of those old-time shoe boxes."

"Let me think about it," Amara reached to tap her locator to cloak her location, thus disconnecting the conversation with Megs.

"Wait! Did you set it up?"

"What?"

"Amara!" Megs's face filled the monitor. "The meeting with the memory specialist. The one Dr. Stone recommended?"

"How do you know about that?" From all the stress at Hope Home, Amara had forgotten all about it.

"You put me on your health notification alerts. Remember? I resent being second to a house bot, by the way. Why do you have an AI assistant as your primary notification anyway?"

"She *is* my closest family member." Why Megs didn't understand the logic of proximity was beyond Amara.

"Have Rosie schedule it. Now!" Megs ordered.

Upon hearing her name, Rosie opened her eyes, ready for a command.

"I'll do it tomorrow. Promise. And, thanks for the job lead."

"Make sure Rosie knows about Christmas, too. You *are* coming, right?"

"Wouldn't miss it," Amara said.

"Kiss. Kiss." Megs blew an air kiss and signed off.

Amara asked, "Rosie, what's for dinner?"

"John and Amara's anniversary special, soy steaks and carrots."

Chapter Two

AT THE CENTER FOR EXCELLING LIFE
MONDAY, DECEMBER 6, 2049

A collector of useless artifacts, John preferred Amara's drafty nineteenth-century Grace Street row house, which she'd inherited from her parents, over the modern design dwellings. Everything in the house reminded Amara of their life together. Her wellness counselor, Dr. Stone, urged her to move out, arguing that its aura kept Amara from recovering from her loss. When the settlement credit from his accidental death arrived, she sold the house with all its contents intact. She walked away from her past life, taking only Rosie and a storage box of ancient photo albums and digital storage drives with her. She vowed one day she'd load everything to her Galaxy cloud account.

The real estate agent called the first-floor apartment an "agile living space." John would have hated its lack of natural wood. But he was gone. Buying the intimate set of rooms with cognitive accessories was the first big personal decision she'd ever made on her own. In spite of her angst for a dead man's approval and the insensitive comments from the apartment systems engineer about first-generation home service robots, she and Rosie had adapted to the roomy flat on Oakwood.

Unfortunately, the move hadn't cured her apathy for living. At her annual good health checkup the previous July, Dr. Stone suggested that Amara try a therapy using biochip plasma. The doctor sold it as a recurring treatment that boosted one's physical energy and helped with cell rejuvenation and weight reduction.

John, and thousands like him, didn't believe in the eternal life craze. He was a founding member of a national organization, Natural Life, whose sole purpose was to disrupt the use of artificial intelligence to extend the natural life span of a human being. To him, the entire world had gone mad for unproven methods of reversing the aging process. "Staying forever young isn't part of our natural design," he'd repeated to Amara each time he saw an ad for age rejuvenation or saw someone they knew who appeared much younger than their actual age. His recurring diatribe included rants against super food diet supplements, vitamins laced with bionic nanochips, and stem cell injections. The companies that produced and promoted these products were crooks and swindlers. To him and Natural Life, all of it cheapened the sanctity of nature and its order.

In her customary way of avoiding confrontation, Amara refrained from stating her opinion on topics John argued against, because he usually would spell out why she was wrong. She'd learned early in their marriage that silence preserved harmony.

But now he was gone and she faced another big decision on her own. Should she do what every woman her age was doing? Use a treatment that defied time and nature. At the doctor's office, Amara tossed her hands in the air and proclaimed, "Why not!" Anything had to be better than feeling the way she did when she sat across from an empty dining chair every night.

The treatments worked. Her body teemed with vitality. Her

clothes fell loose around her waist and the Graves family laugh lines around her eyes disappeared overnight along with the deep creases across her forehead. Even her breasts were responding. They no longer sagged. Recently, a new Hope Home resident had winked at her while he registered for a room.

But, since she'd been taking the treatments, her access contact lenses didn't work as well. Each time she tried to order her favorite smoothie at Juicy Vibes or tried to think of the name of that famous actor who moved in two floors up, the words wouldn't visualize on her optic screens. And when playing Scrabble with Rosie, white pixels hovered over the "a" and "x." For some reason, the lenses and the innovative chips containing what Dr. Stone called "universal elements," or U.E.s, were not playing well together. Somehow her ancient access lenses were affecting her new AI assisted life memory.

Amara scrolled through one of the customer lounge's *Hollywood Zine* tablets as she waited to see the memory specialist at the Center for Excelling Life, or CEL. On the zine, the latest avatar sensation, *i*Hopes, urged Americans to swipe their fractional bitcoins into a children's education fund account. A freak accident involving tornadic winds and a tiny house had pulverized a boy's legs. Controversy arose when surgeons insisted they could save the legs; emphatic that the boy would stand on his own two biological feet. But the child wanted intelligent robotic stilts just like his hero *i*Hopes. The parents were suing the hospital for—

"Amara Vivian Graves. Proceed to cubicle twelve," an announcement floated over the tablet's video story.

Wandering through the maze of cubicles, Amara thought of her own children, grateful that they were functioning adults. The extent of her parenting dilemmas had centered on a teenage Aiden insisting that his parents fund his sound-wave tattoo sleeves. What kind of world allowed a ten-year-old boy to demand that his legs be amputated so he could have robotic appendages? Not one she wanted to be a part of.

"Ms. Graves." Dr. Lydia Coleman appeared on the cubicle's monitor.

"Present," Amara raised her hand. To John's disappointment, she'd kept her maiden name. Keeping it allowed her to feel like she had some say in their relationship.

"Keep your arm in the vita sleeve." The doctor was all business. "Looks like all your vitals are in acceptable ranges. Brain scans normal. Your profile says you use access lenses with your locator. Date of last contact upgrade?"

"Funny story that," Amara said. "My current license expired two years ago."

The doctor stopped what she was doing and gave Amara her full attention. "You've been operating with expired access lenses? That's dangerous for the system."

"Things have been complicated."

"No exceptions. No excuses. There's no telling what kind of nasty malware or viruses they have on them. These new biochip systems are sensitive to common viruses. And, according to your terms of service contract, you can be charged with criminal negligence if you infect the memory networks. Let's get you set up with some new ones."

"Do you think that's what's causing the optic screens to flicker on and off?"

"Maybe." Dr. Coleman was back to reading Amara's biographs. After another minute she said, "I'm sending Moby to you with some new ones. Let's try them on."

An AI arrived and handed Amara a slim quilted case. Opening

it, she removed her old lenses and put on the new ones. Moby scanned her eyeballs with his own.

A signal floated over her right eye, flashing the words "CREATE PASSWORD."

Amara stated Aiden and Kimberly's birthdays. Aiden was born seven months after she and John were married in 2002 and Kimberly came in 2004.

"Have they synced?" Dr. Coleman asked.

Amara blinked a few times and surveyed the bare trees framed by the outer glass walls. "The optic screens are different but I can see much better. Thank you."

"The optic screen designs have optional frames. There's an *i*Hopes look. He pops up in the left lens with helpful suggestions as you go through your day. For example, when you're shopping, he'll let you know about deals nearby. Things like that."

Amara recalled the animated paperclip on her first desktop computer when she was in high school. No way Dr. Coleman would know about the googly-eyed Clippy. She was too young. "The generic option is fine," Amara said. The thin line bordering the optic screens over her eyes flashed yellow, then green.

"The new lenses also come with two free link-ups with Moby. Contact him if you need any adjustments."

A request to accept a follow-up visit with Moby appeared on Amara's calendar view on the optic screen floating over her left eye. She ignored it.

Moby stated, "I see you have an opening in your calendar for Wednesday. December. Twenty-two. Two thousand. Forty-nine. Do you want to schedule a follow-up visit?"

Amara blinked twice to deny the AI access to her calendar.

"Goodbye," Moby said. Smiling, he revealed the *i*Hopes avatar etched into his two front teeth.

"I've ordered you a home vita sleeve. It's covered by your wellness plan. Network it to your home server," Dr. Coleman ordered.

"I like face-to-face visits," Amara said.

Dr. Coleman ignored her comment. "Have your bot install it for you."

Fearing that Dr. Coleman's no-nonsense efficiency could land Rosie in the recycle center out on Goochland Road, Amara flashed two thumbs up at the monitor.

"I see that Dr. Stone and I put you on the latest U. E. chips. Things are good, yes?"

"Ah," Amara hesitated.

"Side effects?"

Too embarrassed to speak of her daytime imaginings of the new thirty-something barista, who looked just like a guy she had a secret crush on in high school, ravishing her on top of the Juicy Vibes counter, she told the doctor about her irrational food cravings. "The first few weeks after starting the treatment I had these constant cravings for peanut butter and jelly sandwiches."

"Old food cravings are perfectly normal reactions. It means the chips are working. They're revitalizing the brain's memory centers. Anything else?"

"Ah, my libido?" Amara eked out.

For the first time Dr. Coleman appeared almost human. "The treatments raise one's libido by stimulating nibs of memory nuggets on a subcellular level. Are you having higher than your normal level of sexual urges?"

"Does having sex with my husband in our autopod while it rolls down Broad Street in broad daylight count?"

"Do you and your husband usually have sex in your autopod?" She grinned at Amara. "It's all harmless. Enjoy it. I'm sure your husband appreciates the new you."

Amara didn't think it necessary to tell the medical shaman that her husband had been dead for two years. The roll down Broad Street was a full on hallucination with a much younger version of John.

As she was leaving the building, a woman grabbed her by the arm and asked, "Amara Graves? Is that you?"

A Grace Street neighbor's image and name popped up on Amara's new access lens. "Celeste. Good to see you," Amara said.

"You've had work done. You look absolutely stunning. Who's your counselor?"

"So do you," Amara gushed. "I'm working with Dr. Stone and Dr. Coleman. Do you really think it works?"

"Are you kidding? You look like that designer," Celeste snapped her fingers, "you know the one. She did this year's fashion show from the Canadian space lab."

"Molli Brands?"

"Yes! I don't know what the doctors have you on but keep doing it, babe. Gotta run. Let's do lunch."

Walking home in the December drizzle, Amara recalled Dr. Coleman's advice and resolved to herself to enjoy the ride.

At home, she took her new access lenses out to rest her eyes. The constant flashing yellow frames on the optic screens were annoying. Something else to adjust to, she thought. As she brewed some tea, she asked Rosie to dig up what she could find on universal elements, memory service treatments, and sexual hallucinations or fantasies.

"Inquiry blocked, John," Rosie said. "Should I remove the triple-X filter?"

"Try universal elements and memory service treatments," Amara said.

"Inquiry too broad, John," Rosie responded.

"Try universal elements," Amara persisted.

Rosie responded immediately. "Universal elements. Term given to elements such as iron, magnesium, aluminum, calcium and potassium mined from ore not indigenous to Earth. For example, universal elements are mined from meteorites found in the Sahara Desert."

Amara thought of her parents, who'd lived most of their lives in a time when a human existing beyond Earth and its atmosphere was the stuff of science fiction. The treatments to revive her aging body's cells were laced with minerals that had once traveled through outer space. "Ted and Audrey would never believe it."

"Mother, turn off your beauty filter," Kimberly shouted. "Wait! What have you done to your face?" Kimberly shrieked into the monitor.

They were holding their annual deliberations on holiday plans. Long-distance travel through hyperloop tunnels and via sonic planes, especially around holidays, intimidated Amara. When he was alive, John shamed the kids into coming home for their annual visit so she didn't have to make the long-distance treks.

Rubbing the side of her face, Amara asked timidly, "Do you like it?"

"Like it?" Kimberly huffed. "I'm glad Daddy isn't around to see what you've done."

"Sweetheart, I'm taking the therapy to help with my depression."

"You look ridiculous. Ingesting biochip plasma? Have you lost your mind? That stuff is soooo toxic."

Ever since Kimberly landed on the adult side of puberty, she mocked and criticized Amara about everything, even going so far as blaming her mother for Kimberly's failings. The early loss of that special mother-daughter bond used to sadden Amara. But now, she felt downright giddy when she learned Kimberly's latest woman friend had run off and wasn't there to dog-sit so Kimberly could travel to Virginia. Amara's daughter and John's princess usually spent the entire Virginia visit sprawled out on an ancient sofa in the Grace Street house basement expecting room and laundry service.

"Don't come crying to me when you get radiation poisoning of the . . . whatever," Kimberly said.

"What's happening?" Aiden asked as he joined the chat.

"Hello, pumpkin." Amara brightened at the sight of her handsome, accomplished son. He favored her people with his lanky limbs and pleasing face.

"Kimberly! Woman of the Great White North! How's the sled dog business?"

"Fuck you, Aiden," Kimberly said.

"Kimberly, don't speak to your brother—"

"Mom's mainlining nanochips," Kimberly interrupted. "Did you know about it?"

"Hi, gorgeous," Aiden said to Amara. "Yep, and doesn't she look grand?"

A painful howl streamed from Kimberly's video frame. "The vet's here and she charges by the hour, so can we get on with this? I'll start. I'm not coming to the land of modern druids this year. You two do what you want." Her monitor image faded away.

"What's got her going?" Aiden asked.

"Something about Karen walking out," Amara offered.

"You mean Deena. Karen was last year," Aiden said.

"Those women take advantage of your sister," Amara said. Before the markets crashed in 2033, Kimberly had cashed out of her Silicon Valley job and joined an Alaska survivalist group called The Cassandras.

"It's her life. Can't live it for her," Aiden said. "Isn't that what

Dad always said?"

"How're Sonia and the kids?" Amara asked.

"All good." Aiden drummed on his desktop with his index fingers. "Sonia wants you to pop over and spend Christmas week with us. Are you up for it?"

Amara adored her daughter-in-law. Sonia and Aiden had two children, both born in London. "Thank her for the thoughtful invitation, but I'd prefer to stay at home."

"We'd love to be with you but things are just crazy with the markets right now."

"I'll be fine, Aiden. Let's chat on Christmas morning," Amara said.

Aiden moved closer to his monitor and asked, "How're you doing, really?"

"I'm fine. Stop worrying. Megs Daugherty has invited me to join her family's Winter Gathering, or fascist patriarchal ritual, as your sister calls it."

"No, I mean, how are you coping with not having Dad around? God, I miss my weekly connections with him." He looked down at his hands.

And here she thought her sensitive child was genuinely concerned for her well-being. "I know it's hard, honey." She longed to put her arm around him.

Sniffing, he said, "Sonia's calling. Gotta go. Happy Christmas, mum. Cheerio!"

The screen cleared.

Actually, Amara was relieved that her grown children had other plans. John was the parent who insisted they all celebrate Christmas under a single roof. Today, Amara rejoiced in the notion that she didn't have to bake five dozen candy cane sugar cookies. During the last two weeks of every year of her adult life, her children and husband assumed that her role as wife and mother included slave to their yuletide whims. Every year when the kids were at home, somehow she managed to clear her horrendous work schedule to do all the Christmas shopping, prepare special meals, decorate the house, and help John host his annual Christmas open house. In all that time, not once had there been a wrapped gift under the tree just for her. Sure, she'd left behind at Grace Street a house full of overpriced, once-used gadgets the kids had given John and her over the years. But her children weren't mindful enough to sense that all she really wanted was a small token or nominal, endearing gift that expressed their love and appreciation for her seasonal efforts.

A new life was revealing itself to Amara Vivian Graves and the titles of wife, mother, and Christmas hostess were no longer required.

Chapter Three

ASHE BOULEVARD CULTURAL CENTER
TUESDAY, DECEMBER 7, 2049

Amara stood on the sidewalk in front of her building. The breezy nip felt sharper than Rosie had warned. She tapped her arm to activate the heat threads in the torso of her "tap" jacket. Megs's co-worker at the cultural center had invited her in for an interview. Afterward, she and Megs planned to have lunch at Juicy Vibes in Carytown.

In spite of the chilly air, the bright sunshine lured her into walking the kilometer or so to the center. Along the narrow side street she took, festive lights shimmered in bare trees in front of the small early twentieth-century row houses that had managed to survive the city's urban high-rise mania. An autopod whirred by, packed with kids and a frazzled-looking dad. With a hover trolley station only steps from her apartment, Amara rarely used the autopod since her move to Oakwood. The last time she did she'd had that wacky hallucination of carnal knowledge with John "the younger."

There he was, naked down to his socks. Stopped on Broad Street waiting for a pod in front of them to turn, he pressed the button to darken the side windows then reached for her as the seats reclined. By the time the autopod had stopped at Fifth Street, she was undressed and straddling a sweating John. Uneasy with the too-real memory, she'd reasoned with herself that John's essence had prompted the illusion. He was everywhere in the little commuter vehicle, the smell of him, his deactivated blockchain tablet in the dash's cup holder, and a vintage Wimbledon bucket hat in the back seat.

Continuing on the walkway, she focused on thinking about something else. As she watched a man and his bot string lights across a porch banister, her optic screens responded by overlaying the narrow side street with a translucent view of the same street from another time. A video she'd made of Aiden, at 12, and Kimberly, at 10, walking in front of her, jelled with the present street scene. The houses looked so different then, covered in emissions soot. She'd forgotten how noisy the gasoline-powered cars were. She tried to recall why they were walking down that particular street.

"Look out!" someone called.

Amara blinked in time to see an autopod coming straight at her. Somehow she'd strayed into the middle of the vehicle right-of-way. She hopped back into the pedestrian lane as the one-seater whizzed by.

"Behind you," a boy on a hoverboard swerved to miss her.

She extended her arms to catch her balance as the board swooped by her. She took in a deep breath and repeated Dr. Coleman's order, "Enjoy the ride, Amara."

At the outdoor mall of the cultural center, Amara watched as an AI mule pushed an internal combustion engine vehicle onto a low platform. Sitting in the driver's seat of the mommy van, Megs Daugherty waved to her friend.

Hopping out, Megs ordered the AI to its home base and turned to Amara. "Whew!" Pointing at the sculpture of an emaciated riderless horse, she said, "They wanted the vehicle parked next to The War Horse. Past modes of transportation. I think it's tasteless."

"It's insensitive. The horse was intended as a memorial to animals that served the country during wartime," Amara said.

"Says you and me. We'll see how long the van stays here," Megs said as she closed the van's door.

"It's just like the one my mom had," Amara said.

"Wasn't every mother *required* to drive one?" Megs laughed.

"I loved driving. I had a flower delivery job during high school." Amara grinned.

"Don't want to make you late for your meeting with Arturo," Megs said, "but did you hear about Jane?"

"No."

"She's pregnant."

"But she's our age," Amara said. "How's that possible?"

"I know, right? It's all over the local streams, and its trending is accelerating. She told me she found out when she went for her monthly renewal injection. She's on the same program we're on. Barry's been calling me all morning. Wants to make sure I'm not, you know," Megs patted her belly. "He wants to represent her." Barry was Megs's lawyer husband.

"That's crazy," Amara said.

"Who would've thought we'd need to use contraception at our age?" Megs laughed. "Juicy Vibes at noon?"

Dazed by Megs's news, Amara waved goodbye and headed for Arturo Santo's office. Maybe Kimberly was right. These medical treatments were unorthodox. But Dr. Stone had assured her that the practice had been mainstreamed for years and historical data showed no negative side effects. She hoped Jane's situation was an anomaly; she'd hate to give up feeling like she could run a marathon, that is, if she wanted to run one.

As she waited for the director in the museum's grand passageway, she watched a young couple take one of the time capsule celebration boxes from a table and walk into the museum's café. The Y2K capsule event in 2000 was Amara and John's first date. When the guide asked them how many boxes they wanted, John had asked for two. At the time, she'd supposed he was being a gentleman, allowing her to have her own. His thoughtfulness at that moment endeared her to fall in love with him. But as their life together progressed, she recognized the gesture as one of his ways of compartmentalizing and separating himself from others in general and her in particular. Not unlike his favorite Dickens' character Ebenezer Scrooge, John guarded his emotions.

Amara's locator vibrated. A stressed Kimberly popped up on her optic screen. She blocked the connection, deciding she'd chat with her daughter after the interview.

As Arturo and Amara sat at a table in the café a few minutes later, Amara interrupted him and said, "Excuse me." She stood and walked away from the interview for a job that wasn't what she'd expected. She tapped at her locator to take Kimberly's second inquiry. "Kimberly, doesn't your screen show you that I'm not available at this very instant?"

"Mom, what's going on down there?" Kimberly's forehead crinkled with worry, just like her father's when he obsessed about inaction toward the latest human indignity.

"I'm in the middle of an interview for a new job. It says so right on my calendar," Amara said.

"No, what's *really* going on? My news stream is saying a seventy-year-old woman is pregnant. And they're going to make her abort it."

Amara stuttered, "I don't know. Ya' got me."

"Moooooom!" Kimberly sounded like her twelve-year-old self.

"I've got to go. I'll call you when I'm out of this meeting."

"I'm coming down there," Kimberly said right before Amara disconnected.

The interview didn't go as Amara expected. On their tour of the musty storage area, Arturo explained that he needed someone to manage the old Gen One androids that packed and stacked the time capsules. The legacy credits he offered were half what she was getting at Hope Home. And, he had the gall to call bots like Rosie old rust buckets. No, this work wasn't for her but she'd need to find something soon. The Office of Fair Housing Rights had posted its new rates and, of course, the rates were going up after the first of the new year. Her housing allotment credits wouldn't cover the rent increase. If she didn't find something comparable to her old position, she'd have to move to a one room flat with no elevator. And steps were a challenge for Rosie since her knee joints sometimes locked up.

Walking out of the museum, Amara overheard others talking about the Bledsoe woman. Amara didn't believe it. How was it even biologically possible? Didn't she learn in biology class, like, a hundred years ago, that a female had a finite number of eggs and they were all gone by menopause? This nonsense about Jane having a baby was probably an attention-grabbing hoax generated by some news contractor looking to boost their trending rates. And, Kimberly. She was always chasing after causes like this one. Telling Amara yesterday that she wasn't coming to Virginia for the winter holidays to be with her family, her daughter was now blazing a trail homeward out of concern for someone she'd never met. Kimberly was just like her father when he was younger, busy saving the world while pushing away the ones who tried to love her.

"Oh, John," she sighed. "Help me through this."

"Watch out!"

Amara turned in time to see the same boy who'd barely missed her earlier, his hoverboard bolting toward her. As the flashing lights in the wheels came up to meet her sternum, she heard a dull thud. The last vision displayed on her optic screen before the light burned out was an image of John in their autopod.

Chapter Four

THE SHOPS OF CARYTOWN
WEDNESDAY, DECEMBER 8, 1999

The flashing terms of service notice fluttered on the optic screen in her left eye. Her right eye had gone fuzzy, as if the lens wasn't there.

"Stay with us. The ambulance is almost here," someone said.

Her chest was on fire. An image of the boy and his hoverboard flickered across the back of her eyelids. Then it broke up into a thousand pixels. She opened her eyes as a chilly breeze brushed at her sweating brow.

"Markus, she's conscious," a woman said as she stooped beside Amara. "Hi, I'm Officer White. What's your name, sugar?"

Frustrated that she couldn't see the person's profile on her lens, Amara was confused. If this person was an officer of the state, as the badge on her bulky jacket seemed to indicate, she should know who Amara was.

"You lie still. We're going to get you out of this cold air," Officer White said as she took Amara's wrist.

Amara pulled back. "Did you see him?" She propped herself on her elbows.

"See who, sugar?" Officer White tried to take Amara's hand again.

"The boy on the hoverboard who ran into me. Is he all right?" Amara tried to sit up but was crowded by a ring of faces, reminding her of that silly *i*Hopes cartoon about pigeons that she and her grandchildren watched together.

"What boy?" one of the faces asked.

"You okay, lady?" another asked.

"Move away," Officer White commanded. "Give her room."

"She was waving her arms around all crazy like and then fell. That's when I came and got you," a small man wearing a baseball jacket said to the officer.

"Everybody clear out. Show's over," Officer White said. "Move out of the way so we can get the ambulance up in here."

Amara rolled onto her stomach and went up on her knees.

"Stay calm. The medics are right here," Officer White said. "They'll take you to the hospital and get you checked out."

Amara brushed the officer's arm aside and stood. Unsteady, she took two steps and stumbled. When the medics grabbed her arms to catch her, she protested, "Leave me alone!" Helping the residents of Hope Home, she knew what happened to those who went to the hospital. Hospital was code for palliative care. People who went in came out in body bags. The last stop, they called it.

The deafening beeps and engine roar of the ambulance was accompanied by a harsh smell Amara couldn't quite place. The putrid odor burned the inside of her nose, making her dizzy. Slumping against the medics, her resistance weakened. A soft tap at the back of her knees caused her to fall back onto a gurney. A rush and a sense of calm followed a prick to her upper arm.

"Relax, everything is going to be all right," she heard as she drifted away.

An intense white glow seeped into the corners of her eyes. She squinted as someone pushed back the curtain surrounding the bed in which she was lying. She pretended she was asleep.

"I'm telling you that's what she said," a voice whispered. "She said she's sixty-nine and we should be able to see her profile on the medical data grid."

"What's a medical data grid?" another voice asked.

"Beats me. Her vitals are solid. I'd say she's in her late thirties, maybe forty. Fit."

"What happened?"

"Told Officer White that a kid rammed her in the chest with his skateboard. There's some slight bruising but nothing's broken. Her breathing and heart check out."

One of them pulled the curtain back into place and their voices faded away.

Amara swung her legs around and sat up. Rubbing her arm, she searched for her tap jacket. She had to get out of this place.

"Oh. You're awake," a nurse joined her.

"Where's my jacket?" Amara demanded.

Pulling the curtains back, the nurse picked up her jacket draped over a chair by a bank of windows. "Here you go. It's not much of a jacket. The temperature is dropping. Weatherman's predicting a foot of snow." Tapping her own chest, the nurse said, "I like how your Christmas pin flashes red and gold. Where did you get it?"

Amara placed her hand over the locator clipped to her shirt as she grabbed her jacket. She asked, "Where's the restroom?"

"Right down that hall. Take a right," the nurse said. "When you get back, we'll take your blood. Doctor ordered some tests."

Amara passed the turn for the restrooms and kept going. In the emergency room lobby, she noticed a crumpled paper magazine on an end table. *Time* magazine was proclaiming Albert Einstein the

Person of the Century. The date on the publication was December 1999. The date on the refolded newspaper beside it was Wednesday, December 8, 1999.

"Calm down," she whispered. "Just breathe. You're having another hallucination. Enjoy the ride. Enjoy the ride." After a hard, deliberate blink, she noticed that her right access lens was missing. The left flashed three red triangles. She tapped her locator and waited for it to wake up and to transmit her coordinates and time of day to her lens. Nothing happened.

In front of the hospital, a sweeping rush of cold air compelled her to slip into her jacket. She tapped the sleeve to warm it up. An old-style street marker at Eleventh and Marshall displayed the name of the fourth chief justice of the U.S. Supreme Court. When Aiden was in high school, he and John attended a city auction. John dragged home all kinds of worthless junk. Aiden had purchased a Marshall Street sign for his bedroom just like the one looming over her head.

Amara turned toward Broad Street to catch the next hover trolley. As she arrived, a giant city bus pulled away from the sidewalk, its exhaust pipes blowing gritty plumes. She spun around, taking in the city: noisy cars and trucks, people bundled in hats and massive outerwear, and a man sweeping the sidewalk with a straw broom. A man brushed beside her, mumbling, "Excuse me," as he shoved envelopes into an oversized metal box. This hallucination was lasting much longer than the others. She snapped her fingers. Seeing all the artifacts in the cultural museum must have prompted the illusion. While waiting for the director, she'd watched a man and his AI cart one of those corner post office boxes across the marble floor. Congress had decommissioned the U.S. Postal Service's physical delivery services in 2027, and it had taken the agency over ten years to sell off all the assets like the big metal boxes. They'd had one just like it in their basement at Grace Street.

Another bus stopped and the door swished stale air at her. People bumped into her as they rushed to get on the bus. Out of habit, she tapped her locator again. No response. It must have broken in the fall.

"I'll just have to walk out of this," she said out loud as she headed west on Broad Street. Her home was about eight kilometers away and the winter daylight was fading. The broad avenue was gloomy with abandoned storefronts. She gagged at the noxious cigarette smoke spewing from people standing on the sidewalk. She was amazed at the vividness of her hallucination.

Fluffy gray snowflakes swirled around her. One landed on her cheek. She looked up into the blowing sky and noticed telephone and electrical cable strung out on uneven poles as far as she could see. This was no dream; it felt too real. It was a nightmare.

By sunset she'd given up on finding an HT station. The blinding snow forced her to keep her eyes on the sidewalk as she cut across Broad Street and into one of the city's oldest neighborhoods. The snow now covered everything. At the corner of Roseneath and Oakwood, she scoured the roofline for her high-rise. It wasn't where it was supposed to be, where she'd left it this morning. Instead, dim streetlights revealed sagging row houses and two-story apartment buildings, the ones she had passed on her way to school every day as a child. Amazed at the hallucination's clarity, she whispered, "It can't be. These places were torn down."

She remembered this because one of John's clients was the owner. She remembered this because he'd left her and moved in with Keekee Biddle, the client who was suing city hall for forcing squatters into homelessness by demolishing the dwellings.

Her feet tingled.

MELISSA POWELL GAY

John's words from that dark night long ago swirled around in the cold wind, whispering, "Amara, I don't know who you are anymore. I can't stay with you."

Chapter Five

ON THE STREETS OF CARYTOWN
WEDNESDAY, DECEMBER 8, 1999
P.M.

Amara wandered the Carytown sidewalks of her youth. Falling snow had whisked excited residents outdoors. The shops teemed with Christmas shoppers. Except Megs wouldn't be there, nor Juicy Vibes. Around nine o'clock she spied Officer White talking to a shivering man at a corner. Amara casually turned and strolled the other way. Her reflection in a dress shop window revealed a glowing face framed by damp hair. The biochip plasma therapy had done its job. Her reflection looked just like a color version of the black and white portrait photo John had insisted she sit for on her fortieth birthday in 2019.

Indian folk music jangled from speakers mounted over the door of a curry shop. Amara's stomach rumbled when she smelled the strong aromas seeping from the place. She'd forgotten all about Bombay's. In the early years of their marriage, she and John had date night there most weeks until its owners Kumar and Geetha closed it and moved back to India. Amara wasn't a fan of curry but went along because it meant she didn't have to cook dinner.

She ran her dry tongue over chapped lips. Her stomach rumbled at the thought of a cup of hot sweet tea and a bowl of lentil stew. Can one taste food in a dream, she wondered. Despite her hunger, she had no cash. Combing her fingers through her wet hair, she panicked. She had no physical ID, no credit card or cash to pay for something to eat. Her legacy credits transferred through her locator and it didn't seem to be working.

Her entire net worth was tied up in legacy credits. After a massive financial market meltdown in 2034, Congress had declared the IRS "obsolete," dissolved the national currency, and set up a mandatory credit account for each of its citizens. She and John had lost most of their life's savings. Thankfully, Aiden's dalliance in cyber investments covered his parent's living expenses, the ones they couldn't pay with their legacy work earnings.

A man, standing inside, waved at her.

"Me?" she mouthed as she pointed at herself.

He waved again for her to come inside. "Would you like to try our special this evening, mum?" the young man asked.

"Is Kumar here tonight?" she asked.

"No, he and Geetha went home for a visit. I'm Ramesh. Where would you like to sit?" Surveying the empty dining room, his lips curled into a warm smile. He said, "I'll try to squeeze you in."

Amara felt his eyes crawling all over her. He knew. Somehow, he knew who she was and where she was from and this caused her to panic.

"Sorry. I'm . . . I'm . . . in the mood for pizza. Sorry." She exited and hurried down the street without looking back.

In desperation, she circled the block where her building should have been but it never revealed itself to her. She felt so alone, so lost, and so tired. Expanding her search, she walked past a church the next block over. Her feet tingled and burned inside her soaked shoes as she slipped through the front door. Organ music filled the sanctuary. Silently, she climbed to the balcony above the narthex, sat, and listened to a choir practicing the Christmas hymns of her childhood. The overheated church and the choir's harmonies soothed her confused mind. Exhausted from walking through snow and slush, she bargained with herself that she'd curl up on the pew and rest her eyes for only a minute, then go back out to search for her home.

Chilly air awoke her from a dream of falling snow and walking on the old Broad Street, before the HT. She opened her eyes to darkness, smelling the musty book she was clutching in her arms. A loud thump of the book's spine hitting the floor was followed by an amplified groan coming from the bench as she sat upright. Shivering, she blinked in the darkness and rubbed her arms to heat up her tap jacket. The reflection of a street light illuminated one of the sanctuary's stained glass windows, the Good Shepherd. "Rejoice with me, for I have found my sheep which was lost," she repeated the scripture she'd learned as a child. "Amara what have you gotten yourself into?" She asked. How long had she been asleep?

She heard muted voices underneath her feet, a deep creaking sound then a door slam shut. She almost called out but caught herself. What would she say to them? She tapped on her locator and the triangles flashed on her optic screen, still no signal.

Back on the street, she continued her trek and, an hour before sunrise, found her way to the old homeless shelter. Thankfully, she didn't recognize any of the staff. But why would she? If the year really was 1999, most of the leaders at Hope Home hadn't been born yet. Keeping to herself, she ate a quick bowl of oatmeal and ventured back out into the cold.

The blankets of snow reminded her of hot chocolate and snow ice cream. In the winters of her youth, her parents would declare a snow day and take Amara and her sister for sleigh rides in the park. She'd forgotten how tranquil the snow made her feel. She'd forgotten a lot of things about her past before John.

She found her way to the library on Ellwood just as the librarian unlocked the door to start the day. The inky newspaper confirmed that she'd traveled in time. The date underneath the headlines read Thursday, December 9, 1999. So it was really happening to her, she was in another time. To calm her breathing, she spread the paper across the library table and forced herself to focus on the words. The smell of the damp ink and thin paper stirred memories of her father and her at their kitchen table sharing funnies and puzzles. The newsprint industry slowly folded once people started consuming news through their locator bands, using ear and eye implants to absorb a constant drivel of unsourced information and outright gossip. Amara refused to have implants. She went old-school and used access lenses with optic screens and earbuds, allowing her to extract them whenever the daily newsfeeds became too harsh, too absurd.

In the newspaper, stories on the pseudo apocalypse called Y2K, an acronym meaning "year 2000," were covered on page two. The city and country were taking extravagant precautions to avoid a digital Armageddon. "If they only knew," Amara spoke softly. As the youngest central office technician at a data transport center at the telephone company, she was required to be in the data network war room when the clock struck midnight on December 31, 1999, her twentieth birthday. Her bosses declared victory when nothing happened. The biggest nonevent of the two centuries was followed by the biggest tragedy. A picture of New York City's recognizable skyline with the World Trade Center loomed on page A-3. Her eyes widened. In another twenty-one months the towers would disintegrate into heaps of concrete dust. Everyone's world would change on Tuesday, September 11, 2001. She raised her head to look around the cramped library annex. If she really had traveled back in time, she could save lives. But who would believe someone who claimed she had already lived through the ordeal? Someone who claimed she was from the year 2049? *She* wouldn't believe it.

Her finger tips and toes tingled with an electric pulse, a buzz.

One of the guys she noticed at the homeless shelter earlier edged in next to her. She shoved the paper at him and left.

A bus stopped in front of the library. Deep in thought about how she might warn people about New York's imminent catastrophe, she hopped on and tapped her locator pin for the bus to credit her account for using public transportation. She headed for the back of the bus.

"Hey!" the driver called after her. "You got to pay." His buggy eyes stared out from the inside rear view mirror.

Her intentional blinking prompted the ever present red triangles in the corner of her left eye to flash. The bus wasn't wired for machine-to-machine connection.

"Lady, you got to pay to ride," he yelled.

The dry heat in the bus burned her nostrils. The buzzing in her toes and fingers flared again. She backed up and took note of his name badge and whispered, "Elijah, I don't have any change. Can I pay you next time?"

"You don't pay, you don't ride," he said as he opened the bifold doors. "Them's the rules. I don't have any say."

An elderly gentleman sitting in the front row wobbled to the fare box and dumped in a handful of coins. "I've got it, love," he said. He reached for her arm like a doting grandfather.

"Thank you," Amara said.

Tipping his golf cap, the man winked. "Anytime, sweet 'art." His accent sounded like a mashup between a Disney chimney sweep and John's grandfather, whom she'd met when they honeymooned in Brighton Beach in East Sussex.

The bus was too warm. Finding a seat, she peeled off her jacket and balled it up in her lap. She closed her eyes and pretended she was in the sauna room at the community center she visited three times a week. Someone sat beside her.

"Don't be mad at Elijah. He's just doing what he's told," the man with the cap said. Thumping his chest, he added, "Farley Dickenson."

"Thanks, again," she said. "I don't have any cash on me right now."

"My treat."

Their eyes met. His were a droopy hazel. "If you don't mind me saying, it's been awhile since I've seen eyes that color blue. Or, in your case, one eye."

Amara hesitated, then said, "Oh! My access . . . my contacts. I lost one of them. As you can see my natural eye color is gray." A thin line of sweat beaded on her hairline.

"Where are you from?" he asked.

Her gasp made her cough. What was she supposed to tell people? She opted for the truth. "Lived here all my life. And you?"

"East London. My missus was from Virginia so we settled here when I retired." He pointed at her locator pin. "Mine's an older model. What year are you from?"

Now her head was buzzing along with her toes and fingers. She covered the pin with her hand. "Excuse me?"

Leaning in, he whispered, "What year's your locator?" He turned the collar of his jacket up to reveal an older style, one like John's, except its indicator lights weren't on.

Amara couldn't speak.

"It's truly a horse of a different color back here. Isn't it?"

She decided to trust him and whispered, "Are there others?"

"You bet."

"What happened?"

"I got lost walking Bonnie one night. Been roaming around here for seven years."

"Seven years?" She gulped.

"Some of us meet at a diner over on Broad Street. Take turns riding the bus lines. It seems to be the first place we all need to go when we find ourselves here." Reading the disbelief in Amara's face, he said, "'Tis a lot to take in, doll. But you'll get used to it." He patted her hand and added, "One good bit of news about living in this miserable time is a body's able to smoke ciggies and drink coffee strong enough to peal the varnish off an oyster boat. Come along and we'll get you sorted."

Chapter Six

AT THE WAY BACK DINER
THURSDAY, DECEMBER 9, 1999

Inside the Way Back Diner, Elvis crooned about having a blue Christmas as Amara followed Farley to the back booth. To her surprise, the young restaurateur she'd spoken to the previous evening was sitting across from a stern-faced woman. Farley gestured for Amara to scoot into the booth next to the woman as he slid in next to Ramesh. He said, "Friends, this is Amara."

"Brenda, ra-*dish* is a pungent yet edible red root. My name is Ra-*mesh*," the young Carytown restaurateur pleaded with the woman.

"That's what I said. Radish."

"Have either of you seen Desi Kurts?" Farley asked. "He's supposed to be doing bus duty today."

"I saw him yesterday outside the diner. He was talking to a couple of tall fellas," Brenda offered. "They left together in a big black car."

"Did you get the license?" Farley asked.

"I did," she said as she pushed away her empty plate.

Farley canvassed the diner for eavesdroppers. "Amara got here yesterday from '49."

Ramesh's eyes popped.

"Great googly-moogly!" Brenda exclaimed. "They're coming farther out. I'm Brenda from '45. 'Cept that's not my real name. Guess Farley told you about changing yours."

Unsure how to react to this brash woman, Amara clutched at her shirt collar.

"You wake up and realize you weren't where you were supposed to be?" Brenda asked.

Amara peered across the table at Farley, her eyes pleading for confirmation that this whole thing was just a nightmare caused by eating too many salty veggie chips before bedtime. "This is all just a hoax. Right?"

Brenda pinched Amara's arm.

"Ow." Amara jerked away.

"Feel that, did you? This isn't the TV show *The Twilight Zone*, kitten," Brenda said. "This is real. Somehow, we've managed to collide with another time channel and got stuck."

"Between the three of us, we know about twenty people who've fallen into the Way Back. That's what we call it," Farley said. "But I believe there may be more of us."

Farley and Brenda explained to Amara the conditions of survival in their shared illusion. She needed to assimilate quickly, get a job, and a place to live. She was told Brenda, a retired genetic scientist in her other life, had wrangled a job at the Department of Health with access to vital records and she'd made friends at the DMV.

Brenda rummaged through her tattered coachman's bag and pulled out a neon yellow accordion folder. "You got any preferences on names? I got a Karen Minor, a Juanita Carson, an Alice Epps." She peered at Alice's driver's license, then at Amara. Tossing the license on the table, she continued, "Close enough. As far as the state is concerned, you're Alice Epps of Fontaine Street. You're five-seven and weigh a hundred and forty pounds, brown eyes, brown hair." She slapped the driver's license and birth certificate on the table. "We done, Farley? I'm late."

"Doesn't look like Desi's coming this morning," Farley said.

Brenda elbowed Amara to move. She scooted out and left.

"Why do I have to change my name?" Amara whispered as she slid back into the booth.

"Think about it, love," Farley said. "There's already someone with your name living here." To lighten the mood, he added, "And she was here first."

Amara folded her bottom lip over her teeth. "I suppose so."

"What do you think, Ramesh? Does the name Alice suit our newest member of the Way Backers?"

Ramesh smiled, revealing crooked white teeth, and acknowledged Farley's assessment of Amara's Way Back name.

Farley tapped Amara's head with a coffee spoon and said, "I dub thee Alice Epps, Fairest of the Way Backers." Sliding out of the booth, he pulled his cap from his jacket pocket and said, "Ramesh is your official Way Back partner. We team up to look after one another. He's going to take you over to his restaurant, where you'll help out until I come 'round to fetch you this afternoon. You'll stay with me until we can get you settled in your own place."

The ride through the city in Ramesh's smoky sedan exposed Amara to the city of her youth. The day had become cloudy and the man's voice on the scratchy radio excitedly projected more snow for the evening.

Amara chuckled. "I've lived here all my life. I remember this place going nuts when the weatherman predicted snow. The stores sold out of bread and toilet paper." Passing a windowless brick structure, she added, "My first job as an adult was in that building."

The car stopped at a light. She turned her head to have another look at the telco data center. "I'm . . . or a younger me? I'm in that building right now?" She felt dizzy.

"It's quite an adjustment. I'd stay away from that building if I were you," Ramesh said quietly.

"What is a Way Back partner supposed to do?" she asked.

He shrugged. "Like Farley said, look after one another." The light changed and the car continued on its path. "To be honest," he said, "I kind of enjoy living on this time channel. Things are simpler here."

"What year did you come from?" Amara asked.

"Forty-five. Same as Brenda."

"So you've been here how long?"

"About a year."

"So the duration is different for each person?"

"We're collecting data. So far it all appears random."

"What did you—or do you—do in 2045?"

"I'm an AI financial analyst manager for the Social Treasury." He checked the rear view mirror and added, "Don't hate me. I was assigned there *after* the '34 default. I was in the private sector when all that went down."

"Do you have kids?" she asked.

"Yes, but they haven't been born yet." Puffing his cheeks and making an explosion sound, he said, "Blows your mind, doesn't it?"

"I was nineteen in 1999. My birthday's on New Year's Eve."

"Wow. Whatever you do don't go looking for yourself," he said. "And like I said, stay away from that building or any place you may have been at nineteen."

"Why?"

"Farley will have to give you the whole 'don't talk to people you knew back then' speech," he said. "I'm no good at explaining what's happening to us."

His arm reached over the back of her seat as he parallel parked on Cary Street. A memory of John doing the same thing ambushed her while a couple, bundled against the cold, navigated a mound of plowed snow in front of the car.

Ramesh pointed at her locator pin. "And that, you should probably deactivate it. The only people with that kind of technology in this age are military types. If it sends out beacon signals, they'll come looking for you and want to know why you have it."

"It's turned off," she said as she put her hand over it.

"I thought the same thing but there's a secondary beacon with its own power source. They came after me. I had to leave D.C.," he said. "Farley took me in."

By the time Farley came to fetch her, Amara was exhausted from busing tables all day. She was surprised that she hadn't encountered any 1999 friends or co-workers since the restaurant was close to the building where she'd worked. But then she remembered she didn't start eating there until after marrying John. In 1999 she was single and always broke from paying utility bills and school expenses. All she could afford to eat was canned tomato soup and mac and cheese from the Safeway down the street.

Farley's Mercer Street house was like all the others in the Fan District: narrow, drafty, and creaky. In his small kitchen in the back of the tidy house, he offered her a cup of coffee, which she declined. Then he poured coffee into a cup that read *World's Oldest Fart* and led her down into the basement. A bare bulb mounted on an exposed joist illuminated the room. On the far wall was an inter-relationship diagram peppered with names.

"Ramesh told me you've been tracking this," Amara said as she examined the map.

He rubbed his bald head. "We ruled out early that it's not a single physical portal situation." Pointing at another map, a map of the city, he asked, "Where did you land?"

"An alley near Cary Street. Here," she pointed. "I was knocked down by a hoverboard."

"The blue pins are where everyone said they arrived. So you can see they're all over the place."

"At the diner, you said there were twenty. There's got to be at least twice that on this map."

"They've moved away or . . ." He sipped his coffee.

"Or what?"

Farley appeared to be wrestling with what to say next. "Look, ah, this time rut we've managed to get ourselves into isn't very pleasant. It's quite nasty, actually."

"How so?" she asked.

"People who've tried to contact themselves or family or anyone who had relationships with them in the past . . . they . . . well, bad things happen to them. By 'them' I mean their future selves, of course. One man tried to go to the house his younger self shared with his parents," Farley gulped, "and as he crossed the street a bus plowed into him." Pointing at a black pin on the map, he continued, "Sam Stokes broke his arm and got taken to the hospital. We never saw him again."

Amara studied the map and fingered a red pin at Fourth and Broad streets.

"Red for vehicular collisions, green for falls, orange for drowning, black for unknown—disappeared. Some of us have just vanished. Here one day, gone the next." Most of the pins were red or black. "Whatever you do, don't try to drop by to say 'hi' to mum and dad."

"All right. Noted. I won't try to contact my family."

"Or anyone who knows them."

"Got it. What caused this to happen?" she asked.

"We've got a hundred theories but that's all they are. Every Way Backer is just common folk, really. Going about their business one day and finding themselves here on this channel the next." He paused then went on with the practical instructions on how to survive their current time rut. "If you see anyone you know from your past, find other people to be with immediately. If things get too dangerous, we'll think about relocating you to another city. Like Ramesh."

"But what if I run into someone, unexpected like?"

"Ah, you'll know, love. Some of us, our fingers twitch, some get tingly all over. One gent described it as his hair and tongue itching. You'll know when it's happening. Your body will sense the danger and will signal you in some way. And, for the Lord's sake, stay away from vehicles and roads when you get those feelings." Without warning, he smacked his hand on his wooden desk and said, "Or, you're tarmac fodder for the turkey buzzards."

"Fingers twitching, bad," she repeated. Taking in his expression Amara knew she wasn't getting the full explanation to the Way Backers predicament.

Farley's description of the time channels and how they were all stuck as if in a bad rut felt true in her case. She asked, "When can we go back to our own time rut, as you call it?"

"Nobody knows. I'm afraid there isn't anything we can do. I'm sorry, love. You're stuck right here."

Maybe they had all died and this was heaven, or the other place.

"You'll get used to it. Look at it this way, you've got a whole new life."

Thinking about the picture of the World Trade Center she saw in the morning newspaper, she asked, "Since we know the future, can we stop bad things from happening?"

"Tried it. Several times. Almost got me-self killed in the

process."

"But, Farley, all those people in the Twin Towers." She rubbed her arm.

"I know, love."

"We could tell others. They could do something to stop it."

"On the night before the '93 World Trade Center bombing, I drove up to New York and went to the security station. They called the police and had me arrested. The next day, amid all the chaos, with the help of some kind people, I managed to get out."

He put his hands on his hips and shrugged. "It doesn't matter what we try. Things are bound to happen. It's like we're wrapped up inside our own personal vortex and can't be of this time. I wish it were different but it's not." He led her up the stairs to the second floor to get her settled in one of the spare bedrooms.

Chapter Seven

Tandy Johnson, a Way Backer from 2043, hired Amara to deliver flowers during the holiday rush. Six days after her arrival in 1999, she parked the Honda Odyssey in back of Tandy's shop La Petite Fleur. In her other life, she spent her time reprimanding bossy AI humanoids and now, in this new life, she occupied her days greeting real people who were actually happy to see her. An added bonus, she was driving, something she loved doing before the world decided service robots like Brad could do it better.

As a teenager, once she got her license, Amara was allowed to do all the family chores that required driving. She picked up her father's shirts and suits from the dry cleaners, shopped for groceries, and drove younger sister Beck to her orthodontist appointments. The summer after her high school graduation, she and her best friend Alesa drove to California and back in her mother's van. It was an Odyssey, too.

Amara had forgotten how soothing driving could be. It required her full attention thus crowding out the anxiety of her unnerving time expedition. The previous day, she'd gone for long stretches of minutes without thinking about John or the kids or Rosie or her spatial situation. Her new job kept her focused on the present, maneuvering through the city and crisscrossing the river that runs through it.

Tandy waved for her to back the van into the warehouse where others helped Amara load her morning deliveries. "We have an expedite," he said. "Some guy wants flowers on his girlfriend's desk by eight-thirty." He handed Amara a stack of paper.

She struggled with the shop's paper processes but kept her commentary about barcode technology to herself. The address for the rush order was across the river. "I'm not sure rush-hour traffic will allow me to make the deadline but I'll try," she said as she hopped back into the van.

"Capitalism is alive and well in 1999, so hustle up. We don't want to lose this account to competition." He smacked the hood of the vehicle and winked at Amara.

At their introduction at the Way Back Diner, Tandy lectured Amara on the death of capitalism in their twenty-first-century life. "The day Congress passed the Guaranteed Income Act, limiting the amount a body can earn, is the day capitalism died. The bastards cut off its head and planted it on a pike at the front gates for everyone to throw rocks at," Tandy preached. Each encounter with him bought a new lament of the slow demise of free-market enterprise. Farley confided in Amara that Tandy was one of the few who were actually happy here in 1999.

Amara's husband was as passionate as Tandy on the topic of private enterprise, from an opposite point of view, of course. His grandparents were tantamount to royalty in the old British Labour Party. His high strung debates with her father on the government's outright takeover of the Gen Ten Cumulus Networks and mandating the collective pooling of intellectual properties usually caused her mind to float to other, immediate, concerns, such as the next round of layoffs her seventy-five-person engineering and project manager group was facing or the leaky roof. Since meeting Tandy, she wished she'd paid more attention to John's arguments because somehow she sensed that Tandy was misinformed. But the old insecurities kept her from challenging her new boss's misguided beliefs so she said nothing.

Exiting the Powhite Parkway on the south bank of the James River, Amara turned left and parked on the road's shoulder. She was lost and the bulky paper map wasn't the optimum way to navigate while driving. A loud, abrupt BLURP caused her to jump in her seat. From the rear view, she saw flashing blue lights and a police officer walking toward the passenger side of the van. Her heart racing, she tapped at her chest to reset her locator. Of course, it wasn't there. She'd stored it and the one remaining access lens in her backpack which was in her room at Farley's.

"Breathe, Amara," she said quietly. The sound of her own shaky voice ratcheted up her anxiety. To calm herself, she whispered, "I'm Alice Epps. I've moved recently from Charlottesville and I deliver flowers for La Petite Fleur." She fumbled inside the console bin for the van's registration and her driver's license.

A tap on thick glass induced another jump. A brawny hand motioned for her to open the window.

"License and registration," came a gentle command.

Amara, her hand shaking like a guilty junkie's, handed over the documents. Her entire body was amped at high alert. White noise screamed in her ears, obstructing her ability to process reasonable excuses as to why she was using poor Alice Epps's identity. She didn't want to be arrested for identity theft, not today.

Finally, after a torturous three minutes, the officer bent over and said, "Ma'am, this road's closed. You mind telling me where you're headed?"

"Ah, ah, no, sir," Amara stammered. "I mean, yes, sir. I'm looking for the Quarry Building, sir. I just started a new job. I . . . I'm still getting used to driving a big car." Be quiet, she warned herself. If she was ever going to wake up from this nightmare, now would be a nice time for it to happen.

Abruptly, the officer's radio hooked through his shirt's epaulet squawked out a ten-something in progress. The license and registration flew back at her through the window followed by, "Turn around. This road is washed out. It dead ends on the ridge of a rock quarry."

Amara watched as the officer rushed back to his vehicle and sped away. She closed her eyes and took in long, deep breaths, willing her heart rate to step down. She slipped off her shoes and rubbed her tingling feet as she studied the oversized roadmap. She'd missed the turn for the expedited delivery address. The road that the van was sitting on wasn't on the map.

As she pulled into the parking lot with acres of cars, a tan sedan appeared out of nowhere and narrowly missed her front bumper. A long arm waved an apology as the car sped away. Sitting in a visitor parking space, the clock in the Odyssey read 8:33. If the officer hadn't stopped her, she'd have driven the van off the road and into a quarry of water far below. Farley's warnings of vehicular misadventure had sunk into her primordial sense of self-preservation, causing her to shudder.

An afternoon delivery took Amara two blocks east of her parents' Grace Street home. After the morning's incident, she drove with deliberate caution to deliver the ugliest evergreen centerpiece ever made.

Her trip out west in the summer of 1998 convinced Amara

that she didn't need a college degree to thrive in the explosive new internet services industry. She aced an engineering assistant aptitude test as part of an interview with the local telephone company and was put to work immediately, monitoring broadband networks. The rosacea on her father's nose flared up when he discovered she'd joined the electrician's union. It didn't matter that the membership was not only a formality but a mandatory requirement for employment. Both Ted and Audrey lectured that as long as she was under their roof, she'd be enrolled at a four-year college. So she signed up for a C++ programming class while working the midnight-to-eight shift at the company's data center.

In the spring of 1999, Ted Graves's company informed him that his job was no longer located in Richmond, Virginia but in San Angelo, Texas. Amara and Beck joined in solidarity to protest a full family migration to the land of tumbleweeds. Reluctantly, Ted moved to San Angelo with every intention of returning to his hometown once he accumulated enough time to retire with full benefits. That Christmas, the girls, nineteen and seventeen, had free reign of the three-story house while their mother spent the holidays in Texas with Dad.

Another delivery took Amara to the street of her parent's home. She slowed as she approached the address. Toes tingling again, she spied Beck and her boyfriend Jared retrieving groceries from the trunk of his car parked in front of the house. They were laughing, happy in the moment. Turning on the emergency blinkers, Amara stopped the van and motioned for the car behind her to go around. She last saw Beck at John's memorial service where the floating three-dimensional Global Conservancy tattoo of Earth's profile from space appropriated ninety percent of Beck's face.

Now, Amara stared in wonder. The young woman across the street appeared fresh, not a blemish on her silky skin. She was in the spring of her life, thin and lithe in her Goth clothes and Army boots, a ring through her nose. She watched the two enter the house.

The need to go to Beck pulled at Amara. Suddenly, she felt compelled to warn her sister of the dangers of dating a doper with unintentional inclinations of sucking everything sweet and wholesome out of her young life. Without forethought, as if a giant magnet had taken control of her body, Amara opened the door.

In one quick blink, the door disappeared.

Cold air rushed around her tingling feet and flushed face. The delayed sound waves of the door being ripped from its hinges flooded Amara's ears. Stunned, she watched as a noisy garbage truck skidded to a stop causing the separated van door to teeter and clang like a giant spinning top.

Chapter Eight

IN THE LA PETITE FLEUR VAN
TUESDAY, DECEMBER 14, 1999

On the dawn of the seventh day of reliving December 1999, Amara dressed and followed the smell of Farley's brewing coffee.

"Sleep well, love?" Farley asked as she entered the small kitchen.

Amara grunted. The last two nights had haunted her. Each time she closed her eyes, her mind played an unending loop of the flower van's door being ripped away by a twenty-five-ton garbage truck in a blink of time.

She opened the refrigerator for her green juice. Farley told everyone at the diner about her spinach and banana smoothies, expanding his face in horrid amusement. She countered with, "This, from a man who eats fried sheep organs"

"I met an elderly couple from down the street," Farley said as he lowered his newspaper. "They're seeking a live-in to share their rather large house in exchange for light housekeeping duties. Interested?"

Amara wasn't. She'd done her last load of laundry the day she'd downloaded the housekeeper app onto Rosie's operating system.

Besides, she was content playing Farley's petulant boarder. She smiled to herself, she was becoming her daughter, dispensing dirty dishes and lippy responses everywhere.

"What's so funny?" Farley asked.

She retrieved a mostly clean straw from the sink and stuck it in the blender's jar half-full of the previous night's green go juice. She sat across from Farley at his breakfast table. "I can't remember the last time I washed linens or dishes."

From behind his newspaper, Farley cleared his throat.

"What are you doing today?" she asked.

"Washing linens and dishes."

"Oh." She stabbed at her goo with the straw. "Tandy wants me to work a double. He's slammed with Christmas orders on top of his regular ones."

"Illusions get dusty, too," came a response from behind a wall of Christmas decoration ads.

"I'll clean when I get home tonight."

"Is that a promise?"

At work, the customer from across the river had ordered another cheapskate special, what the floral arrangers called a vase of asters and baby's breath. Waiting for the light to change, Amara noticed the car in front of her. It was the tan car that had almost clipped the van's bumper the last time she turned into the Quarry Building office complex, the day the police officer stopped her from driving over a cliff of rocks and the garbage truck tore off the van door. The light changed and she followed the careless driver into the parking lot. The car turned right while Amara followed the arrows to visitor parking. As she approached the building, she saw a man get out of the car and head her way. His gait reminded her of someone she thought she should know.

"Better get away from this guy before a file cabinet falls on my head," she half-joked to herself.

The receptionist wasn't at the black marbled counter in the lobby of Chatham & Wright. No way was she leaving the flowers at the front desk. Barton, another delivery driver, had warned her that if customers called to complain about not receiving their flowers, Tandy deducted the second delivery from their pay. She followed a side hallway to a conference room with glass doors. The room was filled with people in business suits. She lifted her hand, ready to knock on the door, when a man's voice from behind her asked, "Flowers? For me?"

Ignoring the person, she peered through the glass panel, searching for the receptionist she'd left the flowers with on her previous visit.

"Who are they for?"

She turned and there he was, the man from the tan car. Her heart skipped a beat as she whispered, "John?"

"That's me," the young man said.

Her throat tightened. She stared in wonder. Yet, something inside urged her to flee. She shoved the flowers into his chest and ran from the office and out of the building. She jumped into the Odyssey. The repaired van door moaned as she pulled it shut. Gripping the steering wheel, she hyperventilated on humid, floral air.

"Ahhhhh!" she yelled. She jumped from the van and rushed to the front bricked plaza. Facing an army of vehicles in the complex's parking lot, her panic rose through her chest. Farley's voice called out to her, "If you meet up with someone from your past, stay away from vehicles and roads." Unable to move, she locked her knees and braced for impact.

A warm hand gripped her arm.

She felt his familiar energy instantly. Her squinted eyes relaxed. "Are you all right?"

She didn't answer him but didn't pull away either.

"Come inside," he said.

She allowed him to guide her but resisted when he tried to escort her through the revolving doors.

"Can I get you some water?" His quiet voice calmed her.

"No," she whispered. She feared that if she spoke any louder, slabs of glass would fall on them both. She permitted herself to gaze at him. Oh, those beautiful, sad, blue eyes. She restrained herself from cupping his face, from brushing his lips with her thumbs.

"You're shaking all over. Let's go in where it's warm. Something has upset you. Is there someone I should call?"

For almost fifty years, he had been her emergency contact. She cupped her hands over her face and wept. Bottled up loneliness spilled into her palms. Unable to stop herself, Amara buried her hands and face into his chest, allowing him to put an arm around her. He smelled of his favorite soap. It took her back to their life and to their bed.

Amara pushed away and wiped her face with the back of her hand. "Sorry. Sorry. Sorry to cause so much trouble." Trying to make light of the situation, she added, "I'm having a day."

His concerned smile evoked such a force of yearning in her that she emitted a high-pitched squeak as muffled sobs tried to escape her body. She tucked her hands into her armpits and held her breath.

"Are you going to be all right?"

She nodded. Where was her bio-relaxer app when she needed it? "I'm fine. My doctor has me on some new medication. It makes me edgy." She buttoned her coat and headed for the van.

"Are you sure you're okay to drive?" John asked as he

followed her.

Now all business, she asked, "Did Battina Laske get her flowers?"

"I'll see that she does," he said.

"Good," Amara said. "I hope she enjoys them as much as La Petite Fleur enjoyed delivering them." Tandy insisted that all the drivers say this, claiming the more a customer heard the name of the business, the more likely she, or he, was to call up and order more.

"It's a prank," John admitted in an attempt to keep the conversation going. "That's why I wanted to take them instead of you delivering them in person. Save everyone the embarrassment."

"I don't understand," Amara said as she climbed into the van.

He raked his fingers through his hair, a habit Amara knew too well. He did it whenever he was uncomfortable with the direction a conversation was headed.

She really needed to get away because she feared she'd do something stupid like kiss her once-dead husband. If Farley caught wind of this, he'd fall into a tailspin and bounce off one of his time channels.

"Some of the guys . . . they're making mischief," he trailed off, then asked, "I'm afraid I didn't get your name. By the way, how do you know mine? Have we met before?" When she didn't respond, he continued, "The guys are just having a little fun. At Laske's expense, I'm afraid. You see, *Miss* Laske in real life is Norman Laske. He prefers a dress and pumps to a suit and tie, if you will."

"Where I'm from, what they're doing is harassment. You'd be required to complete awareness training or go to jail," she said as she started the van.

John looked away, his classic defensive move while thinking up a rebuttal. "It's just a bit of fun. Tasteless really, but quite harmless. Besides, sending flowers is *not* illegal in Virginia. Where did you say you were from?"

"I didn't, Mr. Darnley," she said and backed out of the parking slip.

At the light, she realized her mistake and smacked her forehead. "Smooth move, Graves. How are you supposed to know his last name?" And, at the next light, she pondered the notion that she hadn't experienced any of the warning signs Farley and the others had told her about when meeting someone from her past, no tingling or itching body parts, no rushing sounds of trains.

Chapter Nine

AT THE WAY BACK DINER
WEDNESDAY, DECEMBER 15, 1999

The next morning Amara met up with Ramesh at the diner before her shift at the flower shop. "You're not going to believe what happened yesterday," she said as he slid in the booth across from her. She waited for the waitress to serve their tea, then said, "I talked to my dead husband."

Ramesh rubbed the back of his neck. "How's that work?"

"I made a delivery to the Quarry Building on South Side. And there he was."

"Did the building implode?"

"That's the crazy thing. We talked and nothing happened." She left out the part where she had a panic attack and he consoled her by putting an arm around her.

"That *is* crazy. Does Farley know?"

"No! And don't say anything," she said. "Because of the garbage truck mishap, he's already told Tandy that he doesn't like me driving. I don't want to give him a reason to make me quit."

"Make you quit? You sound like he's your father or something," Ramesh laughed.

"You're right. I'm a responsible adult." After a sip of tea, she asked, "What do you suppose it means?"

"Perhaps he's fallen into this same time channel?"

"But he didn't recognize me. In fact, he asked for my name."

"If that's the case, don't confide in him, Alice. You'll only freak him out."

"My name is Amara." She paused, then asked, "What's your real name?"

"Radish," he shrugged. "I hate it. I prefer my Way Back name. Ramesh."

"You miss your family?"

"My boys talk back. My sister's family depends on me because her husband slithered back to India. My wife's sleeping with someone else. So, no, not really." He looked out the grimy window and added, "I've grown fond of the freedom of no responsibilities. Sweeping crumbs is pleasant enough work for me."

Hearing Ramesh's quest for a more simple life, Amara realized things were just as uncertain here as in the time she had come from. She said, "Farley says our actions don't matter. That we can't prevent or mitigate bad things we know are going to happen. Have you tried, you know, to stop something bad from happening?"

"You mean like, 'Hello, Mr. Kennedy, you don't know me, but you and your wife and sister-in-law should take the ferry to your cousin's wedding on Martha's Vineyard.' That kind of something?"

Amara rubbed the goosebumps on her arm and nodded at his reference to the July 1999 plane crash off the coast of Martha's Vineyard, killing John Kennedy, Jr., his wife Carolyn, and her sister Lauren.

"I called from a pay phone somewhere on Broadway to warn him." Pulling his stocking cap off, he scratched at his hat head. "It's amazing how easy it is to hack into phone systems here. I spoofed a number from inside the control tower of JFK to warn them about that Egyptian flight that just went down in October." He snapped his fingers and said, "Two hundred and seventeen souls. Vanished. Can you imagine what they were all thinking right before the plane crashed into the water?"

"That's a ghoulish thought. You're weird. How do you remember stuff like that?"

"I wanted to be an air-traffic controller. As a kid I memorized every catastrophe in aviation history." He tapped his temple and added, "I used to have total recall. Won the state spelling bee competition four years in a row. But, now, not as much."

"Are you going to try to do something about 9/11?"

"I've thought about it."

"Maybe you could hack the airlines' systems and cancel the flights."

He shrugged. "That's like changing the date of the execution from Tuesday to Wednesday. It's still going to happen."

They sat in silence, then Amara asked, "Have you ever tried to do anything for personal gain? Like betting on an outcome you know is going to happen?"

"You mean like putting all your November rent money on the Yankees to win the World Series this year?"

"Did you?"

"I lost the chit. I put it in my wallet and when I went to collect my winnings, it wasn't there."

Her face wrinkled with uncertainty.

"While we're skating in this other time lane, where we're not supposed to be, we can't affect the future. If I wasn't meant to win big on a ball game, then it's *never* going to happen."

"So, why are we here?" she asked in frustration.

"Not for some greater cause, if that's what you're thinking. I believe something in our own time got hosed up and we're somehow collateral damage."

"Do you have any proof of this?"

"Until you showed up, most of us were from before '45. The first proof of a pattern. But that's all we've got."

"Are there similarities in our profiles?"

"What do you mean?"

"Like, what was everybody doing at the moment it happened to them, that sort of stuff."

"Oh, social engineering? Doesn't work."

Anxious to figure out how she got here, Amara said, "How do you know it doesn't work? We need to have a profile made up of everyone on . . . on . . . everything. What we do, where we live, our family. Everything. Given her background, I'm surprised Brenda hasn't been all over this."

"We tried it. But for some reason the data kept changing or we'd lose what we collected. Like my winning World Series ticket." He leaned over the table. "Each time it seemed we'd uncovered the 'why' and 'how,' things would change."

"What kind of changes?"

"You, for example. Until now, no one's come from '49. And this thing with your husband . . ." he twirled a spoon on the tabletop, "no one, before you, talked to a family member without . . . you know?"

Ramesh had a point. Her encounter with John hadn't erupted into the kind of personal mayhem Farley predicted. However, what it had done was awakened a yearning for her husband that she could not deny.

Christmas 1999 was the first holiday the Graves family had spent apart. Using school and work as reasonable excuses, Amara and Beck stayed at home over the objections of a protesting Audrey who left for Texas two days before Christmas Eve. Beck wanted to invite friends over and raid their parent's liquor cabinet. Amara, the shy and responsible one, hated sophomoric parties and, besides, her parents trusted her to keep the house from burning down while they were away. The sisters compromised. Each invited one person to celebrate Christmas Eve. Beck asked her boyfriend Jared.

A car horn's beep brought Amara's attention back to the road. "Who did I invite?" she asked the dashboard as she turned up the alley behind the flower shop to load the van with the morning's orders. Usually, when it came to recalling names, Amara would ask John or Rosie, or call Megs. Anxiety rippled through her as she realized she was now cut off from everyone she had ever known, everyone who had ever loved her.

Backing the van into the warehouse, she trolled through the graveyard of old school friends' names but came up with nothing. All she remembered about that particular Christmas was catching Jared rummaging through her mother's drawers for something to sell for drugs. She told him to leave. He left, but not until he drove a stone wedge between the sisters. To this day, Beck had nothing but a cold shoulder for her older sibling.

Amara's last order of the morning was near her Grace Street home. To her recollection about her time with Beck at Grace Street, they were both probably out of the house at this time of day so she decided to drop by for a visit. Her encounter with John convinced her that she wasn't like the others. It had bolstered her confidence.

The porch's winter shade felt like the inside of Tandy's flower coolers. The spare key wasn't under the brick by the door so she tried the doorknob. It turned. The door resisted as if a rug or some-thing was caught underneath but finally gave way. Pocket doors to the left were drawn and the Pullman-style hallway created a dark tunnel effect as a spot of light from a transom window in the back of the house blinded her.

Above, two thumps were followed by creaking floor boards.

There was that magnetic pull again, the one she felt when she saw Beck on the street a few days ago. Her toes tingled.

"Beck?" someone called out.

Amara covered her mouth. The voice coming from above was her own.

Footsteps were now in the upstairs hallway.

Her hands burning, she sensed that this would not end well if she stayed. Quickly, she stepped backward and over the threshold. Without her help, the door slammed in her face, rattling the pineapple door knocker. Amara leapt over the brick stairs onto the walkway and bounded down the block toward her van. She dared not look over her shoulder.

At the corner she twirled around in search of the flower van. She'd parked it on the corner, this corner, a corner with no parking restriction or fire hydrant. It was gone. Walking back to the shop, she practiced what she'd say to Tandy when he asked about his delivery vehicle.

Chapter Ten

Tandy and Farley agreed that it would not be prudent to report the vanished van to the police. Two days had passed and it still hadn't turned up. With no van to deliver flowers, Amara was given a new assignment. Sitting on a wobbly chair in the closet-turned-office under the stairs, she was keying work orders into a spreadsheet. She had four grocery bags' worth to go before the journal was current. How archaic. Written retail sales transactions were as obsolete as pencils. When she suggested a point-of-purchase entry system, her employer loudly objected.

The bell on the shop door jingled. She heard Martha, a high schooler working the Christmas season, ask, "Can I help you?"

"Yes, please."

Amara stopped mid keystroke. It was him.

"I'm looking for something for my mother for Christmas."

Tapping young Martha's shoulder, Amara said, "I've got this one. How about restocking the card rack?" She waited for Martha to duck into the back room before she said, "Hi."

"It's you," he said. His hair was tousled as if he'd just toweled it dry from a morning shower. Seeing him like this, the sensation of early morning nuzzlings in their bed trickled through her.

Martha returned with a stack of greeting cards for the revolving card rack. Amara watched John scratch at his chin. She'd forgotten how fair he had been, that smattering of freckles across the bridge of his nose, and how his clear blue eyes turned green when he wore his favorite wool heather scarf, now tied around his neck. She remembered the spicy smell of that neck. Her knees wobbled. She leaned against the counter. "You're looking for something for your mother for Christmas?"

"Ah, yeah. Thought I'd give her a nice plant or something," he said in shy hesitance.

Being married to the man in front of her for forty-five years, Amara usually figured out what he wanted before he, himself, did. He didn't come in here to buy his mother a houseplant. He came looking for her. Neither Farley nor this wacked-out universe was going to like this situation one bit. Why? Because she hadn't gone looking for John, he'd sought her out.

"I live in the Fan. Across from Dusty's Downstairs Grill. Didn't know this place was here until you delivered . . ."

Tandy charged in and stood in front of the flower cooler. "Alice, any amaryllis left?"

John busied himself with the curio cabinet of glass paperweights while Amara helped Tandy.

"Flowering?" she asked John after Tandy went back to the arranging room.

"Excuse me?"

"I bet she likes flowering plants."

He shrugged. "I guess. Could you recommend something? Alice, is it?"

Ignoring his question about her name, Amara pointed to a shelf of potted plants, recalling the numerous pots of African violets his mother tended in her sunroom. Each time they visited Mrs. Darnley pointed out to Amara that the original plant was a gift from a previous girlfriend of John's. A sensation of *déjà vu* crawled up her spine as she said, "How about a nice African violet? A pink one. Should we send an order . . ." she almost asked him if the plant might be shipped to his parents' address in Alexandria, Virginia. But she caught herself. Instead she asked, "Cash or credit card?"

After paying for the plant, he said, "Some friends and I are having Christmas drinks at Buddy's tonight. If you're around, stop by."

The bell over the door jingled and a gaggle of customers in goose down coats waddled into the shop.

"What was that all about?" Martha asked as she waved goodbye to John.

"I think he just asked me out for drinks," Amara said.

"Well, he left his plant. Should I go after him?"

"No, put it on the will-call shelf. He'll be back."

"He's cute," Martha said, "but, isn't he a little . . . ah . . . young for you?"

Resenting Martha's cheeky observation, Amara replied, "Apparently, he doesn't think so."

After locking up at La Petite Fleur, Amara stopped by Bombay's for a bowl of soup. She begged Ramesh to go with her to Buddy's.

"No. No way," Ramesh said, yanking at his apron strings. "I want no part in this. You want to get yourself hurt, that's your business. Besides, that place is haunted."

"Haunted? What do you mean?" Amara asked.

"Just what I said. It's haunted." He flicked off the lights and nudged her to go through the back door. "The place gives me the heebie-jeebies."

"Do you suppose there's someone in there from *your* past?" Amara asked.

"I don't think so. It's just . . . the hair on my arms curl whenever I get near the place."

Teasing, she offered, "Maybe it's a distant relative come to take you back to India."

Giving in, he opened the door of his little sedan and said, "Get in. But if I feel even a little bit queasy, I'm out of there and you're finding your own way home."

At first, the black lacquered door refused to open so she bumped it with her hip and it gave way to a hall of laughter and clinking glasses. They rushed through a gauntlet of smokers to reach the nonsmoking section of the bar in the back.

John sat at the end of a long eight top with six or seven others. Their loud conversations meshed with Van the Man's "Brown Eyed Girl" belting from a giant speaker on a shelf swinging from the ceiling over the booth. He recognized her right away and stood to offer his seat.

She waved and shouted, "Can't stay long," then nodded at Ramesh, who she noticed looked unusually pale for a man of his heritage. Back home in 2049, her next-door neighbor, a woman from Mumbai, had all the melanin eradicated from her skin cells. Like a vampire she couldn't go outside during the day. In the second she looked at Ramesh, she wondered where he would be in 2049. If she ever made it back, she promised herself she'd go find him.

"What's your pleasure for Christmas cheer?" John asked.

"Ginger ale," Ramesh replied.

"I'll have the same," Amara said.

"Caroline, another scotch and two ginger ales," he shouted over the fray to the waitress at the end of the bar. Then to Amara he said, "I'm glad you could make it."

Amara picked up on John's tipsy weave. He drank a lot in their early years. After the kids came along, however, he curtailed his drinking to special occasions and his monthly poker night. Then, as the kids entered high school and grew independent, John renewed his intimate relationship with Johnny Walker. The pair strode, arm in arm, out of her life on her fortieth birthday. A month after he left her, the firm fired him without cause. Amara and John reconciled after two years of separation and he moved back into Grace Street. Their first night back together, he told her that he had forgiven her. She never understood why she required forgiveness. He was the one who had left. He was the one who had an affair. But she didn't want to argue about it. All that mattered was he was back where he belonged, with her.

"This is my friend Ramesh," Amara yelled. She'd let John make up his own mind about her relationship with the man who had brought her to the party.

Abruptly, the Irishman's wailing stopped, replaced by the fast *umf-umf-umf* of a techno beat. As Amara and Ramesh accepted their drinks from Caroline, John went around the table with introductions. Amara nodded, not bothering to keep up with names, their faces hidden by the dark shadow of the mammoth speaker shelf. Then she saw the outline of the long horsey face of her sister's friend from high school.

"This is George and Nancy Biddle and their daughter Katherina," John said as he introduced the last people at the table.

Amara's skin tingled like it did the day she went into her parent's house. Claustrophobia crept up on her as the music changed again. This time Rod Stewart was screaming about hot legs wearing him out. In the background the sound of a distant train roared toward her. Setting her drink on the table, she looked around for Ramesh. Then, *boom!* In an instant, the music's volume dropped and voices muffled as if her ears had been plugged with cotton. She found herself staring close-up at the dirty hexagon-tiled floor. In contrast to the cold, smelly floor, she felt something warm spreading over her forehead.

"Move!" someone yelled. "Get out of the way. Give her some room, you morons."

How did she get on the floor? Amara thought.

The person attacking everyone's character crouched next to Amara and said, "I'm Honey. I'm a nurse so you relax and I'll make everything okay."

"What happened?" John's voice sounded so far away.

"John, you and everybody else need to stand back and give her some air."

"What happened?" someone else called out.

"Stereo speaker, man. I saw it. Just vibrated itself off the shelf," another helpful bystander testified.

"Yuck, look at all the blood."

Through all the haze, Amara was having trouble understanding who they were talking about and why she was on the floor. As she made an effort to sit up, Nurse Honey pressed a wad of paper napkins against her forehead, causing her to fall back. "You stay right there."

Amara pushed at the nurse's arm and wrestled her way to a sitting position.

The nurse pressed on the wound again and pulled the napkins away, blood dripping onto the sleeve of her blouse. "There's a lot of blood but that's normal for a head wound. It's right above your hairline."

"Head wound?" Amara swatted at the nurse's hand. "Where's Ramesh?"

"The guy you came in here with?" Caroline the waitress asked. "I saw him rush out. Looked like he was gonna barf all over himself."

Raising her arms, Amara snapped her fingers at Nurse Honey and Caroline to help her up.

"Take it slow," Nurse Honey said. "You might need a stitch or two. That's a pretty nasty gash."

John was at her side. "Honey, we need to get her checked out."

"Retreat's ER is closest. My car's right outside."

Amara felt John's hand latch onto the back of her arm. "Guys, help me carry her out to Honey's car."

Amara lifted her arm from John's grip and said, "I can walk on my own, thank you." A path to the front door quietly opened. Still uncertain as to what had just happened, Amara left more quickly than anyone had expected. Before the door closed, she heard the braying laughter of Keekee Biddle, the woman John had left her for after eighteen years of marriage.

Chapter Eleven

Nurse Honey and the waitress Caroline sat across from Amara and John in the hospital's waiting room. A couple sitting in the row of chairs behind Amara and John was having a whispered argument. Apparently, he loved her but wasn't *in* love with her. The girl slapped the boy. John winced at the boy's obtuse backpedaling.

The couple's argument sparked a memory for Amara. She hadn't thought of Dr. Debbie in years. Dr. Deborah McLaury was Amara's psychology professor and surrogate parent after Ted and Audrey emigrated to Texas. Amara and the professor had become good friends outside of the classroom. At a campus pub, they drank coffee and yarned on about the fallacies of true love and finding one's soul mate.

Placing his hand on her arm, John asked, "How are you feeling?"

Amara's arm tingled as the ghost of Dr. Debbie whispered to her, "Find the person who'd do anything for you. Donate a kidney. Take a bullet without hesitation."

"Would you donate a kidney to someone you were *in* love with?"

she asked John.

Chuckling, he stood and stretched. "It's been over thirty minutes since you signed in. I'll find out what's keeping them."

Dr. Debbie's presence was back, and she whispered, "Being *in* love is a metaphysical condition that wanes with time. Don't confuse passion for love, Amara. Find someone who loves you in spite of your hairy upper lip and bad habits. That's a real happily ever after story."

"What about love at first sight? Do you think that's possible?" Amara had asked Dr. Debbie.

"You mean like when your eyes lock with his baby blues and," she snapped her fingers, "BAM! the eternal flame ignites?"

"I guess so," Amara had said.

"Fairy-tale drivel. A Stanford study, which I contributed to by the way, has proved that people who married their," she made air quotations, "'soul mates' have a greater chance at divorce than couples who claimed they fell in love over time."

Amara watched John walk toward the nurses' station. If she had to say, their love, at first, wasn't the lusty passionate kind, not in the early years of their marriage anyway.

In his defense, he was attentive to their family's needs. As her career took off and she spent weeks at a time away from home, he became the primary provider to Aiden and Kimberly. To his credit, he cried at Aiden's wedding. As her financial contribution to the family outpaced his, they both agreed he would focus on his work for fair housing laws and other legal aid endeavors. Unfortunately, his passion for helping the oppressed—pro bono clients—led to his dismissal from the firm.

He waved at her from the nurses' station.

Before their brief separation, she sometimes felt like he was somewhere else, with someone else. But afterward, when he returned to their bed, things felt different, as if she was with a different man. Their passion for each other seemed boundless, almost as though their love story had just begun, each passing year bringing more and more of the attentive, and lusty, type of love Dr. Debbie had cautioned her against.

He sat back in the chair next to hers.

"So how do you know Keekee Biddle?" Amara asked.

"You know Katherina?" John asked.

"She's friends with my . . . a girl I know," she said.

"Miss Biddle's father is one of my firm's clients," he said. "And like all the Philadelphia Biddles, she's a handful."

"Are you dating her?" Amara asked.

He coughed over a laugh and said, "She's only a senior in high school."

As if that answered her question.

A nurse called out, "Alice. Alice Epps?"

An hour later, they all politely argued in front of the hospital over who would take Amara home. She told them that she would call Ramesh to pick her up. She didn't want John to know where she lived. As winter winds swirled around them, the two women hustled to Honey's car, not looking back or waving goodbye. John lingered behind.

"I'll wait with you," he said. "Ramesh can drop me off at my car."

"I'm not sure when he'll make it. It'll be awhile. Better catch a ride with them."

"I'll wait with you," he insisted.

Making the excuse of calling Ramesh, Amara went back inside the hospital and found an exit on the other side of the building. Farley's house was only four or five blocks to the east. She'd walk home. The cold air would clear her mind. Her head was on fire where a boyish intern had punctured holes into her scalp for a couple of stitches.

She didn't hear him come up beside her.

"Couldn't get Ramesh on the phone? Why don't you let me take you home?"

Caught in her retreat, she faced him and said, "You're too dangerous to be around."

"Hey, don't blame me for the whims of a stereo speaker." He threaded his arm through hers and walked her to his car. When they got to Grove and Mercer, she said, "I'll just get out here. I can walk the rest of the way."

"My father would have my head if I didn't see the lady to her door," he said as he turned on Mercer. "Which one?"

She pointed to Farley's house and reached for the door handle before the car came to a complete stop.

He gave her left hand, which was resting on the center console, a quick squeeze. "That day you came to my office building, you called me by my name. Ever since, I've been racking my brain trying to recall where we've met. Were you a witness in court, a defendant's family member?"

She froze at his questions. Unable to come up with a reasonable explanation, she bugged her eyes at him with a condescending how should I know stare.

He continued, "I mean, I gotta tell ya, something happened to me when we talked that first day, that day you came to the office. You're a hard woman to forget, Alice Epps. And I'm not just saying this to up my chances of getting a date with you."

"Your name was on the order slip?" she answered with a question. "I just assumed you were the guy. On the order slip. The person who ordered the flowers." She relaxed, happy with her lie.

"But I didn't order the flowers," he said softly, as if to himself.

"Look, it doesn't matter. However it happened, I'm happy we met. I hope you feel the same."

He leaned closer toward her.

In a panic, she hopped out of the car fearing he'd try to kiss her, or something.

"Alice?" he called after her, "I'll come by tomorrow to check on you, all right?"

"No reason to, I'm fine. Thanks for the ride." She waved and hurried up the steps and into the house.

The next morning Ramesh, Tandy, and Brenda greeted Amara and Farley in the back booth of the Way Back Diner. As she mopped up pancake syrup with a half-eaten biscuit bottom stolen from Ramesh's plate, Brenda announced that she had an update on Desi Kurt's friends.

The name Desi Kurts resonated with Amara but she couldn't remember how or why, her head still foggy from the speaker incident. "Desi Kurts? Who is he?"

Brenda squinted one eye and directed her question at Farley, "What happened to her?"

"I can speak for myself," Amara protested.

"Okay, why's there a hospital bandage the size of a cinder-block plastered on the front of your head?" Biscuit bits spewed from Brenda's lips. "Farley, I'm not comfortable talking about our business in the presence of an unknown."

"Stop it, Brenda. You know she's one of us." He leaned over the table and lowered his voice to ask, "Have you gone off the decaf, again?"

"These times call for desperate measures. I need full strength, Far."

Amara interrupted the spat, and joined in the whispering, "A stereo speaker fell on my head."

"Where?" Brenda asked. She rummaged in her worn satchel and pulled out a manila file folder, opened it, and started scribbling. "Well?"

"Buddy's," Amara answered. She felt Ramesh fidgeting by her side.

"Were you around people who knew you before?" Brenda asked.

Here was Amara's moment for true confessions. She hadn't told Farley about John or about him seeking her out at the flower shop. Then she recalled, right before things went off course at Buddy's, John had introduced her to Keekee Biddle.

"Alice?" Brenda asked. "Who. Did. You. See. At Buddy's? Was it someone close to you?"

Amara patted the bandage. She'd gotten a good look at the gash in the bathroom's mirror earlier. It looked better than it felt. Her head was throbbing.

"Alice, love, you with us?" Farley asked.

Ramesh coughed into his paper napkin.

She patted the bandage again. "I'm fine. What were we talking about?"

"You were going to tell us who you saw at Buddy's," Brenda said, her carotid artery pulsing under her fleshy neck.

"Keekee Biddle, Katherina Biddle," she said. "She was there. Someone introduced me to her."

Ramesh rolled his eyes at her. She kicked him under the table, signaling to him that they couldn't know about John, not yet.

"And how did you know this Katherina Biddle person?" Brenda asked. More scribbling.

"She and my sister were classmates."

"There it is," Brenda pointed her pencil nub at Farley. To Amara, she said, "If you know what's good for you, stay away from that person and that place."

Eventually, maybe, Amara would tell them about John, but not now. He had come back to her and she didn't want to lose him for a third time. What the Way Backers didn't know wouldn't hurt them, she reasoned.

Brenda moved on with her progress report, "Desi, real name Desmond Lawrence Kurts, was last seen with what seem to be federal government employees."

"Which agency?" Farley asked.

"Hit a dead end. The vehicle's registered to the federal General Services Administration."

"I'll take a crack at it," Ramesh offered. "Use the same ID and password as last time?"

"Send me what you find to this account." Brenda wrote an email address on a napkin. "The account will self-delete in twelve hours from noon today."

"Has anyone been to his house?" Tandy asked.

"A woman answered his home phone when I called," Brenda said. "She said he hasn't slept there since last Tuesday. We saw him here last Wednesday, so he's left town or somebody ought to be checking the morgue."

"Did he ever give you his locator, Far?"

"Don't recall."

"They got him then," Brenda said.

Amara asked, "Can you describe this guy?" She was thinking about the flashing cultural center marquee in 2049 announcing the futurist Desmond Kurts' appearance on New Year's Eve.

"Small stature, can't miss the tumbleweed of red hair," Brenda said. "Far, do you have a picture of him?"

"At the command center," Farley said, meaning his basement. "Do you know him, or did you know him?" he asked Amara.

"From my time, Richmond is having a mid-twenty-first-century party and a Dr. Desmond Kurts is the guest speaker on the topic of bending time," she explained. "I saw his holograph at a theater marquee."

Everyone, except Ramesh, laughed at Amara's comment.

"That's rich," Tandy said.

"What's so funny?" Amara asked.

"'*Dr.*' Desmond Kurts?" Brenda asked. "Desi Kurts can barely find his way out the front door, let alone matriculate from an accredited institution. I dare say he's doctoral material, especially on a topic as heady as time."

"Maybe you've been living in the past so long that you've forgotten about the advancements in cerebral cortex enhancements," Amara said. "Practical applications were mainstreamed by the late forties. They're called CCEs and are as common as bone regenerations."

Tandy snickered. "Desi would need an entire brain replacement."

"That's happening, too!" Amara said. She'd never met this Desi person and found herself offended at their bias toward a person's intellectual capacity. "Don't you see? If it's the same guy, it must mean there's a way out of this fun house of torture!"

For a moment, everyone seemed to ponder her suggestion.

"Nah," Tandy said, waving her off. "It's not the same dude. No way."

"What year did he say he was from?" Amara asked.

"He told us he came from 2040," Brenda answered.

"So, let's assume he went back to '40. That would have given him enough time to get a CCE and go on to become a rock star on the public speaking circuit, cashing in on his Way Back experience," Amara reasoned.

"Not necessarily," Brenda debated. "Your conclusion that *our* Desi is living in the future is based on an illogical assumption. All the proof you have is a common name. It's a stretch calling it a probable outcome."

"When we find the people Desi went with, we can let them know that there are more of us," Amara said.

"Far," Brenda pleaded, "make her stop."

"Lambchop," Farley said, stacking his hands over Amara's, "there's a terribly wide gap between our muddleheaded Desi getting into a car with two unknowns and your Dr. Kurts who claims to know how to bend time. I'll show you Desi's picture when we get home this evening. If you feel it's the same person, we'll have to figure out what to do about it. Together. Don't go to the authorities on your own."

"Why not?" Amara asked. "What will happen?"

"Did you tell her what happened to Funky Man?" Brenda asked.

"Who's Funky Man?" Ramesh asked.

The waitress appeared with a coffee pot and checks. "Farley, if y'all are finished with your breakfast, y'all need to take all this back to the future nonsense somewheres else. I got customers waitin' for a table."

Chapter Twelve

On her way over to the flower shop, Amara examined why she didn't want Farley to know about John. First, he'd absolutely forbid her to see him again and then go on about how dangerous it was to associate with a person from her past. Then, he'd cite the garbage truck incident when she'd tried to speak to Beck and, now, the speaker falling on her head the moment she was introduced to Keekee Biddle. But nothing like that had happened with John. Each time they met, from the first time, she experienced only mild anxiety and tingling in a place that *wasn't* her toes or fingers.

After entering the last sales slip from the fourth grocery bag into the shop's computer, she found Tandy in the workroom putting together a casket spray of roses and carnations. By 2049, embalming fluids and caustic metal caskets had been outlawed for a decade. Ordinary people opted for cremation with their ashes planted with a tree or placed in a glitzy outer space columbarium. Families with infinite legacy credits opted for organic replacements and eternal life. But, she supposed, the occasion of one's bodily transition would still call for flowers.

"Either let me write some code for a point-of-sale program or get someone else to enter the sales slips," she said.

"Accounting one-oh-one. Paper is proof. You've never been audited by the IRS, have you?" He clipped the stem of a white rose and handed the flower to her.

"At least let me drive over to Circuit City and buy a backup drive. I can write you a simple program to automatically backup each day," she offered. Since the world became enshrouded in all the giant data clouds, Amara hadn't thought about data backup procedures in years. But here she was, thinking about it.

Over the telephone system's intercom, Martha announced, "Alice, line one."

She reached for the phone mounted on a pole beside Tandy's workstation and pressed line one. "Alice Epps, how may I help you?" She sniffed at the rose's sweetness.

"Alice! You're at work. How are you feeling today?"

His voice, so close to her ear, aroused her and caused her to blush. She cleared her throat to stall while thinking of what to say to him. "You forgot your mother's gift. It's on our customer will-call shelf. We're open until six tonight. If you let me know when you plan to pick it up, I'll let our front desk know."

"I get it, you can't talk right now. So listen. I'm just going to come out and say it. Last night. In the car. It felt like we were together, you know, as a couple. Didn't you feel it?"

The autopod tryst with him flashed in Amara's head.

When she didn't answer his question, he said, "I feel like we've made a connection on a very deep level. Don't you?" He waited for her to answer and when she didn't, he asked, "May I take you out to dinner tonight?"

Tandy interjected. "Offer to deliver it and don't forget to say, 'hope you enjoy them as much as La Petite Fleur enjoyed delivering them.'"

"Hold, please." She put John on hold, turned to Tandy and asked, "Are you saying I can deliver the plant?"

Tandy realized his mistake. "We'll get one of the guys to add it to their route."

"I'm going stir-crazy. Please, put me back on deliveries."

Tandy's fingertips rubbed across his cowboy mustache. "The backup thing is a good idea. Get some money out of the register and go buy one. Let me think on putting you back on deliveries."

"Thanks!"

"But get back here as soon as you can. I need you up front. I'm sure you've noticed Martha's not the sharpest knife in the drawer. She struggles with counting out a customer's change."

At the front desk, Amara found Martha at the counter taping silk mums to the ends of the store's promotional pens and arranging them in a glass bowl. Amara went to the phone and picked up on line one. "John?" She couldn't go through with this, torturing them both. She had to refuse him.

"Yes?"

"Look, ah, you're a nice guy but we're not supposed to date customers."

Martha's head popped up from her task. This company policy was news to her. Amara turned her back to Martha.

"That's the silliest rule I've ever heard," John said.

"Yeah, Tandy never told me we couldn't—" Martha pitched in.

Amara looked over her shoulder. "Do you mind?"

"Please have dinner with me tonight," John said. "I can pick you up at the shop. What time do you get off?"

"I'm not sure that's a good idea," she said.

"Last night in the car, I felt something pulling us together. There's something there, even if you won't admit it. Let's just explore it. See where it takes us. Have dinner with me tonight."

"Like I said, I don't think that's a good idea," she repeated. Creative lying wasn't her best skill.

"Come on," he urged, "it's just dinner."

"Our age difference," she mumbled, hoping Martha wouldn't hear.

"Our age difference?" He laughed. "What's a couple of years matter? Come on, what do you say? It's just dinner."

No, it wasn't just dinner, if only she could tell him the whole story.

"Are you there? There's this little place not far from where you live. I'll pick you up at seven."

She caved. "One dinner. I'll meet you at the restaurant."

"Great! You're going to love this place. It's new, called Mama Zoe's and it's on Main at Dogwood. On the corner. Can't miss it. See you at seven?"

"How about eight?" she said.

Farley met her at the door when she made it home at six-thirty. Together they made their way down the basement steps and into his Way Back command center. The top drawer of a metal file cabinet screeched as he pulled it out.

"I've not gotten around to making *your* file. We can do all that before the others get here."

"Can we do this another time?" Amara asked. "I have plans this evening."

"Oh?" Farley asked.

"I've made a friend and we're meeting for dinner at eight. Mama Zoe's? Do you know the place?"

"Is this person a Way Backer?" Farley asked.

"No. Does it matter?"

"I advise you not to get involved with people outside our group.

Too easy for things to slip out, you know, about our situation. Imagine what it would do to the person's sanity when they discover you're from another time. And I do mean *when* and not *if.* They always find out. And the damage it causes can be formidable." He pulled out a cardboard folder with "KURTS, D" written on the tab.

Together they sat at the wobbly card table beside his desk.

"Ah, here he is." Farley pushed an Instamatic photo in front of her. "Is this your Dr. Kurts?"

"There is no *my* Dr. Kurts. I was only reporting what I saw. I never met the man." She studied the picture. The unshaved man in the photo looked as if he was wearing every stitch of clothing he owned. Gnarly, sun-bleached tangles spewed from a broad swatch of dirty yellow bandana covering his forehead. His eyes had that lost stare that Amara was all too familiar with from her work at Hope Home. For the self-exiled, time had no relevance.

"As you can see, Desi had trouble adjusting to his new life," Farley said. "Funky Man made sure he got food and a place to sleep when it was cold out. He stayed away from people."

"This man looks mentally ill."

"Funky Man helped him," Farley said. "Usually, if you saw one, you saw the other."

Amara heard the faint catch in Farley's voice.

"Who is Funky Man?"

"Was," Farley corrected her. Then he went on, "What do you think? Is this Dr. Desmond Kurts?"

"It's hard to say. I only saw the marquee for a second as I passed it on my ride home from work." In her other life, the optic screens over her eyes replayed anything she needed to recall. Not having them now, she realized how dependent she'd become on her personal assistance services—the locator and contacts, her smart apartment, Rosie. "Where's the guy you call Funky Man? Maybe he can tell us where Kurts is."

"Funky Man's—"

BOOM, BOOM, BOOM! Someone was pounding on the front door.

"That's probably Tandy and Brenda," Farley said. "Look through Desi's file and see if you can uncover anything that may tie him to Dr. Kurts." Another round of pounding prompted him to call out as he mounted the stairs, "'Ang on. I'm coming!"

Amara's focus on Desi's picture was interrupted when she heard raised voices. She went to the bottom of the stairs and listened. Farley said something, then an unfamiliar voice responded. The front door slammed. When he appeared at the top of the stairs, he seemed anxious. She asked, "Not Tandy and Brenda?"

"Where is it?" he asked as he descended the steps.

"Where's what?"

He aimed his long finger at her. "This is not a game. People's lives are in danger. Give it to me."

"What are you talking about?"

He pointed at the ceiling. "Do you know who that was?"

She tossed him a shrug.

"Richmond Police. Detective Armstrong and one of his goons."

Amara shrugged, again. "So?"

He grabbed her by the arms. The strength in his thin hands surprised her. "This isn't a game, love. There are things . . . people who want us to disappear. Our memories erased, permanently deleted."

"I wouldn't mind disappearing from this place and going back to my real life."

"You don't understand. *This* is your real life now. Believe me when I say, you can't go back. And it's people like Detective Armstrong who'll see that you don't."

"I'm confused. Are you saying it's possible to go back but there are people preventing that from happening?"

He eased back into one of the folding chairs and said, "Come sit with me."

Out of habit, Amara blinked, expecting to see her news crawler and the time flash before her eyes. But there was nothing. "What time is it? I've got to go."

"You can't," he said.

"What do you mean I can't? You can't hold me here."

"Sit down," he commanded. "Listen. For your own safety, do as you are told."

She quietly sat.

"The man who was at the door just now? He came looking for Funky awhile back. Then the next day, Funky was found splayed out on a median strip on Route One, dead."

Amara watched as Farley's shaking hands neatly stacked the contents of Desi's folder.

"They tracked him by his locator and ran over him like an animal. They're tracking you now."

Amara swallowed. "That can't be. I turned it off."

"The more advanced locators have a built-in homing signal. It runs on a secondary power source. You must have one of those."

She retrieved the locator. Placing it on the table, she said, "I keep it in my room in a backpack I found in the closet."

"Thanks to Detective Armstrong's ineptness at flattering judges during their dinner hour, we've got until tomorrow morning to get rid of it."

A half hour later the entire Way Back Diner club sat around Farley's card table. The locator lay open and disemboweled. Ramesh, wearing a jeweler's magnifier, poked at the device with a pair of tweezers.

"It's pretty clever what they've done," he reported to the group.

"These nano-letters are some I've never seen."

"Never mind the techno-commentary, do you see the kill switch?" Brenda asked.

"Yes, I think so. I'll have to flatten an air path."

"Wait!" Amara exclaimed. "Will you be able to reactivate it?" This device was her only connection to life in 2049, her token of proof that her life with John and her children and Rosie existed, that she existed. She couldn't allow them to destroy it.

"Not without the proper tools," Ramesh said.

"Before you disconnect it, let's think this through," Amara stalled. "Farley, you said someone tracked my signal to this house. If we kill the signal now, they'll know this is where the trail ends."

"Kill it, Ramesh," Brenda insisted.

"No!" Amara demanded, surprising even herself. "Look, I'm expected at Mama Zoe's. Why not take the locator and disconnect it somewhere along the way. It gets it out of this house."

"She's got a point," Tandy said to the group. To her he added, "Now you're thinking like a Way Backer."

Chapter Thirteen

Standing on the sidewalk in front of Farley's, Amara pulled the scratchy wool collar of her Goodwill coat up around her neck. She missed her tap jacket. Wearing the jacket would raise questions, questions she couldn't answer without sounding like an alien from another galaxy, Farley had pointed out to her.

Lying in bed that morning, she'd tried to remember a life where a tap jacket was as common as down vests were here. She missed her environment-controlled apartment, Juicy Vibe smoothies, riding the odor-free HT, hologram clothes shopping, and 3D tel-chats with her grandchildren. She even found herself, at times, wishing she was back at Hope Home apologizing to bossy Brad's owner about shutting the bot down.

The plan called for Ramesh to take the locator to the library on Franklin Street and physically deactivate the back-up signaling channel. He promised to return it to her when he had finished his task.

The walk to Mama Zoe's took longer than expected. Despite

her brisk pace, she felt her core temperature dropping and missed the warmth of her own jacket all over again. Steamy air greeted her as she entered the bistro. The smells of caramelized meat caused her to heave. Aside from the occasional cultured chicken, what John called petri meat, she hadn't eaten animal protein in years. She placed her mitten over her nose as she searched for John.

"Alice! Over here," John called out. As she sat, he said, "Thought you were going to stand me up."

"Am I too late?" She asked.

"I've ordered us a bottle of wine and an appetizer. Do you like fried calamari?"

"I'm vegan."

"What does that mean?"

"Only plant-based protein," she said.

"Oh." He sounded disappointed.

"A glass of wine would be nice," she offered.

He filled her wine glass and then opened the oversized menu. "Let's see if we can find something for you. How about a nice cheese lasagna?"

"I'll have a small salad."

After the waiter left, John raised his glass and toasted, "To you and me." After a pause, he added, "And our future together?"

Amara lifted her glass to his toast and sipped the Chianti.

During the meal, John chatted excitedly about his hobby, collecting eighteenth- and nineteenth-century artifacts. Under the influence of most of the bottle, he proudly imparted to Amara his ancestors' role in the American War of Independence, turning from Tories to spies for General Washington. She'd heard it all a million times before and, yet, this time the story seemed to sound like the first.

"What about you?" he asked. "What are your passions?"

She hesitated. While they were dating, John had once accused her of having no zeal for life, no sense of adventure. The harsh judgment had cut deep, leaving her to believe he wasn't in love with her. She'd wanted to break up with him, but a few days after the argument, she discovered that she was pregnant. As years passed, she'd decided what he meant by his proclamation was that she wasn't like him. She wasn't a dreamer; she was pragmatic in every way. Through their relationship, she'd learned that about herself.

"I like to drive," she offered.

"I guess that's why you deliver flowers," he responded.

"I suppose." Amara worried about Ramesh. If someone was tracking her locator, he could be in danger. He could end up like Farley's friend Funky Man.

"Surely you've done more than drive a delivery van. Did you go to college?"

Yes, she went to college and earned a BS and Ph.D. in electrical engineering and an MBA but she saw no reason to tell him all that. It would only lead to mocking comments about being overqualified for her current job. She settled for, "I'm quite adept at computer hardware and software design. I suppose my passion is that I like to learn. And to read."

Together, they embarked down the rabbit hole of great literature for the next hour or so. She leaned toward fantasy and science fiction. He enjoyed poetry and the Bard, of course. But after law school he had time only for contracts and municipal codes. Crossing his eyes at her, he said, "Now you know why I drink."

She smiled. The glass of wine and his company had warmed her.

After the waiter came with the check, John asked if she'd like to go somewhere for a nightcap.

Thinking of Ramesh, she feigned a yawn and said, "I have a

long day tomorrow."

He stood to join her. "This was nice. Can we do it again?"

She pretended she didn't hear his question. He followed her to the sidewalk. Ramesh was parked across the street, waving at them.

John asked, "Well now. Are you and the Raja a 'thing'?"

"Excuse me?" Amara asked.

"Are you and this Roger character dating?"

"His name is Ramesh. I told you, we're friends," Amara said. As she crossed the quiet street, Ramesh rolled down his car window. Seeing his worried face, she asked, "What's wrong?"

Ramesh nodded, indicating that John had followed her.

"Hello, Roger," John said.

"I saw you come out of the restaurant as I was driving by. Thought I'd offer you a ride home," Ramesh said. Like her, he wasn't any good at lying. He appeared nervous.

John snorted. "Isn't that convenient. You just happened to be driving by."

"Thanks for dinner. Ramesh can take me home," she said to John.

At the same instant she turned to go to the passenger's side, John reached for her. They fell into an awkward embrace. John held onto her arms to steady them both. He stole a kiss from her cheek and whispered, "I'd really like to see you again."

"I know," she replied

"Come away with me this weekend," he whispered while rubbing her arms.

"Tempting as that sounds, I can't," she said.

Waving goodbye, he called out to her. "I'll come by the shop tomorrow."

Ramesh put the car in drive and pulled away from the curb. "You've got to stop seeing this Romeo," he insisted.

"I know, I know," Amara said. "But I can't help myself. You don't know how lonely I've been since he died. Seeing him like this makes me want to be with him."

"Soooo, stop seeing him," Ramesh reasoned.

"You've never been in love, have you?" Without waiting for his answer, she continued, "When we get to Farley's block, drive down the alley and I'll go in the back way. It's quieter," Amara said.

"We're not going to Farley's," Ramesh said. "They came and got him."

"What? Why didn't you say something?"

"In front of Lawyer Lover Boy? He'd insist on me telling him what happened. He'd want to go with us to bail him out," Ramesh said.

"So they took him to jail?"

"If we're lucky, that's where he is."

Ramesh drove to the third precinct on Meadow and pulled to the curb.

"Why would they arrest Farley? I'm the one they're looking for."

"He wants to protect us. You, Tandy, me," Ramesh said. "They haul him in to scare him, or so that's what he's told me. He said they think he'll tell them what they want to know."

"Local police know what's going on with us?"

"Farley suspects one or two."

Their side-street location rendered a view of the back parking lot of the precinct. Officers and others were entering and leaving the building. "Must be a shift change," Ramesh said. He got out of his car for a better view of the lot. Getting back in, he said, "Not good. Let's go."

"Wait! What about Farley?" Amara cried. "If he's in there, we've got to get him out."

He put the car in gear.

"What's happened?" she asked as he raced away.

"The car Brenda saw? The one Desi rode away in? It's in the parking lot."

"That's not a reason to abandon Farley," she said. "Did you get anywhere with the license search for Brenda?"

"Hit a dead end. Which tells me it's National Security or some rogue outfit. Something's wrong. I can feel it. This thing, whatever is happening to us, it's changing again."

"Why fear it? Maybe it's a good thing. Maybe we get back our old lives if we talk to these guys."

"Are you the kind of person who always sees the tea pot half full?" Ramesh asked, daring to smile.

"I get it. We're in danger. So, what do we do now?"

"Let's go to Brenda's. She'll know what to do."

At Brenda's South Side high-rise apartment, Amara and Ramesh sat on a small sofa, squished together between oversized pillows. Amara sneezed. She was allergic to cats.

"Brutus, get off Alice," Brenda exclaimed. "Go play with Cassius and Cornelia." She set a service tray on the coffee table. "Help yourselves." After a taste of coffee, she cleared her throat and asked, "What happened? Did you squash the locator?"

"When I got to the library to disrupt the back channel path, I discovered I'd left the jeweler's loupe at Farley's. I drove back and saw a couple of patrol cars out front. All the lights were on in the house. I saw Farley leave with them."

"Where's the locator now?" Brenda asked.

"In some bushes on Grove Street," Ramesh said.

"What!" Brenda squawked. Shaking her finger at him she said, "You go back and get it. Tonight. Now, you said something about the unmarked vehicle?"

Nodding at Amara, he said, "When we went to the precinct

headquarters looking for Farley, I saw it parked in the back lot."

Brutus was back, nudging Ramesh's hand with his head, begging for a scratch, to which Ramesh obliged.

"Did you see them taking anything from the house? Stuff from the command center?" Brenda asked.

"I didn't stick around to find out," Ramesh said, "And, after we left the police station, we came straight here. I assume they're still watching the house."

"I know a way in without attracting attention," Amara offered. "He keeps a basement window off the alley unlocked."

"You're not going back to that house, toots. Not tonight anyway. Too risky," Brenda insisted. "You can stay here with me."

"I can't," Amara said. She sneezed, then pointed at Brutus.

"I got a drawer full of antihistamines."

"I'm using biochip plasma therapy for depression." Trying to exaggerate her condition, Amara said, "Taking allergy medicine probably isn't a good idea. I'd hate to have a negative reaction on top of everything else that's going on." Truth was she'd rather not stay with Brenda at all, even if she had no cats.

"There's a spare room over the restaurant," Ramesh offered. "It's closer to the flower shop. You can walk to work."

"She'll stay here until Farley gets back," Brenda insisted. "I'll call Tandy and see if he'll go over and bail Farley out."

Amara sneezed.

Chapter Fourteen

THE JEFFERSON HOTEL
SATURDAY, DECEMBER 18, 1999

The next morning Tandy reported that one of his biggest customers, a divorce attorney, had made inquiries at the jail.

"A divorce attorney?" Brenda complained. She and Amara were at her breakfast nook staring at the telephone. "What the hell? We need big guns. Let's call that loudmouth shyster who's always screaming on WRVQA."

"Did he confirm that Farley has been arrested?" Amara asked the speakerphone.

"No, he's not getting any straight answers. But, I'm inclined to give him a chance to work his magic."

Brenda muttered, "Magic my foot."

"What about the command center?" Ramesh's voice came softly through the speakerphone. "Should I go over there and see if anything was taken?"

"No," Brenda barked. "You stick to the plan we put together last night. If he hasn't surfaced by this afternoon, I'll go by the house tomorrow. Have you contacted everybody?" She stood and stretched.

"I sent out a broadcast alert on voicemail last night requesting a response. The ones who confirmed are worried about what's going to happen to their new families. They want to know what they should do," Ramesh said solemnly.

Brenda rubbed her chin. "Hmmm, maybe calling everybody now wasn't such a hot idea." She bent over the table and yelled at the speakerphone, "Send another message telling them to stand by but be prepared to vacate the city." Her right eye twitched.

"What?" Tandy's strained voice streamed from the speakerphone. "I'm not going anywhere. I got people depending on me. I got orders to fill, deliveries to make. Good God, woman, have you looked at a calendar lately? It's the height of my busiest season."

"Tandy," Brenda tried to speak over the florist's excitement. "Tandy, Tandy. If we don't leave, they'll find us. Now, let's all pull ourselves together. We're going to get through this."

"Through what?" Amara asked. She'd had enough of Brenda's vague warnings of doom. "What are we expecting? The Four Horsemen? Do we have concrete proof that some dark state is out to get us?"

Flapping her hands up and down, Brenda said, "Kid, I don't have time to go over this with you right now." She stuffed her purse with two apples from the fruit bowl on the kitchen table. "I'm late for my Saturday volunteer gig at the center. But trust me, you don't want to get invited to visit any government facility right now. Not with what you've got floating around inside of you. Radish, can you give her a ride over to Tandy's shop?"

"After I open up the restaurant, I can swing by," Ramesh said.

"Why don't I just get my own car?" Amara protested. She wasn't sure she could take another twenty-four hours with Brenda and her cast of cats. "I mean if I've got to leave the city, I'll need wheels." She sneezed.

"I think we all know that you getting behind the wheel of an automobile ends badly," Tandy said. "Besides, if they were looking for you and snared Farley instead, you need to lay low for a day or two. Stay with Brenda until tomorrow and we'll see how things look at Farley's."

After Brenda left for her Saturday gig as a domestic violence counselor at a neighborhood community center, Amara paced around the tiny apartment. She spied Brenda's worn leather satchel hanging from a kitchen chair. Inside, she leafed through the tabs and stopped on the one labeled "Incident Reports." The first page showed a summary and graph of incidents involving each Way Backer. Only one was trending sharply upward, the last one, number sixty-three, which was highlighted and underlined. A yellow sticky note in the upper right corner read: "Far—I don't like the direction this is taking. We should isolate this one." Sixty-three had to be Amara. She shoved the report back inside the satchel.

If she was going to be forced into isolation, she'd do it where there wasn't a layer of cat dandruff on everything. She picked up the phone receiver to call Ramesh to come and get her. She slammed the receiver back into its cradle when she realized she didn't know his number. She picked it up again and dialed directory assistance. Ramesh wasn't answering his phone, nor was Tandy. She called a cab.

Wrestling with her winter coat, she twisted the doorknob but it wouldn't turn. Seeing the deadbolt lock, she punched the door with the side of her fist.

"Awwwww," she cried.

Brutus, Cassius, and Cornelia sat in the middle of the apartment and watched as Amara ransacked every drawer in the place. She finally found a set of keys hanging from a peg in the kitchen. Waving the keys in front of them, she hissed, "Thanks for nothing."

A cab ride got her back across the river. She asked the driver to circle the block on Mercer Street. A black sedan and patrol car were parked across the street from Farley's. The side of her hand throbbed. She'd lost her nerve and was too timid to confront them. She ordered the driver to take her to Bombay's.

The restaurant was closed and Ramesh's car wasn't parked out back. She waited on the back stoop for him to return while brushing orange cat hair from her black coat. When Ramesh hadn't returned after an hour, she walked across the street and called another cab from the tea house on the corner.

She checked into the city's only five star hotel The Jefferson and ordered room service as she took in the view from her fifth floor room.

"You want me to isolate," she said to herself as she ate the strawberry yogurt and granola parfait. "This is how I isolate."

The oversized tub filled with bubbles and warm water as she stripped from her smelly, cat fur-clinging clothes. Under the muted lights of the bathroom mirror, she marveled at her rejuvenated body. She raked her fingers through her light brown hair. It seemed thicker now than it did when she was twenty—the year she'd met John. For a second, she thought of calling him. Instead, she slid into the tub and resigned to enjoy the solitude. Tomorrow, she'd deal with the Way Backer fallout: Brenda's screeches about her disappearance and Tandy's disapproving glare after telling him she'd used La Petite Fleur's gas credit card to pay for the room. She'd pay him back, she promised as she dozed. She dreamed of other hotels, other luxury baths; she and John celebrating New Year's Eve and her forty-fifth birthday in a tub for two at The Park Hotel in New York City.

Later, while wearing the lush bathrobe, she rubbed scented oils, complements of the hotel, over her long legs. The plasma treatments had worked better than she'd been led to believe. However, Dr. Coleman had warned that failure to take the supplemental injections each month could result in rapid regression, back to the body's native state. Sitting on the edge of the bed, she counted on her fingers the days since her last injection and wondered how long it would be before her eyelids and other body parts would begin their downward migration.

Chapter Fifteen

The next morning, as Amara had predicted, Brenda and Tandy were not amused by her act of defiance. They sent Ramesh to retrieve her from her reverie of luxury. As the little car puffed toward the flower shop, she said, "Take me to Farley's."

"Brenda said to stay away from there."

"Did you do *everything* your mother told you to do?" Amara asked. "I need to change clothes."

Ramesh parked in the alley a block east of Farley's house and they got out of the car. After locking the door, Ramesh blew into his hands. A man appeared in the alley at the far end of the next block. Dressed in black jeans and a leather jacket, he walked with purpose down the middle of the cobblestones toward them. Amara sidled up to Ramesh and threaded her arm through his.

"Don't look at him," she whispered to Ramesh. "Keep your head down."

The man turned onto the sidewalk and disappeared.

Amara felt her friend shaking.

At the back of the house, she stooped and pushed against a

basement window. "Good, he didn't lock it," she said. She pulled herself through the window and went to open the basement door for Ramesh. Together they surveyed the room. Someone had turned the furniture upside down. All the posters of the Way Backers' appearances and locations had been torn from the walls.

"Someone was looking for something," Ramesh said.

They stood over the rust-stained outline of the file cabinet on the carpet.

"Looks like they found it," Amara replied.

Sounding lost, Ramesh said, "Now all of us are known to them."

Not all, Amara thought. Farley had yet to make a file on her.

"Here, help me," Ramesh said as he grabbed the side of an over-turned bookcase and stood it upright in the middle of the room. "Farley told me to check underneath the wall-to-wall carpet under the bookcase if he ever disappeared."

"Don't say that," Amara said. "We don't know if he's gone. For all we know, he's doing his bus circuit gig or over at the diner smoking and drinking a cup of his death drip."

Ramesh pulled an oversized envelope from under the carpet. "This must be what he meant for me to find." Pointing at the return address, he said, "Looks like something from his bank." He pulled a single piece of paper from the envelope.

"What's it say?" she asked.

"Bank account and safe deposit box numbers."

"Deposit boxes? What's in them?"

"How would I know?" He peered inside the envelope and said, "Two sets of keys. Like deposit box keys? Maybe?"

"Let's take them with us," Amara said as she surveyed the ransacked room again. Everything, all the evidence the Way Backers had accumulated about their existence, was gone. As she climbed the stairs, she said to Ramesh, "Check the front to see if anyone is watching the house." In her bedroom, she changed clothes and tossed what she was wearing in a corner, vowing never to touch them again.

A few minutes later, Ramesh stood at her bedroom door, appearing concerned. "That man. The one in the alley? He's sitting in a car out front." He followed her down the stairs to the parlor.

Amara peeked from the side of the parlor window and asked, "Is it the same car as the one Desi got into?"

"I can't tell," Ramesh said. "We should go. The longer we stay, the more opportunity they have to discover us." Ramesh's heightened accent revealed his uneasiness. He was on the verge of fleeing, as he'd done at Buddy's.

"Chill," she said. "We'll slip out the back door. You walk over to Floyd Avenue and circle back to your car. Pick me up at the corner."

On the sidewalk, she considered Ramesh's unreasonable fear. She, for reasons she couldn't explain or understand, felt no anxiety whatsoever. In her other life, her timidity kept her from questioning anything or anybody. Could it be that the nanochips altered her personality, turned her into a different person? For a second, she thought about approaching the guy in the car.

"Hey!" Ramesh was waving for her to get into his car. "I got the license number. It's not the same. I'll get another temporary pass code from Brenda and do a DMV check."

They found Tandy and Brenda sitting at the florist shop's break room table. Tandy was on the phone, "Uh-huh. I see. Uh-huh. I will. I owe you one, friend." Hanging up the phone, he said, "They have no record of him coming into the station."

"What?" Brenda asked. Turning her head, she blew cigarette smoke away from the others and fanned her face.

"That was the lawyer friend I asked to help us. He says the police are now denying Farley ever came in."

"How is that possible? I saw him get in the police car," Ramesh protested.

"They could have taken him anywhere," Brenda said.

Tandy ran his thumb and fingers over his mustache and in his low voice asked, "What'll we do now?"

"We found this in Farley's basement," Ramesh said. He tossed the envelope on the table. "Someone's taken the file cabinet with all the data we've collected. So much for our idea of going old school and using paper."

"I told you all to stay away from Farley's," Brenda warned again.

"It was my idea," Amara said, shielding Ramesh. "What's in the bank boxes, Brenda?"

The older woman appeared more frazzled than usual. The Way Backers' biochip plasma must be thinning as Dr. Coleman had explained to Amara. They were struggling to cope with this crisis of friends disappearing with no explanation. The ordered life they had woven around themselves was coming unraveled. On top of the constant anxiety of something big falling from the sky and landing on them, they feared being sucked away from a life they'd built for themselves, just as it had happened the first time. They were terrified. Amara, strangely enough, had no fear.

Answering Amara's question, Brenda explained, "Our locators, tablets, bitcoin dongles, our legacy credit ID cards, stuff that came with us. Technologies we can't let anybody get a hold of. It was Farley's idea to put them in the bank boxes. He said we can't let our coming here jeopardize the future."

"If he was so concerned with how we could impact the future, he must know that we *can* go back there," Amara reasoned.

"Not me, I don't want to," Tandy said. He stood to put the break room in order, stacking newspapers, pushing chairs under the table.

Amara turned to Ramesh. "What about you? Do you want to

go back to your real life?"

"Honey, this *is* his real life," Brenda spoke for him.

Watching for Ramesh's reaction, Amara said, "I'm asking you. Don't you want to see your family?"

Ramesh said, "I don't know. I'm afraid of what I'll find." He fiddled with the zipper on his jacket. "Besides, I'm not that person anymore." He hung his head.

Amara wasn't sure if he was scared because of Brenda's blunt assessment of their current situation or of him finding his family doing fine without him. They all seemed to have reasons to want to stay here in the past. And, as each day passed, she feared Brenda's proclamations. If this was her real life now, Amara would never see her kids or home again. Or Rosie. Rosie, an outdated bot, was the one she missed the most.

She asked, "So, all this Way Backer stuff about trying to figure out what's going on and how we're going to get back to our old lives is . . . what?"

"We . . . it's . . . ," Ramesh stuttered.

"We do all that malarkey to help the newbies," Brenda blurted out. "Give them hope while they adjust."

"Adjust to what?"

Brenda spread her arms. "To the fact that this is it. This miserable day-in, day-out existence is all there is. All it ever will be."

The front door bell jingled.

Amara rose from the table. To Brenda, she said, "Then explain why I saw Desi Kurts' face on a 2049 billboard claiming to have traveled to the past."

"I don't know who you saw but it wasn't Desi Kurts. Maybe a second cousin. But I guarantee it wasn't him."

"I don't believe you," Amara said. She left to serve the customer who had entered the store.

The man from the alley stood at the counter. His stature was a rack of bones, his face pocked and chinless. The man liked styling gel.

"I'm looking for Farley Dickenson," he said.

"No one here by that name. May I interest you in some poinsettias?" The guy had seen her with Ramesh near Farley's house. He must have followed them to the shop.

"Sam Jennings. *New York Post*," he said.

"How may we help you today, Sam? The poinsettias are nice this time of year. We've got a two-for-one special."

"Farley Dickenson stood me up. We were supposed to have coffee at a diner on Broad Street."

"And you'd like to send him a bouquet of forget-me-nots?" she asked.

"Funny. He said that if he didn't show I should come and find you."

"He did?" That was a lie, Amara thought.

"A friend of his told me that the police were accusing him of stealing trade secrets. Guy's street name is Funky Man? Do you know him?"

"No, I'm afraid not," she said.

"We were going to meet at a place," he glanced at a small spiral notebook, "the Way Back Diner for breakfast this morning. I drove down from D.C."

"The Way Back Diner *is* a popular spot for eggs and coffee." The guy was bluffing. No way would Farley speak to the press about their dilemma. "And this Mr. Dickenson told you to speak with me?"

The reporter looked around the shop. "That's what he said."

"I'm sorry, but I can't help you."

"Is it true?" he asked.

"Is what true, Sam?"

"About Funky Man being a time traveler?"

"Who?" she asked. She straightened the pens with the silk flowers tapped on them, which Martha had arranged. Getting cute, she said, "If I had to guess, you'll find a time traveler or two bunking up with J.E.B. Stuart and Napoleon Bonaparte down at the homeless shelter on Canal Street."

The front door bell jingled. John Darnley stomped snowy slush from his boots.

"Let me know if I can help you with our two-for-one poinsettia special," she said to the reporter as she watched John pretending to show interest in the flowers in the cooling cases.

"Here's my card," Jennings said. "I'm staying at the downtown Marriott."

Amara took it, assuming they were done and the guy would leave.

But Jennings lingered at the counter.

Now, Ramesh was at her side, too close. Placing his hand over hers, he leaned into her. While eyeing John, he whispered in her ear, "He's a dog with a bone, that one. You're welcome to stay with me in the room over the restaurant. Bunk beds, we can play like we're at camp." As he walked by John, he brushed shoulders with the lawyer. The bell over the door jingled again. Ramesh was gone but the heat from his words lingered in her ear.

"Listen, what time do you get off work? Can we go for a coffee?" Sam Jennings asked her.

John raised an eyebrow and left the shop.

He was always leaving her.

Whenever things weren't going his way, throughout their marriage, he'd leave a room, stomp upstairs, slam a door. The first time he left the marriage was before the rash of troubles with his law partners and into the arms of his lover Keekee Biddle. Without warning, he walked out on their lives one frigid January night. With the kids insisting on their independence, she'd found herself alone for the first time in her life.

A few days before, at Christmas, they'd argued over something silly. What was it? The dumb plastic Christmas tree. She bought and decorated it while he was away on business, thinking he'd be happy to see it, and the house, trimmed out for the holidays upon his return. Instead, he lost it. He acted as if she'd betrayed some arbitrary ancient yuletide rite by using synthetic fiber instead of real fir. He'd been drinking, of course.

She'd fired back, accusing him of stealing money from the children's college accounts and giving it to people they didn't even know, the kind of people who took advantage of others' kind deeds.

That's when he slapped her.

Chapter Sixteen

IN THE LA PETITE FLEUR VAN
SUNDAY, DECEMBER 19, 1999

One of the delivery guys, a Way Backer, didn't show up for his Sunday shift. Tandy found Amara at the front counter making bows for wreaths and thinking about John. Seeing one man whisper in her ear, causing her to blush, then hearing another ask her out for coffee must have scared him away. Perhaps his leaving was for the best.

"Barton's gone," Tandy said in a matter-of-fact tone. "That was his girlfriend on line three. She said he didn't come home last night. Wanted to know if he showed up for work."

"That makes two," Amara said. "Farley and Barton."

"Three. Barton's Way Back partner's missing, too."

"Has anyone heard from Farley?" she asked.

"I fear we've seen the last of Farley. You can have his house," Tandy said.

"How's Brenda?"

"She's a wreck. He was her Way Back partner, you know. She's beside herself worrying about what's happened to him. And she's worried that she's next."

"You make it sound like an execution. Who knows? Maybe there is a way back and that's where everyone is disappearing to."

He tossed her a ring of keys. "I don't have time to interview for new delivery personnel. Job's yours if you want it."

She snatched up the keys. "I'm fully qualified. I'm an engineer with a Ph.D., and an MBA."

"Just because you got an entire alphabet behind your name doesn't mean you have enough common sense to drive," he said. "Orders are in the truck." Then he warned, "The minute you start getting tingles and hearing trains, you leave wherever you are. Promise?"

"Promise," she said. She peeled off her hot pink and green La Petite Fleur apron, reached for her wool coat and headed for the van out back.

"We need you," he called after her. "Don't do anything stupid like get run over by a city bus."

If she didn't know better, Amara thought, Tandy had already forgiven her for running up charges on his credit card at the fancy hotel.

Early morning rain had washed away some of the snow and left the roads slick with patches of black ice. Tempering her excitement to be driving again, Amara kept the van below the speed limit. Turning the radio on, she discovered that Barton liked heavy metal jam. At a stoplight she searched for another station and landed on one with a pop diva pouting about being a naughty girl at Christmastime.

From her time, radios and headphones were obsolete, except at the Graves-Darnley house. John collected analog and digital radios, cell phones, and elaborate high-fidelity stereo systems. Most people used their locators or cochlear implants to listen to music or news programs. Not John. He had converted Aiden's bedroom into a soundproof studio and listened for hours to anything from

Beethoven to grunge rock. "With my own ears," he'd emphasized. Amara tried implants but had them removed. She hated that feeling of being connected every minute of every day. She relied on Rosie to find music and books that she'd like. But mostly, since John's passing, she enjoyed the ringing sound of a good silence.

At the next stoplight, she turned the knob again and found a local news program.

A male voice announced, "Time for the news on the hour. Earlier this morning, police detained a man who was running down Main near Twelfth Street. Wearing only running shoes and a stocking cap."

Another announcer, a woman, added, "Jeff, an emergency medical professional on the scene stated that the man appeared severely dehydrated and unaware of who he is. The source told our station the man was screaming, 'I don't want to go back to 2042.'"

Amara looked up from the delivery list she was studying and stared at the radio. Someone behind her tooted the horn. The light had changed to green.

"Go back to 2042? What does that even mean? Was there a full moon last night?" The radio jockey joked.

"Who knows, Jeff. Maybe he was talking about a street address."

"You never know, Darla. Y2K is next week. Bizarre predictions on what could happen are flying around everywhere."

"Well, let's not add to the hysteria and hope this man gets the help he needs, Jeff. Speaking of predictions, the weather for the last two weeks of the year are forecasted to be cold, cold, cold. Brrr. Wrap up for chilly weather, with highs only in the high thirties."

Assuming this man had been admitted to the city's medical center, Amara took the downtown expressway to the hospital. After parking, she placed a flower arrangement on a hospital meal cart and rolled it into the visitors' lobby. She called Tandy from a guest phone.

"What's wrong?"

"I heard on the radio that a naked man was picked up on Main Street and taken to the hospital. He was yelling that he didn't want to go back to 2042. Who's missing from forty-two?"

"Barton."

"Could it be him?" She asked.

"His Way Back partner, Trevor, is missing, too," Tandy said. "This isn't good."

"I'm at the hospital now. What does he look like?"

"Well, you know Barton's lean and blond. Trevor has a mop of curly brown hair, facial hair."

"If it's not Barton, what do I say to the guy, you know, so he'll recognize me as a Way Backer?"

"Just tell him Farley sent you. That should be enough." Then he repeated, "This isn't good. See if you can get to him without stirring up too much attention."

She rolled the cart toward the ER, an area she'd visited on her first day back to 1999. As she walked the noisy halls, she congratulated herself for remembering the layout of the place without using her locator.

Loud voices boomed down from the other end of an expanded corridor. The nurse she'd skipped out on during her previous visit was helping a man get out of his bed parked against the wall. The nurse saw her but didn't recognize her. Amara dared not look away.

The man fit the description of the one Tandy called Trevor.

Here goes, Amara thought. "Trevor, there you are. Farley and Tandy have been looking all over for you."

"You know this man?" the nurse asked.

"He's a friend of a co-worker," Amara said. She turned to the man in the hospital gown and said, "We go way back."

Except Trevor wasn't having any of it. "I don't know you."

Amara addressed the nurse, "I heard about what happened on the radio. I'll call his friends and let them know he's here."

"And you are?" the nurse asked.

"She's one of them," cried Trevor, getting his legs tangled in the tube dangling from the IV pole.

"One of who, Mr. Griff?" the nurse asked as she helped untangle him. Suspicion shifted from the crazy indigent to Amara.

Amara said, "Trevor, we met at the Way Back Diner. Remember? I'm a friend of Farley and Brenda?"

"Brenda?" Trevor asked, his eyes becoming more lucid. "That woman's a tyrant." He pulled away from the nurse and grabbed at his hospital gown. "Where're my clothes?"

Amara extended her hand to the nurse and said, "Alice Epps. I work for La Petite Fleur." To Trevor she said, "I'm happy to call someone to bring you some clothes." Calmly, she rolled the cart by them and scanned the corridor for another telephone. What a nuisance, having to find a telephone every time she needed to talk to someone outside of shouting distance.

"Tandy, it's Trevor," Amara said. "He's in the ER. When you come to pick him up, you need to bring him some clothes."

"I can't leave the shop," he said. "You've got to get him out of there before they take him."

"But—"

"Handle it." He hung up on her.

Watching the nurse help Trevor settle back into the bed, Amara overheard her gently remind Trevor that he had come to them as naked as the day he was born and, for now, he needed to settle down and rest.

Amara pushed the cart down the hallway. Turning a corner, she found herself in another corridor with rooms on each side.

Pretending to match the room number to a delivery ticket, she stopped at each room and browsed for street clothes or a suitcase. At a nurse's station, she watched a man toss a duffle bag underneath a desk and put on his white medical coat. He spoke to a passing tech and, together, they walked away from the station. Without hesitation, Amara pushed the cart to the station, lifted the bag, and tossed it on the bottom tray of the cart. Circling the cart around, she went back to the ER to rescue Trevor.

The area where the nurse had parked Trevor was empty. She got lucky at the ER command station, a different nurse was there.

"I'm here to see Trevor Griff." Lifting the duffle, she added, "Got his clothes."

"Are you a relative?" the nurse asked.

"Half-sister," she lied. "Got here as fast as I could."

The tech's fingernails clicked against the computer keys. "Says here he's being transferred to Central State Hospital."

"What?" she asked as indignantly as a half-sister to a crazy naked man would. "Doctor's orders were for him to be discharged to me."

"Sorry. You might be able to catch them. They just left."

Something wasn't right about this, there was no way an urban hospital operated that quickly in a non-emergency situation. Someone had snatched Trevor.

Back in the van, she turned right on Broad Street. She spotted him. Trevor, wearing only his hospital gown, was running west on the frozen sidewalk. Traffic lights were all green for at least four blocks. She passed him, turned at the next corner and yelled. "Get in!"

He hesitated, looking around for another route of escape.

"I'll take you to Farley's house. Get in!"

They both saw the late model black sedan a block away, slowed by traffic and the changing light.

"Lady, if you're lying to me, may a plague of lice infest your body parts where the sun don't shine."

As soon as his hairy legs were in the van, Amara punched the gas.

"Who are those guys?" she asked.

"Are you really a Way Backer?" Trevor asked, breathing heavy.

"Forty-nine," she said. "They tell me you're from '42."

"That's what I believe most days," he replied.

Smelling the fear on him, Amara decided to wait to ask him what compelled him to run naked down the street in the middle of winter. She sensed he was operating from the Desi playbook, he wasn't coping well with his new time. She checked the rear view mirror for suspicious black cars and saw none. To set Trevor at ease, she said in a calm tone, "I was walking over to the Shops of Carytown for a smoothie. Next thing I know a police officer is loading me into one of those awful ambulances to bring me here. Buddy, I can relate."

She took her time weaving through the city neighborhoods. Over the smooth Christmas jazz on the radio, she asked, "Mind if I make a couple of deliveries before we meet up with the others?"

Trevor had loosened his he-man grip on the door handle.

She asked, "You hungry?"

"I could eat."

She pulled to the curb and reached behind the console. Tossing the pilfered duffle at him, she said, "Put these on until we can get you something else."

Trevor stepped over the console into the back of the van. The sound of a zipper was followed by grunting snorts from Trevor. A pair of clown shoes and a red curly wig sailed over the console. "Really, man?"

Two minutes later, they were both wiping at their eyes. "A good laugh does a body good," Trevor said as he sat up in the back of the van. "Can you help a guy out? My boys are freezing back here."

She took off her coat and tossed it to him. "Let's swing by Goodwill and get you some pants." A call to Tandy, while Trevor tried on clothes, instructed her to meet up with Brenda and the rest of the Way Backers at Farley's at four o'clock.

After she finished her deliveries, Amara and a fully clothed Trevor were hunkered down in the back booth of the Way Back Diner. Trevor inhaled his pinto beans and cornbread as Amara sipped at a mug of hot tea. Whether she liked it or not, Amara had become the new Farley, guardian to the hapless time traveler.

Chapter Seventeen

FARLEY'S HOUSE
SUNDAY, DECEMBER 19, 1999
P.M.

After confirming that the coast was clear, Amara took Trevor back to Farley's. As the two straightened up the basement command center, Amara broke the news about the sudden disappearance of their leader.

When the others arrived, they all gathered at the card table. Brenda spoke first. "Here are your new credentials. You're now Thomas Woff." She pushed the papers across the table to Trevor.

Trevor pushed them back. "Nope. I like the name Trevor. I'm keeping it."

Brenda frowned at Amara. With that sour nod of hers, Brenda had assigned the responsibility of Trevor over to Amara. Brenda said, "You can keep the name 'Trevor' but you've got to use your new ID when asked for it. If you don't, it will be easier for them to figure out who you really are. Do you want that?"

"Bring it," Trevor said. He folded his arms over his chest.

"Tell us what happened," Amara said.

"The lanky one, the one with the funny mouth, grabbed me.

Right while I was talkin' to Blow Hole about his Harley in front of the Rainbow Inn. They stuffed me in the back seat. When they stopped at a light, I bolted, man."

"Where's Barton?" Tandy asked.

"I don't know. You tell me. Last night I went over to his house. He and Sissy and me were going to have a little Christmas party. When I got there, he wasn't there. Sissy kicked me out, told me to go over to the Rainbow and bring Barton home. That's when they tried to nab me, man. They told me I had to come with them."

"Come with them? Did they say where to?" Brenda asked.

"They said they was sending me back. Said I was gettin' my other life back. Then I said to them, 'What if I don't want to go back?' That's when it got ugly and they stuffed me in their car."

"What do you suppose they meant by getting your other life back?" Ramesh asked.

"Oh," Trevor said. "Y'all don't know my real name." With his thick hands he pushed his bushy hair away from his face. "My beard has you at a disadvantage." Tandy, Brenda, Ramesh, and Amara stared at him. "No clue?" He chuckled. "I am, or was, or will be, Sargent Harry."

Their silence informed him of their ignorance.

Raising his eyebrows, he said, "Sargent Harry? King of the Bots? You know, 'You leave 'em, we'll love 'em?'"

"Oh! Oh!" exclaimed Brenda, jumping up and down in her chair, "You're the recycle guy."

"That's me. I was doin' a bang-up job until the city decided to contract their repurpose department out to an outfit called Fourth Revolution or something like that. Business dried up for me. Lost my home, my wife, kids. Started abusing U.E.s."

Ramesh persisted, "Did they explain how they planned to get you your other life back?"

"Said I'd have access to unlimited legacy credits. That's when I knew they was lying. Lying to get me to go along. Don't no moss grow on Sargent Harry."

"Then what happened?" Tandy asked. He appeared curious but haggard. The free enterprise flower business, complete with herding unlucky Way Backers, was wearing on him.

"That's when I waited for the car to stop and jumped out. Took all my clothes off and went running down the street. Got all the way to the Capitol building before they caught up with me."

"Why did you take your clothes off?" Brenda asked.

Trevor flashed a toothy grin. "To get the local boys' attention."

Ramesh persisted, "Did they say *how* you'd get back to your other life?"

"They said it would all be clear when we got to where they was takin' me." Then he asked the group, "That sound right by you?" Trevor shifted in his chair. "Besides, the drugs are better in this time, more organic. U.E.s was burning out my organic circuits. If you know what I mean."

"You were abusing chips with universal elements? As in bio-nanochip U.E.s?" Ramesh asked, sounding in awe as much as incredulous.

"Worse. I was heppin' up on junk grade. Stuff used for second class AIs," Trevor admitted. "I was hard core with nowhere to go but to hell. Somehow I ended up here."

They all seemed stunned by Trevor's bravado.

To nudge Trevor on, Brenda asked, "About the people who claimed to want to take you back?"

Trevor shuddered and said, "Wouldn't trust them to dig a hole."

"Human?"

He nodded, then joked, "Unless AIs are wearing aftershave now. Two men and a woman. She seemed to be in charge. They called her Coleman."

"Lydia Coleman?" Amara asked.

"No, just Coleman."

Amara rubbed her hands together in worry. Dr. Lydia Coleman was her biochip plasma therapy administrator. Maybe she would come for Amara.

"What are you thinking?" Brenda asked Amara.

"Lydia Coleman assisted my wellness administrator with my biochip therapy. The nanochip plasma they injected in me has a new pharma combination, including a higher level of universal elements."

"So what. We *all* were injected with those lil' demons. But it can't be the reason we're here," Brenda assured her. "If those treatments caused all this," she waved her arms frantically, "all this would be an illusion. A massive shared illusion? That's impossible."

Tandy added, "And how do you explain the fact that most of us have not had supplements in years. And, what about the chips? They're bound to have been flushed out of our systems by now."

"There's got to be a correlation. You can't deny it," Amara said.

"I can and I do," Brenda said. "I'm not a figment of your imagination, nor you mine. I'm real." She smacked her freckled arm. "Flesh and bones and blood. Organic. Besides, if this is a controlled experiment, we'd be back in our old ruts by now with no memory of this ever happening to us."

Ramesh rolled his eyes at Brenda's comment. "How can we be having a discussion about a theory of our very existence that includes erasing the memory of that existence?"

"Exactly," Brenda argued.

Everyone waited for her to explain the logic of her comment but the confusion in her eyes told them she'd lost track. Brenda was teetering off her rocker.

To bring Brenda back from the edge, Amara picked up the debate by asking, "Why all the intrigue? Why are they kidnapping us one at a time. Why don't they just call a meeting and tell us what happened?"

"Farley suspects some type of conspiracy," Brenda confessed. The lights had come back on in her eyes. "And if he's right, there's no going back to our previous lives. Don't you see? They can't have that. It'd be an admission of failure of whatever they've hosed up. And think of the cost."

Amara said, "I don't know about the rest of you but I want to find out why and how I got here. If these people know something that will help me understand, I want to talk to them. If they have a way for me to get back to the life I was living, I'd like to know about that, too."

Tandy spoke, "Y'all do what you want. I'm staying here."

"Me, too," Trevor chimed in. "I'm happier here than I ever was in that other life."

"Would you go, Amara?" Ramesh asked.

"I thought I wanted to but, right now, I'd just like to know what my options are."

"Is it because of John Darnley, your husband?" Ramesh asked.

Amara kicked him under the table.

"What's he saying?" Brenda asked.

Reluctantly, Amara decided it was time to share with them her encounters with John. "I've met the man I married in 2002."

Brenda sucked in air. Pounding the tabletop with her fist, she shouted in her teacher voice, "We expressly forbid Way Backers from getting involved in their past lives. In any way. Period."

"It's that John person who keeps coming by the shop, isn't it?" Tandy insisted.

Amara shrugged. In a way, she was grateful to Ramesh for

bringing up something she was having trouble reconciling.

"Do you realize the danger you've put yourself in? And others?" Brenda asked.

"I've seen cars plow through storefronts, fall on people's heads from roadway overpasses," Tandy said.

"I seen a woman pinned between a brick wall and a trash dumpster. Smashed her like a bug," Trevor added.

Amara sat straighter in her chair. "When I'm with him, I don't get the bio-warnings like the tingling or hearing the rushing sounds." She stopped there. She wasn't about to share how she felt whenever he looked at her. Their attraction had nothing to do with what was happening to the Way Backers. No way. "It's like we didn't know each other in my other life."

"Wait a minute," Ramesh said. He leaned in, "You said you were married in '02. What year did you meet?"

Amara thought on that one.

"Most people know what they did on their first date," Trevor offered his help. "I took my first wife to the Steely Steeds concert in Vegas. Back in '05."

"It was so long ago. I've known the man my entire life, it seems." Amara rubbed her temples. "We dated for a while, then I got pregnant with Aiden, our first, so we got married."

"That's it!" Brenda yelped. "Amara's not met him yet. This is bad, Tandy. Bad, bad, bad."

The others quietly waited for her explanation.

"Don't you see? The young you, the first you, hasn't met this John person yet. When she does, I guarantee, something's liable to happen. Something not so good. The damage has been done."

"Why do you say that?" Amara protested.

"This older you has met this man. You've built a history of memories with him, albeit a short one. Have you two had sex?"

"Hold on, that's none of our business," Tandy interrupted.

"There's no time for niceties. We're in uncharted waters here. I can't believe you ignoramuses don't see how truly bad this is. Oh, darn it, Farley, why'd you leave me?" Brenda lit up a cigarette and blew smoke over the table. She tried to explain. "What if we could go back? What if Alice just keeps after this man, traipsing all over her past." She took another hard drag on her Virginia Slim. "When this John-boy finally *does* meet the young Amara, here in 1999, he won't be the same person because of his involvement with the *old* version. You, Alice! Your meddling increases the possibility that they may never meet. Let's pretend that you could go back now. It would be a whole different place for you. Maybe no kids. Maybe no husband. No life as you know it to be."

Ramesh scratched at his beard stubble. "That could happen," he said. "Alice, if you keep messing with this man, you could wreak havoc on your life. It might not be the same if you ever get back to 2049."

"I'm lost," Trevor said.

"That makes two of us," Tandy chimed in.

"It makes perfect sense," Brenda said. "For the sake of our collective futures, it is pure folly for you to talk to anyone here you may have known in your past." Stamping out her smoke, she warned Amara, "And it's downright stupidity to talk to people who claim they can take you back to your other reality."

"Why?" Amara asked.

"Look what happened to Farley!" she exclaimed. Her logic had retreated back to the foggy side of her brain again.

Pulling at his hair, Ramesh cried, "But we don't *know* what happened to Farley!"

"'Look what happened to Farley?' That's your proof?" Amara asked. Then, she continued, "Aside from disappearing into thin air, we don't know what happened to him. We have no evidence that he's suffered the same fate as Funky Man or gone back to walking his dog Bonnie in 2042."

"Everybody calm down. We're talking in circles here," Tandy reasoned. "I say we take a break and meet up tomorrow. Pray that Farley comes back. Who's on bus duty tomorrow?"

"I'll take it," Trevor volunteered. "Can't go back to my job fixin' boilers. Can I bunk up here 'til I get me a new situation?"

"You're right, Tandy. I've had a day, too," Amara said. "But I'm tired of walking down the street thinking that any second I could die a gruesome death. When Coleman and the others approach me, I'm going to talk to them. Trevor, you can have Farley's room."

She left them at the table and went upstairs. As she climbed into bed, Amara agreed with Brenda on one thing. Why did Farley have to leave?

Chapter Eighteen

Loud grunts came from the second floor bathroom. Apparently, the new boarder saw little purpose in closed doors.

In her bed, Amara stretched. The Way Backers' heated discussion from the previous evening was zipping about in her head. They were confused about the effects of the biochip plasma they'd received. And, without any reason or proof, they suspected the strangers meant to do harm. She didn't know what to believe. She hugged her pillow and thought of Rosie. She missed Rosie. When Amara asked, Rosie always had the answers.

Another fart erupted from the bathroom.

Rosie would like Trevor in spite of his coarse manners. When the others recalled Sargent Harry and his robot reclamation business, she'd drawn a blank. She'd never heard of him or his business.

She'd tossed and turned all night, worried about Brenda's claim that Amara, the younger one yet to meet John, may never meet him. That would mean no Aiden or Kimberly. And, possibly, no Rosie.

Trevor was helping himself to a cup of Farley's coffee when she joined him in the kitchen. Holding up a mug that read *Awesome Water*, he said, "Yes, sir, this is so true. Farley made good coffee. We both hated that crap everybody wanted to pass for coffee in our other time. Whose idea was it to ban coffee anyway?"

"Same people who banned tobacco and high fructose sugar, I suppose," Amara said as she inspected a glass she pulled from the cupboard.

"Can I have this mug?"

"It's all yours," Amara said as she stood in front of the open refrigerator.

"Ain't nothing in there. I already looked."

"What's your story, Sargent Harry?" she asked Trevor.

He stirred a heaping teaspoon of sugar into his coffee.

"First thing I'd do with a donated bot was place my hands on its head. You know, like what those little Asian ladies do when they come in your house to tell you what to do with all the junk your mama's hoarded for fifty years. I'd do the same thing with the bot. Like this." He cupped his hands around the coffee mug. Closing his eyes, he continued, "Then, I'd think about the bot—not its metal components but its software, why it was made, what its purpose was. If its purpose still made sense to me, I'd restore it and find it a new home. If the purpose was no longer there, you know like those crumb snatcher vacuum sweepers, I'd help it find usefulness. Very rarely did I decommission and deconstruct one completely."

"Just like us humans when we go through major life changes," she mused.

"You could say that. One time, I converted a '32 Sweeps & Clean janitor into the first nonhuman school crossing guard. Look it up in the news archives. It made the top ten list for forty days when the story posted. Hmm. I guess you can't do that now. It ain't happened yet."

"We need a plan," she said.

"A plan? For what?" Trevor asked.

"We need a plan to figure out whether the guys in the sedan mean to harm or help us. Maybe you and Ramesh could plant a bug in their car."

"Like I said last night, they said they was taking me back to my other life where I belonged," Trevor said. "'Cept I don't believe 'em. They liable to be cartin' us off to some funny farm."

"Well, before I make it on their radar, I'd like to hear what they're actually saying while driving around," she said. "Think you could get a bug in their car?"

"Sunshine, if they're like most retrievers, all they know is how to fetch. A bug in the car is a waste of time. All you'd hear were farts and burps." Trevor shoveled in another spoon of sugar and stirred his coffee. "If it's really possible, would you go back?"

Someone pounding on the front door interrupted Amara's consideration of Trevor's question. As she'd done the day before, she peeped out the parlor window from behind the curtain. Sam Jennings, the reporter, stood, shifting from foot to foot and blowing into his hands.

"Who's that?" Trevor asked from behind her.

"A reporter. He's looking for Farley," she said.

"Ain't everybody," Trevor said. "I'll let you handle it. I got a bus to catch. You got any change?"

The reporter pounded again. "Farley, come on, man, I know you're in there. Open up."

To Trevor, she whispered, "Check the junk drawer in the kitchen. That's where he keeps his bus tokens. What do you think? Should I answer the door?" She turned in time to watch Trevor slip out the back door.

Since Trevor wouldn't bug their car, Amara needed another plan to find out what the stalkers in the black sedan wanted. Teaming up with a reporter might be a decent strategy. But it could just as well backfire. If he was simply out to exploit Farley for the sake of selling sensationalism, she'd need to learn of his intentions quickly.

"Here goes," she said and opened the door.

Showing surprise at seeing her, the reporter asked, "Is he in?"

"Nope, didn't come home last night," she said, no turning back now. "To be honest, I think he's moved on."

"Moved on? Where to?" The reporter appeared desperate.

"If I knew, tell me why I'd tell you," she said. She leaned against the door frame and crossed her arms to ward off the chilly air.

He gazed out at the street, his hands crammed in his coat pockets. "Look, Farley still owes me a cup of coffee. You gonna invite me in?"

Ignoring all the relentless warnings her parents and husband had pounded into her head, she invited an unknown man into her empty house and led him down the dark hallway to the kitchen. She motioned for him to sit at the table while she poured coffee into a cup that read *I May Be Wrong But I Doubt It* and placed it in front of him.

"How do you two know each other?" she asked.

He took a long sip. "I'm gonna level with you. Farley and I never actually met. But we talked on the phone. Someone gave me his name and number."

"Who?"

"Are you aware of your housemate's unique history?"

"I just moved in a few days ago. We don't really talk that much."

"Funky Man, the guy I told you about, told me that Farley claimed"—he paused, weighing what he would say to her—"he was from another time."

"Come again?" Amara asked as she sat across from him. So,

Farley and Trevor's friend Funky Man spilled the beans to this reporter.

"He claims Farley's from England from the future. Twenty forty-two."

"He told me he moved here with his wife and that she'd died," she said.

"He never mentioned things about the future?"

She shrugged. "Like I said, I just met the guy."

"Someone told me that he said he was living his life and one day he woke up and he was in 1993. Doesn't have any recollection of how he got here."

"Wow, that's some story. I know Farley's a little forgetful because of his age and everything, but I didn't—"

"Are you a Way Backer?" he interrupted her.

"A what?"

"The day before he got run over, Funky Man told me about people who call themselves Way Backers and about Farley being the ring leader. Are you part of it? My paper will pay you good money for the rights to your story."

She laughed. "Way Backers? What are they? A band? I don't sing."

"You know something," he said, "otherwise, you wouldn't be living in this house. Funky Man said he, and others, came here from another time. And that some of you weren't adjusting. Crashing into things, heads exploding."

"Heads exploding?" she said. "Wow!" She'd made up her mind, this guy was fishing. Not only that, he was dangerous. "Which paper did you say you worked for?"

"The *Post*," he said. He pulled out what looked like a wallet, flipped it, and flashed something too fast for her to read.

"Farley's been gone since Saturday and you're here to talk with him about exploding heads?" Amara shook her head.

"Stop playing the dumb innocent, Miss Epps, if that's even your real name."

Amara wiped imaginary crumbs from the table to hide her reaction of him knowing her alias. Martha must have told him.

"Samuel Joseph Jennings does his homework before he comes knocking on doors, accusing people of time travel. I happen to know that Alice Epps from Charlottesville died last August. Want to see a copy of her obituary? And I know that the man you live with is not Farley Dickenson but Farley Davis from England, married to one Dorothy Davis, but she died. Want to see *her* obituary?"

The refrigerator motor kicked in as Amara considered how to answer the reporter's inquiry. Her response would impact her and the others. What would Farley do to distract a reporter? How about a nice government conspiracy? Farley and Brenda were always arguing over the topic and reporters loved a juicy cover-up narrative. Slowly, she said, "Maybe I know some things."

"If you're not Alice Epps, who are you?"

Ignoring his question, she said, "I'll tell you what I can if you agree to help me."

"Anything," he said.

Perhaps the Way Backers could identify the men following them by using Jennings as a decoy to poke around. She leaned in and asked, "Did this Funky Man say anything about someone following him around. Someone trying to kidnap him?"

Jennings took another gulp of his coffee and said, "He did act a little paranoid the last time I saw him. Said he was being followed."

"Did you follow up on his claim?" she asked.

He slowly shook his head. "What are you saying? Are you being followed through time by some type of time traveling G-man?"

Jeeze, this guy had a one tract mind. "That's some imagination you've got, Sam. You sure you're not a sci-fi novelist?"

So what if Jennings reported on claims of having met time travelers, she argued with herself. That sort of nonsense was reported daily in supermarket tabloids. Aside from his own mother, no sane person was going to actually believe Jennings.

Except. Except, the people in the sedan with the government plates.

Chapter Nineteen

DRIVING AROUND TOWN
MONDAY, DECEMBER 20, 1999

Trying to deflect the conversation away from the Way Backers, Amara said to Jennings, "I can tell you what I know about Farley, but you've got to do something for me."

"Shoot. Anything," Jennings said.

Laying the groundwork for a conspiracy story, she said, "Don't ever come here again. From what I've heard, Farley ran with a tough crowd. They might not appreciate you poking in their business. You could get killed."

"I can handle myself. How do I get in touch if I have follow-ups?"

She considered his request and said, "Call the flower shop, tell whoever answers you're calling for Alice and give a time and place to meet. If I can, I'll come."

"Okay. Now, answer my question. Are you from the future?"

"You're wasting your time on the time-travel angle, bud. There's no such thing and how do you prove something that doesn't exist, anyway? You can't."

"I've interviewed someone who's experienced it. Funky Man.

That's first-hand testimony. Proof enough for my editor." He added, "If I could find a traveler from the year 2999, it would be the scoop of the century. What year are you from?"

"If I had an inquiring mind, I'd want to know *who* was making Funky Man, an unstable individual with claims to have time travelers as friends, paranoid." She plopped this in front of him.

His eyes jiggled. "You think it's some kind of cover-up?"

Hoping he'd bite, Amara said, "You're the reporter."

He surveyed the faded poster of *The New Yorker* magazine cover hanging on the wall. "How would I start?"

"Write this down," she said. "A friend of Mr. Dickenson's told me that they saw two men help Funky Man's buddy into a government-issued sedan and drive away. The guy's name is Desmond Kurts, goes by Desi. No one's seen him since. Another friend said they saw Mr. Dickenson talking to the police in front of this house the night he disappeared. When he didn't show up for a coffee date, his friend went to the police station looking for him. The same government vehicle was parked inside the squad's lot." She stood to pour Jennings more coffee, then said, "Wait right here."

She left Jennings scribbling at the kitchen table and went downstairs to Farley's command center. Quickly, she shuffled through all the papers on the table and found the scrap with the license plate number Brenda had snagged from Desi's kidnappers. Somehow, Farley's captors had missed it. Back upstairs, she recited the number to Jennings as he wrote it in his notepad.

"You're thinking Dickenson and the Kurts guy were kidnapped by a government organization?"

"Find out which agency those tags belong to and you've got a solid lead on a government conspiracy."

"Are you from the future?" he asked.

She laughed. "I'm from Richmond, Sam."

"Be serious. What's your real name?"

Thinking about the day she tried to speak to Beck as a garbage truck careened by her, ripping away the van's door, she said, "My name is Alice Epps and I'd rather not get involved."

"How did you get here? Did you walk through some kind of portal? Where is it? Does it work both ways? Can I travel to the future?"

Fighting the temptation to tell this guy everything, she heeded Farley's warning to tell no one about her experiences.

"Think about it, kitten," Farley had said. "The world's crazy *now*. What would happen if everyone—or worse, a handful of people—knew the events of the future? For one thing, the world economic markets would implode."

"But, Farley," she'd replied, "they *did* implode. In '34, remember?" She didn't have time to noodle through that revelation at the moment. She needed to stay focused on the reporter. To Jennings, she said, "Can you travel to the future? Hardly. You've been reading way too much science fiction, space cowboy." She rubbed her chest where the hover craft hit her, the one that had bumped her over into another time channel.

"What year did you come from?" he asked with persistence.

Not wanting to give him anything, she busied herself with re-arranging Farley's coffee mugs on the curio shelf hanging above the kitchen table.

He pulled out a small, hand-held recorder. "Come on, give me something," he whined. "Does everybody have their own jet pack? Do the Cubs ever win the World Series again? No, don't answer that last one. I don't want to know." He paused to think of another question. "What's it like? What's a typical day like?"

She hunched her shoulders. "Beats me."

"Give me something concrete," he said. "Like, will cancer be cured? Will there ever be a woman president? Do we make it to Mars?"

As the reporter went on with his futile questions, she got up from the table to put the coffee creamer in the refrigerator, then winced at the sink full of dirty dishes. When she got back home, her real home, she was going to find someone like Sargent Harry and upgrade Rosie so she could retire from service at Oakwood.

"Alice?" the reporter spoke from behind her. "Are you listening to me? I need something concrete."

Snapping on rubber gloves, she said, "Think about it, Sam. There's no way you can verify answers to any of your questions. And if you reported answers to those questions without verification, what kind of journalist would that make you?"

Aren't we being bold, today.

"But if I had to guess, cancer won't ever be cured. Like every other malady before it, there'll be treatments that allow people to live with it. And, NASA has had its sights on Mars for decades. We'll make it, hopefully, in our lifetime. As to a female president, in my opinion, it can't happen soon enough."

The phone rang.

Before picking up the receiver, she said to Jennings, "Your best lead for a blockbuster story is that license plate number. Find out who's driving the car, kidnapping people off the streets." Then, to the receiver she said, "Hello?"

"It's Ramesh." He sounded nervous, like the night they went to Buddy's nervous.

"What's going on?"

"The sedan is back."

"Where are you?"

"I'm at the bank. With Brenda. She's inside. She said we needed to change deposit boxes since Farley left. They've been following us. What do we do?"

"Which bank?"

"The branch at Gardenia and Grove."

"Hang tight, don't go anywhere. I'll be right there." Hanging up the phone, Amara glanced at Jennings. He was watching her. "Give me a ride?" she asked.

"But we haven't finished this interview," he protested.

Tossing the rubber gloves in the sink, Amara locked the back door, motioned for him to follow her to the front and said, "We can talk in your car." Grabbing a coat and Farley's keys, she shooed the reporter onto the porch and locked the door.

"Something's happened," he guessed as he led her up the block to his rusty two-door Civic.

"My friend spotted the car I just told you about. We're going to follow it while it follows him," she said. Inside the car, there was just enough room for her to squeeze in amid all the clutter. Handing Jennings a bowl of half-eaten oatmeal, she said, "I don't know what to do with this."

He tossed it into the back seat and started the car. "Where to?"

"West on Grove."

As the car slowly skidded through ice and slush, Jennings asked, "When you go back in time, can you talk to yourself? You know like in that *Star Trek* scene where Spock talks to himself?" After a few seconds of silence, the reporter asked, "Ever wanted to tell your younger self how you've royally messed up your private life for a meaningless job full of endless dead ends?" The car crawled to a stop light.

"Can't this thing go any faster?" Amara asked. Without thinking, she jumped out, dashed to the driver's side, and opened the door. "Move over."

"What?"

"Move over. I'm driving," she commanded. After they buckled in and were back on their way, she said, "We need to get there before next week."

Six blocks later, Amara slammed on the brakes as she skidded by the bank. Taking the corner like an Indy driver, she saw Ramesh's car in the parking lot. Both doors were wide open. She sped past and circled the block again. To Jennings, she said, "Look for a late model generic style sedan with the license number I gave you. Parked or moving." Seeing nothing, she circled again.

"I'm not seeing it," he said.

She parked in the bank lot and walked over to Ramesh's empty car. The doors were still open, keys in the ignition, motor running. "What the . . . ," she said softly to herself. Catching her breath, she forced herself to casually stroll into the bank and scan for Way Backers.

"Excuse me," she said to a teller, "did a tiny lady with puffed up hair come in to see her safe deposit box? Brenda—." She didn't know Brenda's last name.

"Mrs. Bruce?" the teller asked. "She just left. If you check the parking lot, you might catch her."

"I just came from the lot and didn't see her." Amara took a deep breath. Things were getting ugly. In her mind she heard Brenda saying, "Bad, bad, bad, Tandy." To the teller, Amara said, "She asked me to meet her here. She was going to upgrade her lock box. There was something she wanted me to have. Do you know if she got anything out of her box?"

"You'll have to ask her about that. She did go into her box and she paid for another one." The teller's mouth formed an "Oh" as she covered it with her hand. "I'm not supposed to say anything."

Amara gave her a thumbs up. Outside, she stood next to Ramesh's car and scanned the area as if her optic screens were on and her locator was signaling them. No ubiquitous sedan. She was too late. They took Ramesh and Brenda. She blew out a puff of air and quoted Brenda, "This is bad, bad, bad, Tandy."

"What just happened?" Jennings asked.

"The government agency you're investigating just kidnapped two more people."

"Are you going to call the police?" he asked.

Ignoring his question, she got into Ramesh's car and, before closing the door, she said, "Call the flower shop when you have something on the license plate."

As she changed gears, her knee bumped against her locator swinging from Ramesh's key ring. Amid all the excitement, did Ramesh ever get around to deactivating the homing beacon on her locator? It didn't matter. They had him now, and Brenda, too.

Chapter Twenty

On Tuesday, Barton was still MIA and his girlfriend Sissy called the flower shop every half-hour for updates. Eventually, Tandy refused to talk to her, delegating the task to Amara. She was getting better at coming up with new euphemisms for "he's not coming back." The poor woman, like all the other local people involved with missing Way Backers, had become consumed with endless worry and would never learn the truth of her loved one's fate.

According to Farley and Brenda's theory on the Way Backers' situation, Barton was either roaming the streets of Richmond in another time channel or being committed to a mental institution. Until she spoke to the men in the sedan, she had no way of knowing the fate of her friends. One thing Amara knew was true: Going back to their previous lives was what they feared most. But not her. Why was that?

When Amara shared with Tandy the news of the disappearance of Ramesh and Brenda, she asked him if she needed to contact their loved ones.

He replied, "No, thank God, they were smart enough not to get involved with a local."

She found herself thinking about Ramesh. She'd grown fond of him as a friend.

Since her arrival in 1999, Amara craved junk food. Her favorite Juicy Vibes drinks must have been spiked with something because her homemade smoothies left her craving more sugar and salt. At lunch she pulled into what was becoming her favorite restaurant's drive-through lane. Before she could order a large chocolate shake and salty fries, the van's two-way radio bleeped.

"Van six? You there? Tandy wants to talk to you," Martha announced.

She spoke into the push-to-talk radio handle, "Van six, here."

Tandy's voice squawked loud and clear, "Midday news reports a body found in Byrd Park. Make your way over to the morgue."

She came back with "My job description doesn't include looking at dead people."

"Somebody's got to. Farley's not here. How many deliveries you got left?"

"Finished with the morning run," she said.

"Call the shop if you run into trouble. On a telephone line."

"They're not going to let me waltz right in and—"

Her protests were greeted by an ear-splitting squawk-hang up over the radio.

An hour later, Amara sat in the van near the loading dock behind the downtown state building. She glanced around, expecting a security guard to order her to state her business. She rubbed the bulging belly of the plastic Buddha mounted on the dashboard of Barton's delivery van. Barton's van had never lost a door to a garbage truck whizzing by, Barton's van had never been stolen.

Toying with cover stories, in case police knocked on her window, she contemplated who would send flowers to a morgue.

A few minutes later, a white van arrived and backed up to the loading platform. Then a car, a black sedan, rolled in beside it. Two men got out of the sedan, one much taller than the other. They watched as a tech rolled a gurney from the medical examiner's van and followed him into the building.

"Hello there," she said softly. The sedan's license plate number matched the number she'd given Jennings, the number Brenda recorded when Desi was taken. If these were the same guys harassing Way Backers, then whoever was on the gurney was probably someone she knew. Please don't let it be Ramesh or Farley, she prayed to the plastic Buddha. Watching a security guard lumber down some steps, Amara turned the ignition and slowly rolled out of the parking lot and onto the street.

"Where does Barton's girlfriend live?" Amara asked Tandy. She was calling from a pay phone.

"Why?" he asked.

"I'm thinking the body is Barton's," she said. "The sedan Brenda saw showed up at the morgue as they were wheeling in a body. We can get the girlfriend to go down and ID it."

"That's *your* job," Tandy ordered.

"The girlfriend has a better story to get inside," she insisted.

"Farley doesn't like getting regular folk involved," Tandy said.

"Farley's gone, Tandy."

Across the river, she parked the van on a Manchester neighborhood street and knocked on Sissy Eubank's door. A pair of anxious eyes stared out from above the door chains.

"Sissy?" Amara asked. "I'm the person you talked to on the phone. From the flower shop? You can call me Alice."

"Did you find him?"

"I think we did. Can I come in?"

"Are you alone?"

Amara stepped back and held up her hands.

Sissy shooed away her cats as Amara entered and stood by the door.

Cats. Why do there always have to be cats?

"Where is he? Is he in jail?" Sissy asked as she tightened the kimono's sash around her narrow waist.

From a hallway skylight, the afternoon's winter sunbeams spotlighted Sissy's face and neck. Blue-inked reptile scales around the woman's neck gave Amara a fright. She steadied herself. A serpent tattoo encircled the girl's scrawny neck, its beady black eyes staring at Amara. Amara rubbed her own throat in sympathy.

"Well?" Sissy insisted. "Where is he? He's had me worried sick."

"Tandy, that's Barton's boss, is still asking around, calling Barton's regular customers to see if they've seen him."

"But you said you know where he is," the girl said.

"I do." Then, Amara clarified herself. "That is, I think I know where he is."

"So where is he?"

"Sissy . . . are you and Barton legally bound? Married?"

"Why? What kind of trouble is he in? Do I need to hire a bail bondsman again?"

What a life this woman must lead, Amara thought, talking about interacting with a bail bondsman like he was an ATM machine. "Has Barton mentioned to you any characters following him around?"

"Characters?"

"You know. Guys in unmarked sedans, police cruisers?"

"I don't think so. Why?" Sissy's toe nudged at a cat that was rubbing against her leg.

"Have the police contacted you about your report?" Amara asked. She sneezed.

"Why the twenty questions, lady?" Sissy's impatience was causing her to scratch at her arm underneath the oversized sleeve of her robe.

"I think he's at the morgue," Amara blurted out.

"At the morgue? What's he doing there?"

She really can't be that dumb, Amara thought. "I think he's a"—sneeze—"a guest?"

"A guest?" Sissy's eyes lit up with recognition. "What? He's dead?"

"I'm not sure, that's why I asked if the police have contacted you."

"No," she squeaked. "What happened? Can I go see him?"

"I'll take you there," Amara said. Thinking of her encounters with moving objects while driving and Sissy's safety, she asked the young woman, "Do you have a car?"

"Sold it last week to, ah, pay rent," Sissy said.

"Get dressed and I'll take you. Did you say you and Barton were married?"

"What does that matter? My man's dead," Sissy huffed.

"If you two are married, you'll have a better chance of getting in and confirming it's him," Amara explained. "Or not," she quickly added.

"But you said he was at the morgue. Are you saying it might not be him?" Sissy was scratching again.

After the ride downtown, Amara managed to get a confused Sissy out of the van and to the morgue's front entrance. Business hours posted on a bulletin board indicated they had fifteen minutes before the building closed to the public for the day. The chilly stillness of the cramped reception area calmed Sissy into a comatose state. When asked who she was, Sissy offered up a zombie stare.

Amara spoke for her, "I'm a friend of the family. I drove her down here. This is Sissy Eubank. She believes her significant other might be here."

Tossing daggers of suspicion at the pair, the receptionist consulted a monitor. "What's the name," she asked.

"Barton Armistead Hobbs," Sissy proclaimed softly.

"We believe Barton is the body that was discovered this morning in Byrd Park," Amara added.

Hearing this, Sissy flailed her hands in the air, flopped onto the floor and wailed, "No, noooooooo! This can't be happening to me again."

The receptionist stood and peered over her monitor at Sissy, who was now slowly rolling on the floor. "You want to help your friend get straightened out?" She ordered Amara. "I can't take all this noise, not when it's almost quitting time."

A Polaroid picture of a freckled bicep with a tattoo reading *My Be Loved,* was shown to Sissy. She confirmed to an assistant medical examiner that the tattoo belonged to Barton. She was with him when he got it. She was his beloved, she'd explained. She added that the plan called for a red heart, with her name in it, to be inked in below the words when Barton got his Christmas bonus money.

A police detective questioned Sissy while Amara waited in the reception area. On her way back from the ladies' room, she detoured to the loading dock area. The sedan wasn't there.

"Did they say how he died?" Amara asked Sissy as she drove her home.

"They wouldn't tell me anything. Every time I asked about him, they answered with one of their dumb questions."

"Such as?"

"Like did Barton ever talk about his past or about things that were gonna happen, like he could predict the future or something?"

"I don't follow you," Amara said.

"They said his name wasn't really Barton Hobbs. That it was Christian Thomas." She added in a squeaky cry, "But I know my Barton and he'd never lie to me. He'd never *not* tell me something like that. We shared everything."

At a stop light, Amara glanced over at Sissy and asked, "Did he? Did he say things to you that sounded, you know, out there?"

"Barton Hobbs is *not* crazy," Sissy insisted. Hearing her own use of the present tense in reference to her lover's life status, Sissy wailed, then blew her nose and wailed some more. "My beloved is gone."

"The flower shop will cover his funeral expenses. Let us know how we can help," Amara said.

"Doesn't matter. They won't let me have his body. Said he was part of some kind of science project," Sissy said. She blew her nose and stared out the window.

No one spoke until the van stopped in front of Sissy's house.

As she jumped out of the van, Sissy proclaimed, "They won't tell me what happened to him. I'm hiring a private investigator." She dashed away before Amara could clarify who "they" were.

Traffic was heavy with holiday shoppers and evening commuters. A half a block ahead Amara saw them. Keekee Biddle and John were walking briskly down the wide boulevard's sidewalk with Keekee latched onto John's arm like a barnacle. A frame of the scene of John and Amara's first meeting flashed at her. It was one of Keekee's infamous all-nighters at the Biddle mansion. Keekee was clutching at John's arm just as she was doing on the sidewalk up ahead. Amara shook her head to deflect the memories. But they kept coming.

New Year's Day 2000, the first day of the new millennium,

Amara had come off her midnight shift at the network center. Y2K had been a major bust but she'd earned double time plus holiday pay, enough money to cover spring semester's tuition. Before she could get her coat off that morning, Beck pounced, offering to do her laundry for a month if Amara would take her and Jared to Keekee's "Hair of the Dog" party that evening. Beck never got around to doing her laundry, as she'd promised, but took full credit for introducing Amara to John.

Needing to be part of the "in" crowd in high school, Keekee financed most of Beck's friends' parties. She'd emotionally black-mailed her father to hire John when Jared was arrested for cocaine possession and distribution. Beck once said to Amara, "It's like her parents pay her to stay out of their way. I feel sorry for her. Nobody likes her but they go to her parties and drink her booze and snort her cocaine."

At Keekee's that night, everything and everybody around John had fallen out of focus for Amara as she watched him peel Keekee off his arm and walk across the posh, low-ceilinged den with its panoramic views of the James River. All eyes were on him, the adult in the room. Like a real prince, he bowed in front of her, took her hand and said, "John Darnley. Have we met? I feel as if we have."

Punch drunk from too little sleep after working the Y2K shift, her head was muddled, like it was stuffed with cotton. And here was this handsome man staring at her, asking her a question that made no sense. To her, it felt like Prince Charles was asking her to pass the French onion dip. Unable to form a response and not wanting to embarrass herself, she mumbled shyly, "No," and went in search of the dinner buffet everybody was excited about.

Chapter Twenty-One

t wasn't love at first sight, exactly; it was more like love at first sight, interrupted. For young Amara, the aura of instant infatuation had been interrupted the second John pulled out that tired non sequitur about knowing her. And now, fifty years later, and in another dimension, she discovered why he'd asked her such a clichéd question. He had met her before, or the older version anyway. And to his credit, he had recognized the resemblance between young Amara Graves and the poser Alice Epps.

For all the years they were together had John known about Alice Epps and her true identity? Sissy was adamant that her man shared everything with her. But he hadn't. He hadn't shared with her his real name. And he hadn't revealed to Sissy his past—being from the future.

What if John had somehow learned about her concealed duality and kept it to himself? Perhaps he was protecting her, like Barton obviously was protecting Sissy. Had he insulated her all these years from an incomprehensible truth? Her lower lip quivered as her eyes teared up.

"Keep it together, Amara," she said as she backed the van to the shop's loading dock.

"Well?" Tandy asked as Amara entered the workroom. "How did it go?"

"It's Barton all right," she said. "What do we do now?"

"We bury the poor bastard and hope his soul can have some peace," Tandy said.

Amara rolled her eyes at Tandy's reference to an afterlife. He'd been in 1999 too long. By 2049, belief in an afterlife and a holy spirit had fallen into ambiguity. The divine and its relics had been replaced with walking dead souls, faith in the cosmic universe, and infinite black holes. Community centers and housing alternatives like Hope Home had moved into the church buildings.

"Are we going to find out what happened to him? I mean, what if there is a cover-up and they're killing Way Backers on purpose?" Amara asked.

"We have no evidence of that," Tandy said. "Funky Man's death was witnessed. He got run over."

"But what if he was pushed?" Amara suggested.

"And God help us if that's true," he replied.

"Yes, it means our government is committing murder to hide all this," Amara said.

"Martha gave me this before she left." He handed her a "while you were out" pink form. "Said some guy said you'd know what it meant."

Sitting in Ramesh's little sedan in back of the shop, Amara took in its smell—curry and burnt motor oil. She missed him already. Not familiar with the address scribbled in the message, she thumbed through the worn road map Ramesh used for restaurant deliveries. She noticed as she flattened the map on her lap that she'd stopped patting her chest to reactivate her locator, which was safely tucked back inside the backpack in her room at Farley's.

A knock on the car's window caused her to jump. "Ahhh!"

John was blowing into his gloved hands and stamping his feet. She rolled down the window. "You scared me."

"Where are you headed?" he asked as he pointed at the map.

"I have to go to Craig Street. Not sure where it is."

"East or west?" he asked. "It's divided by Chamberlayne over on North Side."

On the map, her finger followed Chamberlayne until she found Craig Street. "Thanks. Why are you stalking me today?" she asked, glad that he hadn't lingered with Keekee.

"Was in the neighborhood. Thought I'd drop by and see if you'd like to go for an after-work drink." A light breeze lifted his wispy bangs. He flashed his helpless little boy look at her, the one that melted her resistance.

"What is it with lawyers? Always wanting to drink," she teased.

"Okay, then let's skip the drinks and go for a light sex," he said.

"Excuse me?" she asked.

"I mean . . . . I mean . . . . light supper . . . supper."

His cheeks flushed from the verbal slip. Or was it the cold air?

"How about it, then?" he asked in his light English lilt.

"I've got to be somewhere," she said.

"Tomorrow?" He wasn't giving in.

Borrowing from Tandy, she replied, "You do know we're in the middle of our busiest season, right?"

He crouched and folded his arms on the bottom of the car's window frame, then leaned inside the car. His face so close to hers, she smelled his sandalwood soap. "Don't make me beg. It's not pretty," he whispered. Then he grinned at her.

He was going to kiss her, she just knew it. "Gotta go," she said as she fumbled with the ignition.

"Can you give me a lift?" Not waiting for an answer, he rushed to the passenger side and hopped into the car. Buckling up, he asked, "Where's your friend? Ramesh, is it?"

"Gone home to India to visit his family," she said.

"He's got a crush on you, ya' know."

"We're just friends," she said.

"I'd say he wants more than your friendship," he teased.

In front of his rowhouse a few blocks away, he said, "Now you know where *I* live. I'm having friends over tomorrow night for Christmas dinner. Join us?"

Amara hesitated. What could it hurt? Other people would be there to keep anything from happening between them. Now that Farley and Brenda weren't around to nag, what was stopping her? "I'll think about it," she said.

"Good. See you around six."

The address Martha had scribbled on the pink slip was a run-down affair amped up on flashing neon. Shorty's was open for business. After watching the place for a few minutes, she went inside. Jennings was sitting at the bar, staring into an empty shot glass and smoking a cigarette.

"Who grated your face?" she asked.

"Your friends with the license number," he said.

"What did you find out?"

"After you left the bank, I drove over to the police station where you said you saw them. They were there. Parked out back talking to the station chief."

"And?"

"When I asked about Dickenson, they all stopped talking. The chief went inside and the two men followed me back to my car. Told me to drop it. Then, the stumpy one did this." He lightly touched the gnarly gash over his right eye.

She winced. "That needs stitches."

"That's what I told him," a short barrel of a woman behind the bar complained.

"Nothing Jack Black can't fix," he said as he tapped the bar with his empty glass, signaling Shorty to pour another.

"Look, if this is how it's going to be, I don't want to be the cause of you getting your head bashed in permanently. You need to back off—"

"You were right," he said. "The license plate checks out. My source at DMV said the numbers indicate federal law enforcement. I bet they're covering up time-traveler instances. This could be big."

"Sounds like you've already made up your mind as to what the truth is. And now you're just looking for evidence to back it up."

"People have a right to know what their government is doing," he said hastily.

She patted the bar with her open palm and said, "All right then. You go all Fox Mulder and chase *X-Files* all you want but leave me out of it." She slid off the bar stool and leaned in so Shorty couldn't hear. "Never contact me again."

As she opened the door to leave, he called after her, "I'll go where my leads take me."

Her plan had failed. Jennings was still obsessed with finding time travelers to interview for his story of the century. She drove to the McDonald's on Broad Street and ordered her new favorite dinner. Sitting in the parking lot, munching hot, salty fries—darn they were good—she thought about what she should do about him.

A Christmas card, wedged through the mail slot of the front door, fell on the floor as she let herself into Farley's later that night. On the inside, a persistent John had written, in his flowing cursive, a reminder of his dinner invitation for the following evening. Seeing her name written by his hand stirred memories of another letter, one he'd written to her, asking to come home after two years of separation. He'd stopped drinking and apologized for slapping her. In the letter's last paragraph, he admitted that he was weak. He wrote, with his flair for the poetic, "I'm not like you, my darling A. I'm a bumbling mortal who knows not the depths of the universe. Forgive my failings to doubt you and our love." There was no mention or reference of an affair with the Biddle woman.

Seeking affirmation that she'd done the right thing by reconciling with John, Amara had shown the letter to Megs.

"Bumbling mortal?" Megs asked. "What's he mean by that?"

"I don't know," Amara said. "He's really changed. It's like he's not the same person. And he promised me that he's stopped drinking."

"So you're letting him move back in?"

Amara nodded.

"You're so blind when it comes to loving that man," Megs said as she hugged Amara.

Amara took John's Christmas card with her to bed and reread the note on the back. "Be mine at Christmastime."

She nodded off to sleep.

He was back, this time in her bed, whispering, "In spite of what's happened to us, I never stopped loving you."

She raised her arms and arched her back. His warm breath on her neck was accompanied by his soft lips, tracing a path from the base of her throat to her ear. His lips nipped at her lobe then made their way to her lips. The kiss was sweet and slow.

A sensation of falling rushed through her. Her heart beating erratically, she kicked at something binding her feet. She blinked at the darkness and called out on her way down, "John!"

A stream of light seeped in as a toilet flushed and the mumblings of Trevor brought her back to her 1999 reality. Placing her hand on her chest, she patiently waited for her heartbeat to slow. She closed her eyes to search for her husband but the dream had melted away.

The next morning at the Way Back Diner, Amara reported her visit to Shorty's to Tandy and Trevor. They discussed Jennings' confirmation that someone in the federal government was indeed following and harassing Way Backers.

"I tried steering him away from Farley and the time channels but he seems insistent on finding someone who'll talk to him about it." After describing to them the state of Jennings' rearranged face, she added, "Maybe the guys looking for us will keep him quiet."

"Don't count on it," Tandy said. "You stay close to this guy and make sure he doesn't write anything about us."

"It doesn't matter," Amara said. "Think about it. The only people who'd believe anything he wrote are people like us and the guys looking for us. Did Farley say anything to you about talking to a reporter?"

"No. He'd say we don't need that kind of attention."

"I'll agree to that," she said.

Onto other business, with Brenda gone, there was no one to process the new arrivals. The three argued over who would assume the role of identity creator. Trevor drew the short straw.

"There're five identity profiles in there," Amara said as she handed over Brenda's brown leather satchel which she'd recovered from the back seat of Ramesh's car.

"What are we gonna do when that sixth person gets here?" Trevor asked.

"Can we recycle the others?" she asked Tandy.

"Too risky. We'll have to get someone on at DMV or Vital Statistics downtown," Tandy said. "Did anyone show up yesterday?" he asked Trevor.

"Nope." As Trevor stood he gulped down the last of his coffee. "Guess I'm off to the races. By way of the Greater Richmond Transit Authority."

"Trevor, you're a trooper for stepping up to these new responsibilities. I appreciate what you're doing, man." Tandy said.

"It's what Farley would do," he said. "I'm doin' this for him. And for Barton. And for Funky Man." He retrieved what he called his "blow rag" from his back pocket and blew his nose. Amara noticed that it looked a lot like one of the tea towels that complemented Farley's tea service on display in the dining room. Better that he wasn't coming back.

Chapter Twenty-Two

ON DELIVERIES
WEDNESDAY, DECEMBER 22, 1999

Three days before Christmas, holiday songs blared from everywhere, in the shop's arranging room, on the van radio, in elevators, and from customer's offices and homes. It seemed to Amara that the ghosts of Christmas past were channeling radio DJs to play "Santa Baby" at least every thirty minutes.

She switched off the radio after parking Barton's van in a downtown loading zone. In the silence of the cab, she watched as workmen wrestled with a windblown artificial tree, laden with snow and ice. The Graves-Darnley fake tree appeared in her mind. The one she'd decided to use in place of real Christmas greenery, the one complete with lights and an "authentic" conifer scent. As she had predicted, the kids didn't care. On Christmas Eve, John discovered her traitorous act and sulked for the remainder of the holiday season. The fake fir, or, if she was being honest, John's reaction to it, had helped her to understand for the first time in her life that the only person she could truly make happy was herself. She finally admitted to herself that she'd never shared John's passion for the Christmas holiday, not his version anyway. For her, the anticipation of the long winter darkness after too many sugar plums always left her dreading the January blues.

Arguing with the silent radio, she said out loud, "You'd think if they could colonize the moon, they could do something about the January blues." She got out of the van, went around to the back and opened the doors. While pulling the delivery order from the floor of the van, she decided, in spite of her doubts and Brenda's warnings, to accept John's offer. Why not take an evening away from Trevor and his open-door bathroom practices and spend it with John and his friends? She found herself wanting to be there with him when the last guest said goodnight. "Why not?" she said out loud to no one. "It's not like I'm being unfaithful." On her way back to the shop, maybe she'd drop by the Village House of *re*Design and find a secondhand party outfit for the occasion.

A familiar tingling in her hands prompted her to set the huge crystal bowl of forty roses back on the floor of the van.

A strange *POP!* sounded over her head. Before she could react, a powerful force engulfed her and lifted her entire body off the street, slamming her onto the sidewalk. She landed on her butt. What she took in burned onto her retinas and haunted her for days. A metal box, what a reporter later described on the local news as a multi-ton air handler system, ripped the van's back doors from their hinges a split second after a man dove toward the pavement.

Reverberations from the crash bounced against her. Warped sound waves rippled in front of her, distorting her senses. She blinked as silence enshrouded her. She felt trapped inside a slow motion video bubble. When the bubble burst, sounds rushed at her in hurricane windspeed: the awkward creaks of the hulking mass settling, people yelling, tires squealing, and more metal crunching. A loud rhythmic wailing caught her attention. She looked up. Swinging from a crane's jib was a mammoth hook with a broken cable whipping around like a kite's tail.

A woman screamed from across the street. "Somebody call an ambulance!"

Amara pushed herself up and wobbled over to the man. His foot had gotten caught underneath the gnarled doors. Ignoring the confusion, the man calmly pulled his leg from the fray. Unable to look away, Amara expected to see pulsating blood and an exposed tibia. Instead, a steel rod jutted from shredded black flannel trouser. The foot, enclosed in a rubber-soled wingtip, dangled from tiny threads of fiberoptic cables.

Too stunned to speak, she watched the man reconnect the prosthetic foot to the jutting metal rod. She bent down to pick up her shoe, which had flown off her foot. Standing, she looked his way but he was gone. He'd not given her a chance to thank him for saving her life.

Refusing care from the EMTs, Amara tried to focus on the police officer's questions.

"Did you see or hear anything that might have caused the cable to break?"

"Did you know the man who pushed you out of harm's way?"

"Why did he leave the scene of the accident?"

These were all reasonable questions. Amara had no answers.

Sitting on the curb, she watched the workers reattach the HVAC unit to the crane's hook. A worker came over and asked, "What do you want us to do with these?" Seeing the doors crumpled on the pavement, Amara's shock took her back to the split second when the unit crushed through the doors on the spot where she'd been a nano-second earlier.

The man moved so quickly. He pulled her away so fast with no effort at all, as if she weighed nothing, a feather.

Tandy arrived with Evan, a new Way Backer. She recognized

his dazed and confused stare, the same gawking look she'd made when she arrived.

"This is Evan," Tandy said.

The boy nodded at Amara.

Tandy gently placed his hand on her arm and quietly said, "The boy claims to be an AI developer genius. But for now, he's taking over your deliveries and I'm taking you back to the shop."

After Evan drove away in the breezy van, Tandy and Amara got in Tandy's 1988 Lincoln Town Car and rode back to the shop in silence.

Amara sipped hot cider as she answered the phones. Still on edge, she was unable to stop thinking about her near-death experience. The scene repeatedly played in her head: The sensation of flying through the air, seeing the man dive for safety, then the mother of all air conditioners crashing down on the exact space where she had been standing. Her upper body wilted onto the stool behind the front counter.

The man's push, and the sensation of flying through the air, felt like the pounding she'd taken when the hoverboard knocked her in the sternum the day she ended up here in 1999. Her shaky state was now accompanied by a thin bead of sweat trickling down the side of her face.

Was she in shock? Or, had she traveled to another time channel?

In a panic, she went to the computer workstation in the closet office and pressed the "enter" button on the keyboard. Her heart pounded in her ears. Paranoia kept her from asking Martha what year it was. Impatiently, she tapped on the keyboard, cursing the slow response time of the monitor. Finally, she clicked on the toolbar at the top of the screen.

"What's wrong?" Martha asked. "You're as white as a sheet."

Ignoring her coworker, Amara clicked on the date icon.

It flashed: Wednesday, December 22, 1999.

Amara pushed her bangs away from her brow. "I'm having a day," she said to Martha. Reaching for her coat, she said, "Can you handle the front? I'm leaving."

The temperature was on its way down to freezing. Out of habit she tapped her sleeve but her funky Goodwill coat didn't respond. Feeling all was lost, she cried all the way to Farley's.

A warm bath soothed her jangled nerves. But later, as she lay in her bed, each time she closed her eyes she relived the incident. Giving up on sleep, she got dressed and went downstairs where guests from Barton's wake had extended the party to Farley's front room. Trevor was holding court, regaling everyone with his nude flight from the police. Sissy and others were smoking pot and helping themselves to Farley's single malt scotch and Irish whiskey.

Then she remembered John's invitation and her plans to attend his dinner party. She went back upstairs and changed into a blouse and velvet slacks she'd bought for the shop's Christmas party and packed a toothbrush in her backpack, just in case. She locked her bedroom with the house's only skeleton key and left through the front door. Evan, the new Way Backer, greeted her on the front steps. It was official: Trevor had turned Mr. Dickenson's home, a shrine to his cherished Mrs. Davis, into a frat house.

Chapter Twenty-Three

Walking toward John's house, Amara picked up her pace to keep warm. She'd be unfashionably late for the dinner party. She wasn't hungry but she could use a drink, a strong one, and some normal company.

Her other self had been to John's house before, many times. In fact, they lived there a few months after their wedding. After Beck followed Jared to Baltimore, they moved into the much larger Grace Street house. By then, Audrey and Ted had "emigrated to the great Republic of Texas," as her father had joked. Aiden was a newborn. At John's insistence the house was restored to its Victorian splendor of exposed wood paneling and marble accents. The young family moved in, sharing the expansive row house with a hefty mortgage and ghosts of the Old South.

"Hi," she said a little nervously. "Am I too late?"

"Come in!" John said. "We're having a night cap." He invited her into the foyer and hung her coat over the stair's newel post.

In the living room John introduced everyone to the late arrival.

The four names sounded familiar, the names of the people at Buddy's. In a quick panic, Amara scanned the room for Keekee, but she wasn't there. She tapped the healing cut on her head.

Along with Christmas tree lights, a glow from a television sitting in a built-in bookcase illuminated the room. The volume set low, the late news was playing.

"Did you hear about this?" Talia asked, pointing at the set.

"What happened?" John asked.

"Some schmuck forgot to secure a lead on a crane hook. A cooling unit dropped a hundred feet onto a delivery truck," Duncan offered.

"A miracle no one was hurt," Sandy said, placing his empty glass on the coffee table. "Talia, my darling love of my life, it's time we went home to our perfect angels."

Talia laughed as she stood to leave. "Sweet talk all you want, Buck-O. It's still your turn to walk the babysitter home."

"John? There's a case with your name all over it," Duncan said, bringing the conversation back to the downtown crash.

"Oh, yeah?" John said. His hand brushed hers as he handed Amara a heavy tumbler of scotch. Their eyes met, both knowing why she'd come.

Ellen Ann motioned for Amara to sit next to her on the sofa.

While John saw Sandy and Talia to the door, Ellen Ann asked Amara, "Aren't you the friend who had the stereo speaker fall on her head? John said it was a nasty gash."

Tracing the raw scar with her cold fingertips, Amara said, "Oh, it wasn't too bad. Two stitches. They're out now." They weren't just out, her skin healed so quickly the stitches had fallen out the next day. Trevor and Brenda could criticize this new life therapy all they wanted, but Amara was going to keep using Dr. Coleman's miracle cure—that is if she ever made it back to Oakwood.

"Let me take on your case. I can get you free beer for life. Ha!" Duncan was weaving in front of her. "Can you imagine, honey? Free beer at Buddy's for life?"

Ellen Ann rolled her eyes at her drunk husband. To Amara she whispered, "I don't know if you realize it but John is smitten with you. You're all he talks about. His mystery older woman. I've never seen him so . . . infatuated."

Duncan said in yawn-speak, "You got him under your spell, woman."

When John re-entered the room, Ellen Ann stood and said to him, "We'll say our good nights."

When Amara and John were alone, he switched off the TV then asked, "Another drink?"

"Maybe later," she said. The warmth of the first one had relaxed her tense shoulders. The deep downy sofa cushions absorbed all the day's stress. Resting her head on the back of the sofa, she watched shadows dancing on the ceiling. She closed her eyes. The alcohol had muted her doubts of being there.

A moment later, she felt his body next to hers. She drew in his warm scent of cologne and scotch. His arm tunneled its way behind her neck, causing her heart to skitter. He gathered her in his arms and nuzzled at the side of her neck, exactly as he had in her dream the night before.

Unable to hold her desire inside another second, she kissed him with a passion she thought she'd lost forever.

They were both tugging at her blouse, him nuzzling at her neck. As Amara allowed herself to savor the mounting throbs of her body, a loud repetitive beep echoed from the foyer.

"What's that?" Amara whispered.

John, his face now buried in her cleavage, groaned and said, "Nothing." His lips found hers and they kissed with renewed intensity. She moaned as his fingers brushed over the silk of her bra.

The beep sounded again, this time seeming more urgent.

"What *is* that?" she asked again.

"A coitus interruptus device," he mumbled. As he gently pulled her blouse back over her shoulders, he continued, "And it will not stop until I pay heed to its demand."

"Ah, a pager. Remember when—" she caught herself from asking if he recalled a very young Aiden insisting that John page his mommy and demand she come home and make him pancakes.

"Remember what?" he asked, fondling a strand of her hair.

She reprimanded herself for the slip. He wasn't her husband, not now.

He cried out in frustration as the beeper sounded for a third time. He pulled his arm from under her neck and said, "Don't go anywhere. I'll be right back."

She nestled into the cushions as he spread a throw blanket over her, the one he'd gotten on a trip to Mexico with his law school buddies. From the adjoining room, she heard John's loud protest, "What?" then a door closing. His muted voice lulled her into a deep sleep, one without dreams or fears.

A distant ringing awoke her. Seeing crystal tumblers at eye level brought her back to John's living room. Under the scratchy blanket, she checked, she was still dressed. Where was he?

No one seemed to care if the phone went unanswered. The ringing stopped as she found the bathroom off the kitchen, which was in a state of nuclear meltdown. She recognized the kitty cat clock his sister had given him his first year of law school. Kitty cat reported the time at five-thirty-ish. She was due at the Way Back Diner at seven.

Returning to the foyer, she stopped at one of the photographs hanging on the wall. The first time she had seen the photo, John had told her about his older brother and younger sister. The brother, the favorite son, lived on the West Coast and they had lost track of him. Myra lived in Alexandria.

By the stair landing, she called out, "John?" She placed her hand on the stair handrail. The familiar time channel warnings of tingling feet and fingers caused her to step back. Like at her house on Grace Street, there was someone or something upstairs that she shouldn't see.

Chapter Twenty-Four

In the misty predawn light, Amara carefully tiptoed around the patches of frozen snow on the sidewalk. A block from John's house, she became aware of footsteps crunching on the ice behind her. She stopped at the corner refraining from looking over her shoulder. The crunching stopped. She trotted across the street and continued west toward Farley's. She heard footsteps again. Someone was definitely following her. Her mind jumbled with possible escape routes. There was a coffee shop two blocks north. No, it won't exist for another ten years. To crush her fears, she focused on her next move. She quickly calculated her route to Farley's, two blocks west, one south and one more west to safety. The crunching was getting closer. No way she'd make it to Farley's front porch in time.

She spun around. Dredging up her empowerment training from eons ago, she stood like a superhero, legs spread wide and hands on her hips. The stalker stopped. In the dim light it was hard to make out his features but she immediately recognized the tattered trouser leg.

"You," she said. It was the man who had saved her from the

killer A/C.

The man said nothing as he came closer.

"Who are you?"

"My name is Moby," the man answered.

"Why are you following me?"

The stranger blinked but said nothing.

"Who are you?" she asked again.

"My name is Moby."

"Yes, you've already said that." She took him in. Where was his winter coat? The temperature had to be below freezing. No hat, no gloves. His nose and ears weren't red from the extreme cold, like a normal human. Moby was a robot. And not just any bot. He was Dr. Coleman's assistant. The one who installed her new contacts and locator.

Sensing she was in no immediate danger, she asked, "How did you get here?"

Moby didn't answer.

"Stop following me," she shouted at him. She continued on her way to Farley's, the sound of Moby's heavy footsteps ever present from behind.

Amara sipped at her tea in the front room as she watched Moby standing on the sidewalk across the street. Trevor joined her.

"He still there?" he asked. "Let me go over there and shut him off. Takes two seconds."

"Let's think about this first," she said. "Why is my wellness counselor's assistant following me around in 1999? How did he get here?"

"Maybe somebody injected him with a bad batch of nanochips, like the rest of us," Trevor said. He took a pull on his coffee, then lifted the mug to toast the missing host, adding, "Found Farley's private stash of Kenyan."

"But his being here, what does it mean?" she asked.

"Maybe to shut us up, make us disappear." Raising his bushy eyebrows, he added, "A robot assassin."

"Don't be silly. A bot can't be designed to harm," she said.

"Maybe they're afraid people back in our other time will get wind of what's happening and will want to stop taking their treatments."

"Hardly," Amara said. "Biochip plasma is the veritable fountain of youth. No one's going to want to stop using the program. And if it gets them a trip down memory lane, they'll see it as an added bonus." She set her empty mug on a crowded end table. "Surely they've located the cause and corrected it by now. Maybe that's why Moby's here."

"Right. And pigs fly on Jupiter," he said.

"Maybe Moby's here to reset everything and make it right."

"Or, maybe they want us taken care of. Don't want us blabbin' on about what's about to happen," Trevor said as he tossed empty beer bottles into a trash bag.

"Maybe," Amara admitted as she watched the unmoving robot.

"Can Sissy move in?" Trevor asked. "She got evicted."

"Let's go. Tandy's waiting," she said.

Driving Ramesh's car, Trevor continued his pitch for Sissy's cause. "She can bunk with you. I gave that new fella Evan the back room. Did you know he did a tour on the moon at Armstrong Research? Math whiz. How 'bout it? Sissy, I mean."

Amara ignored his petition, hoping it would disappear on its own.

The reporter Sam Jennings was sitting at the Way Back Diner's counter. He slightly raised his coffee cup to Amara as she passed. The place was packed with regulars and holiday celebrants, the air stuffy with grill vapors, human sweat mixed with cigarette smoke, and a whiff of pancake syrup. Amara pulled her sweater up over her mouth to filter the air she breathed. Tandy, Evan, and a young man in Army fatigues were already chowing down on their Maggie Walker specials: johnnycakes, eggs, and bacon.

She slid in beside Evan as Trevor pulled up a chair at the end of the booth.

"Guys, this is Nadar," Tandy said as he pointed to the newest new guy.

Nods and grunts all around, then Tandy asked Amara, "You feel well enough to work?"

"Tell him who you ran into," Trevor insisted.

Amara glanced at Nadar, then Tandy, and asked, "New recruit?"

"Nadar says he missed the last HT out to Fort Lee and fell asleep on a bench. Woke up on the sidewalk. A homeless man was stealing his boots. While he was still wearing them."

"What year?" Amara asked.

"Forty-nine," Nadar said. "Is it really 1999?"

"Keep your voice down," Trevor said. "This place has more cockroaches than Moscow's American embassy." On cue, the waitress appeared with Trevor's coffee and menus.

"Can I get some more bacon?" Nadar begged the waitress. She winked at him and flitted away.

Squinting at the young man, Trevor asked, "How old are you, guppy?"

"Old enough," Nadar said.

Amara said, "Now's not the time to act cute. What year were you born?"

"Twenty-five," he said.

They all did the math. The time travelers were getting younger. This was a new data point.

"Were you undergoing any type of medical treatments?" she asked him.

The waitress placed a plate of bacon in front of Amara. Like a hungry pup, Nadar snatched the fried meat from the plate and wolfed it down in a couple of chews.

"Answer the woman," Trevor insisted.

"I lost my foot in a training accident," he said. "They grew me a new one."

"Were you required to use biochip plasma for treatments?"

"Ma'am, they poked at me so much, I have no idea what's inside of me. All I know is my foot works and I can run again," he said. He lifted his plate and licked it clean.

"Why were you off base?"

"Checkup at the CEL clinic."

"What is the name of your wellness counselor?" Amara asked.

He shrugged. "Whoever's there?"

"Do the names Stone or Coleman mean anything to you?"

"Nope," he said.

"Were you ever treated by a bot named Moby?" she asked.

"Don't recall the name. You gonna eat your biscuit?"

"What day and year were you last treated?" Amara asked.

"What is this? A black ops interrogation?"

Trevor bopped the back of the young man's head. "Stop acting cute. Answer the lady. What was the day and year of your last visit?"

Nadar rubbed the back of his head. "I got fitted with new contacts yesterday, Wednesday. The twenty-second?"

"And the year?" Amara asked.

"Two thousand forty-nine. Like I already told you."

"Your contacts are no good here," Trevor said. He pointed at the boy's wristband and added, "The locator doesn't work here, either. Hand it here."

Everyone at the table felt Nadar's reluctance to give up his locator. It was a portal to his life, his finances, his security clearances, his avatar identities, and life memories. Tandy reached for Nadar's wrist but the young man was too fast for him. The older man raised his hands in surrender.

"Are you aware of a futurist named Desmond Kurts? He is supposed to speak at Ashe Boulevard Cultural Center about time travel?" Amara asked.

Nadar nervously adjusted his locator on his wrist. "I saw him on local newsfeeds. The governor wants to ban him from speaking. Says it would stir people up. But some nut job group called the Black Hole Society is protesting to let him speak. They feel like if the state wants to put a muzzle on this guy there must be some truth to what he's saying." He asked, "So this Kurts character ain't lying? This is crazy. How do I get back? I don't want my sergeant to think I've gone AWOL."

"Son, letting your sergeant know where you are is the least of your worries," Trevor said. "Come on, let's get you squared in your new quarters and assignment."

Tandy slid out of the booth to allow Nadar to leave with Trevor.

"Don't take him to any bars," Amara warned as the pair made their way through the diners standing around waiting for a booth to open up.

"Don't turn around but your friend the reporter is having coffee at the counter," Tandy said as he counted out a tip.

"I saw him," she said.

"What did Trevor mean earlier? You meeting somebody?"

"I was out walking this morning and someone followed me home. It was the guy who saved me from the A/C crash."

"That's weird," Tandy said.

"No, what's weird is that he's a bot who works at CEL where Nadar gets treatments for his foot. What's weird is he's the bot who installed my new locator and contacts."

Chapter Twenty-Five

A persevering Moby located Amara at the flower shop. At noon it started to sleet. She and Tandy watched as the robot stood like a sentry while pedestrians, with their heads down, bumped into him.

"I managed an entire team of AIs," Tandy said. "Worked as a manager at Patty and Fry's over on South Side. Seeing him makes me wonder if there are others like him. You know, looking for us."

"Let's bring him in," Amara said. "He's going to attract the wrong kind of attention standing out there with no rain gear on."

Handing her an umbrella, Tandy said, "I've got a feeling he won't listen to me."

She quickly crossed the narrow street and stood in front of him. A yearning for home swept over her. Here was someone from her time. Someone whose data storage content was not unlike her own, full of sights and sounds of everyday life in her time. Except Moby wasn't organic, flesh and bones and organs and arteries and fluids. They had one thing in common: They both needed electromechanical nits to help them make it through the day.

"Hello, Moby," she said.

"Hello, Amara Vivian Graves," Moby said.

"Moby, smile," she commanded.

He spread his broad lips, revealing perfect teeth complete with pop diva *i*Hopes etchings. "I see you have an opening in your calendar for Friday. December. Twenty-four. Two thousand forty-nine. Do you want to schedule a follow-up visit?"

Moby's question was an ordinary question, one he asked his clients every day. However, his question stirred her longing for connection to her world. She hugged him around his waist. Squeezed him like she did Aiden whenever he came home to visit. Even though she'd only connected with Moby once, on a health maintenance related occasion no less, he felt like an old friend, a dear friend. "Moby, follow me," she commanded.

Amara ordered Moby to sit on the chair in the office under the stairs. And when Martha showed up for her shift, Tandy gave her the day off to avoid explaining Moby's presence. After the arrangers and delivery drivers had left for the day, Amara led him to the workroom.

As he swept the day's clippings, Tandy said to Amara, "His eyes follow you, like a puppy's. He's here for you."

Amara caught the sadness in Tandy's voice. She took the broom from him and handed it to the robot, saying, "Moby, sweep." To Tandy, she assured him, "We're going to get through this."

"While I was arranging a casket spray this afternoon, I was thinking. Do you suppose Moby could find my van?"

Together they watched as the AI, with exact precision, gather up each petal and stem from the floor.

"I reported the van stolen to OnStar but they don't have much interest in finding it until I file a police report. And I'm not going there."

Amara followed him to the front and stood by as he rummaged through an overstuffed file cabinet in the tiny office under the stairs. "Here it is," he said. He handed her the van's bill of sale. "Let's ask him to locate it."

Back in the workroom, she held the document in front of Moby and said, "Moby, scan."

"Scan complete," Moby responded. "Nineteen ninety-eight GMC utility van, white. Last scheduled maintenance. Monday. November. Twenty-nine. Nineteen ninety-nine."

Tandy studied the van's service folder. "Danged, if he's not on the money."

"Moby, report location by nearest street intersection," she commanded.

The AI's eyes brightened as he stood straighter. They watched for a few minutes but Moby seemed to have fallen asleep with his eyes open.

"He must've hit a light deflector," Tandy said, referencing a security barrier used to block content access.

"It was worth a try," Amara said. "Maybe Trevor or Evan have a work-around."

"The diner tomorrow morning at seven?" Tandy asked while standing at the back door waiting for Amara to gather her things to leave.

"Vehicle 3RBFJ32KZNM584933 GMC van in idle state. Location coordinates as requested: 2000 Brewery Street, Richmond Sector, Virginia, USA, North America." He even supplied its global positioning system coordinates.

Tandy and Amara were speechless. Moby had located the vehicle on a street that would not be in existence for another twenty-five years. In 1999, an apartment complex, part of the city's public housing, existed at the coordinates Moby recited. The complex was torn down and the city's popular Brewery Mall was erected, naming the main thoroughfare Brewery Street.

Tandy said, "I'll drive by those apartments on my way home. You know, see if it's parked on the street. On this time channel."

"And if it's not there?" Amara asked.

They both looked at Moby and Tandy said, "Wonder if Moby could go get it for us."

"It means he'll have to leave this time channel and go into another one," Amara said.

"He's already proved he can do that," Tandy said.

"But can he move the van from one channel to another? That's the question," Amara said. "Do we risk it?"

"On second thought, I say no. If he goes wandering off into another channel, we may never see him again. Somehow, I feel he's your way back. We don't want to jeopardize that."

Amara faced Moby and asked, "Moby, can you bring the van from its current location of space and time to this location on this day? If yes, what are the risks? If no, state the reason why."

Moby's eyes blinked twice. "No. Reason: I do not have valid permission settings to operate an internal combustion engine powered vehicle."

Tandy let out a loud "Ha!"

"I guess driving without a license falls under the AI creed of 'do no harm'," Amara laughed.

"Let's call it a day," Tandy said.

As they were buckling up in Tandy's Lincoln, they watched Moby walk toward the car. "Like I said, he's a puppy that wants to follow you around. Might as well take him home with you."

Farley's house was ablaze with light, partiers, and head banging rock 'n' roll. She asked Tandy to pull into the alley so she could escort Moby into the basement without any witnesses. The headlights illuminated someone on the back porch, peeping in the windows. Tandy edged the front of the Lincoln to block the peeper from leaving the porch.

"Hey!" Tandy shouted from the car. "What's going on here?"

The man trampled over the car hood, then jumped and slipped on uneven icy snow.

Amara leapt from the car and managed to grab a handful of the fleeing intruder's hair.

"Awwwww," he cried out as he went down a second time, "aww, aww, aww, let go!"

Amazed at her strength and fearlessness, Amara yanked a little harder before she released her hold. "Meet Samuel Joseph Jennings, reporter and all around stubborn creep," she said as she rubbed her hands on the sides of her pants.

"My shoulder," Jennings wailed.

Tandy squatted to help Jennings to his feet. "You ought not go around snooping in other people's windows. Did you hurt yourself?"

Jennings stood and rotated his shoulder forward and back. "I was looking for you," he nodded at Amara.

"Thought we had a deal. I gave you information and you promised to stay away," she said.

"You weren't as forthcoming as you led me to believe," he retorted.

Walking away from him, Amara mumbled, "It's Christmas. Shouldn't you be under a rock with the rest of your family or something?"

He called out to her, "I finally tracked down the agency. The one that chased after Funky Man."

She stopped in her tracks and pivoted to face the reporter.

Tandy leaned in to the reporter, getting in his face. "Keep your voice down, son."

"I'll talk as loud as I want, old man."

"And get yourself killed," Tandy stammered in a loud whisper.

"Let him talk," Amara said. "Who's going to believe his nonsense?" She pulled at Tandy's arm and said quietly, "Come on, just walk away."

Tandy straightened himself and got into his car. Amara joined him. "Start the car but wait to see what he does."

"Samuel Joseph Jennings. Reporter. Freelance on topics of the paranormal, extraterrestrials, conspiracies, and unexplained occurrences. Born. Nine. April. Nineteen sixty-four. Died. Two. January. Two thousand," Moby reported from the back seat.

"Moby, mute audio," Amara said. Moby's report chilled her as she watched Jennings approach her side of the car. If the data were accurate, Jennings would be dead in ten days. She had to warn him. She rolled down her window.

"I caught up with those knuckleheads again. They're rounding up you guys."

"I'm sorry. Who are 'they,' Sam, and who are they rounding up?"

"Come on, Mrs. Darnley, don't play dumb. I know you're from the future." He lowered his head and asked Tandy, "Are you one of them, too?"

"What's he talking about, Alice? And why did he call you 'Mrs. Darnley?'"

"Because he's deluded," she said. Flashing her hands in the air, she went on, "He's got this crazy idea that I've traveled from the future and some spooky government agency is out to get me." She laughed. Laughed because when she spoke the truth out loud, it sounded beyond ludicrous. If she ever got back, Megs wasn't going to believe her, ever. "Stay away from me. No, better yet, leave. Leave town or somebody not as nice as me is going to have you arrested and thrown into a rubber room."

"Go ahead. Report me," Jennings said. "And we'll see whose story they believe, yours or mine."

She signaled for Tandy to drive on. The long car lumbered down the alley, its undercarriage scrapping on the packed, icy snow in the alleyway. The car circled the block twice. Before Amara and Moby got out, she said to Tandy, "We'd be wasting our time trying to persuade him to leave. Right?" She felt guilty leaving Jennings knowing she could possibly do something to prevent his imminent death.

"We'd have to introduce him to Moby and have him listen to Moby's report. And I don't think that's a good idea," Tandy answered.

"Right," Amara said. When Amara and Moby arrived at Farley's back door, Jennings wasn't around.

Inside the basement, Amara commanded Moby to sit at Farley's desk. She asked him, "Do you require a recharge?"

The robot responded, "Charge is at full capacity."

"Really? Rosie has to recharge, like, every night."

"Rosie says, 'Hello,'" Moby said.

"Wait. What?" Amara asked.

Party noise burst from overhead as Trevor opened the basement door and trotted down the stairs, a Jamaican spliff behind his ear. "Oh, you're home. Didn't see you come in. We're runnin' out of beer. Gotta break into my private stash." He hefted a case of beer from a far corner, the place where Farley used to keep his file cabinet. "Oh, hel-lo," he said as he noticed Moby. "So you decided to come in from the cold."

For Trevor, Amara said, "Moby, repeat your last sentence."

"Rosie says, 'Hello.'"

Trevor's eyes widened. He slammed the beer on Farley's desk. "Rosie? As in the zero gen house bot you're always pining for?"

Amara nodded. "When did you last interface with Rosie?" she asked Moby.

The robot was silent for sixty seconds. "Ten. December. Two thousand forty-nine."

"Did you try to contact me for a follow-up session?" Amara asked.

"Yes."

Amara explained, "About a month ago, I went into the clinic for new contacts and locator. I never got a chance to schedule a follow-up appointment. They must have scheduled Moby to ping Rosie for a response." She paused, then asked, "Moby, did Rosie ask you to find me?"

Trevor slid into a chair across from Moby, his mouth gaping.

Amara clutched onto the desk waiting for the answer.

"Affirmative. Rosie says, 'Please come home.'"

Chapter Twenty-Six

FARLEY'S HOUSE
THURSDAY, DECEMBER 23, 1999
FRIDAY, CHRISTMAS EVE, 1999

Someone from the first floor called down, "Trevor! Where you at, man?"

Amara motioned for him to tend to his guests.

"I'm shutting it down," he said of the party. "Be right back."

As the noise of scraping chairs and clunky footsteps clattered from above, Amara contemplated how to ask Moby her next question. She was anxious about the answer. Was he here to take her home? If he acted on her inquiry immediately, she might disappear like Ramesh and Brenda. She wasn't ready to leave. She wanted to say goodbye to the others. She needed to see John again, just one more time. To say goodbye, forever.

When all was silent overhead, Trevor bopped down the steps and sat across from Moby. He commanded, "Moby, state your make and model."

Moby's eyes did not respond to the command.

Amara said, "Apparently he only cares for the sound of my voice."

"Then you ask him," Trevor said.

"I don't think any of that sort of stuff matters. I think he's here to find me. Maybe to take me home."

"That's stupid talking. No self-respectin' AI of Moby's caliber is gonna take commands from a zero genner. But, hey, I never thought I'd be runnin' around downtown in my birthday suit in the middle of winter either," Trevor said. "Ask him if that's why he's here."

Her throat dry, Amara gulped and then asked, "Moby, why are you here?"

The robot did not respond.

She said to Trevor, "Maybe, you're right. Let's start with the basics. Stuff we know he knows." She patted her chest with her palm and asked, "Moby, what's my name?"

He turned to her and said, "Hello, Amara Vivian Graves."

Placing her hands on Trevor's shoulders, she asked, "Moby, who is this?"

"Harold Simmons Beauford. Known as Sargent Harry, the Bot Fixer. Born. Four. May—"

In a panic, Amara quickly commanded, "Moby, delete inquiry." She relayed to Trevor what Moby shared about Jennings's impending death.

"Damn!" Trevor exclaimed. "Ask him who sent him."

"When I asked him that question this morning, he didn't, or couldn't, answer." She leaned on the table, her face close to Moby's, and asked, "Moby, did Rosie send you?"

Moby's eyes lit up and he said, "Rosie says, 'Hello.'"

"Sounds like Rosie's got some type of hold on him," Trevor said. "I'd like to meet the old gal."

"So you think a utility robot like Rosie couldn't issue commands to a bot in Moby's class?"

"Not that I'm aware of," Trevor said. "But, it could be some kind of machine-to-machine behavioral learning. You know, they absorb more of each other's content and system code each time they exchange transmissions. If he's been pinging away at her for a while, I'd say they've gotten to know each other pretty good. It's the same principle as when a system interacts with us. It learns our preferred settings, shopping habits, what brand of toilet paper we prefer. Stuff like that. Just a theory." He massaged his bushy hair, as he was fond of doing.

The pair spent the next hour attempting to gain information about how Moby traveled to 1999. The bot went silent when asked questions about physical movement from one time channel to another, where he came from, or who sent him. However, Moby knew about events, people, and places, and he warmed up to answering Trevor's questions about football teams and scores. When Amara asked him to recite the highlights of the daily news feeds from December 10, 2049, two days after she arrived in 1999, Moby slipped into his now familiar power-save mode and closed his eyes. They'd reached the end of Moby's content, which ended at 12/10/2049 and from his other time channel. The AI had followed her into the world of the past.

Exhausted, she retired to her bedroom and discovered Sissy and a rather large party guest twisted up in her blankets. She returned to the basement and settled on the sofa as Moby hovered next to her. As she drifted into sleep, she thought of John. He never called to explain why he'd left her stranded on his sofa. Trying to convince herself, she mumbled, "It's for the best."

The next morning, Christmas Eve, Amara grabbed a parka from the hall tree and handed it to Moby with instructions for him to put it on. Trevor and Amara decided to skip breakfast at the diner and headed to the flower shop in Ramesh's car. Moby came along.

"How many of Brenda's identity packets do you have left?" Amara asked Trevor.

"Three," he said. "But I'm working on a way to get all I want. Can I borrow Moby later on tonight?" He opened the door for the bot to get out of the back seat and added, "Me and Moby's gonna watch a little football from Farley's easy chairs."

"If you're thinking of using Moby to bet on games, it won't work," Amara said.

"Why's that?" Trevor asked.

"Ramesh tried it. Something always prevented him from collecting."

"Well, I ain't Ramesh," Trevor said. "Spot me a couple of Bennies."

Amara and Tandy sat Moby in the closet office under the stairs so Martha and the other locals wouldn't see him. Hoping John might come by to pick up his mother's African violet, she set it on the counter next to the cash register and thought about him each time she rang up a sale. Chaos prevailed until noon. By two, anyone who was ordering Christmas arrangements had already done so. La Petite Fleur's family gathered around the work table and shared a glass of Champagne and Tandy's homemade fruit cake. After all the locals left, Evan and Nadar announced they were taking over Brenda's apartment and asked if Tandy and Amara needed a cat or two.

And so, it was Christmas Eve and all was calm. At Mercer Street, Sissy had left a barely legible note stating she was off to parts unnamed for her obligatory annual dinner with her father and his wife. Trevor entertained himself by dressing Moby in Farley's smoking jacket and ascot and ordered him to sit in Farley's favorite wingback. Together they watched the last half of the NFL's

Christmas Eve game—Dallas at New Orleans.

Trevor strutted his best victory dance on his way to the refrigerator to get another beer. He invited Amara to join them in watching the recorded broadcast of the 1999 Christmas parade. The city stopped having parades in the 2030s. Group protests about Santa Claus's portrayal as a "benevolent capitalist" and reduced funding were the excuses city officials gave for the cancellation.

Whatever happened to just having a bit of whimsy? Amara mused. Watching the campy parade with teens dressed as elves and clown cars buzzing down Broad Street saddened her. She excused herself. Moby tried to follow her up the stairs but she ordered him to stay with Trevor. She burrowed under the bed covers with her lingering sensations of John's kisses and caresses from two nights ago to keep her company.

She awoke to the sound of Trevor and a woman singing. The illuminated alarm clock read 1:30 A.M. "Inviting people to the house with Moby here, he's gonna get us all shipped off to the asylum," she swore to herself. Cinching the sash of her flannel robe, she floated down the stairs and into the parlor.

"And a par-tri-e-geeee in a pear treeeeeeeeeee," wailed Trevor and Moby. Moby's voice had been set to "female soprano." Still wearing the ascot, the bot was naked from the waist up. Cables ran from his side to the TV. Arm in arm, the pair was singing Christmas songs, karaoke style.

Amara couldn't stop smiling. Maybe Moby was her Christmas gift. Maybe Rosie sent Moby here because she couldn't come herself. Maybe Rosie sent Moby to help Amara in her new life.

Around eight o'clock the next morning, Amara luxuriated in the delight of sleeping in on Christmas Day. Before she and John separated, every year her plea for a quiet, simple Christmas morning with the kids was ignored. Instead, John insisted they break out the silver and china and host a brunch buffet for family, neighbors, friends, and, sometimes, a client or two. She stayed in the background with her reticent in-laws while John flitted about as host and bartender.

After 2019, the Darnley Christmas brunch waned in popularity because of their separation. Plus, John had sued the city and a couple of their Monument Avenue neighbors. When the city condemned Keekee Biddle's legacy of college student slum rentals, a tract of four Victorian apartment houses, she got her daddy involved, who, in turn, got John involved.

On behalf of Keekee and her rental management company, the lawsuit accused neighbors of colluding with city officials to impede Ms. Biddle's right to rent her own property. The line had been drawn. Keekee's intercity activists, mostly her non-paying tenants, riled about the "injustice of a tyrannical government violating an individual's right to housing space." They called for an "end to discrimination against temporary occupants."

The defendants, surrounding homeowners, just wanted city hall to clear out the blighted tinder—once stately Victorian suites that, unfortunately, had been neglected far too long and were beyond restoration.

A judge ruled against Biddle's defense and ordered the buildings razed.

The case was a turning point in John's legal career. He started drinking the hard stuff again. Citing the mishandling of the case, George Biddle dropped John from his company's legal roster of outside counsel.

In his late night drunken diatribes against the unfair justice system, John pledged to Amara that he'd continue his fight on behalf of the downtrodden. And, as a result of his self-destructive efforts, his cases quickly transformed from resolving issues of common dispute to creating a firebrand of legal chaos. Kimberly cheered for him. Aiden wanted to know if his dad was having a midlife crisis or something. Wearing her positive public persona, Amara told the kids that their role was to support Dad in his new endeavor. His higher purpose, he'd called it. But when she learned that he'd used the kid's college fund to bail out a group of protesters, she told him he'd gone too far.

Their argument ended in his angry slap across her cheek. The blow had left a bruise.

Without saying another word, he moved out the next day. A messenger delivered a check for the full amount to replenish the college fund. The check was drawn from Keekee Biddle's personal checking account.

"Amara!" A hungover Trevor stood in her bedroom doorway.

Amara pushed aside the sad memories of that rocky time in her family's life. She sat up in bed and asked, "What is it?"

"They're baaaaack," he sang as he put on his Army field jacket.

"Who?"

"Our friends with the shiny sedan," he said. He went to her bedroom window and looked out, saying, "After you went back to bed last night, I found Moby's back channel signaling option and turned it off. Found communication files confirming he's pingin' your locator. That's how he found you. I thought Ramesh turned yours off?"

"That explains why he showed up now instead of earlier. Ramesh had the locator clipped to his key fob. I found it when I found his car."

"According to the file data, Ramesh never shut it down," Trevor said.

Someone pounded on the front door.

Acknowledging the interruption, Trevor said, "Bet they're upset 'cause I'm monkeyin' with Moby's SOS signaling. I turned off your locator, by the way. Moby and I both agree you need a better hiding place than your little rucksack."

"Wait! What's going on?"

"Moby's headed out with me," Trevor said as he fastened his coat.

"Where are you going?" She got out of bed and pulled on her floppy sweater over her pajamas.

"I got winnings to collect. We'll be in touch."

Amara watched as Trevor walked to the end of the second floor hallway and crawled out a window onto the roof of the back porch.

He yelled, "Moby, catch!" Then the wild man cannonballed off the second story roof and was gone.

Chapter Twenty-Seven

Stalling to give Trevor time to get away, she called out from the top of the stairs, "Just a second." She finished dressing and descended the stairs. Her hands shook as she held onto the doorknob and slowly counted to ten.

Someone banged on the door and called for "Mrs. Darnley!"

Trevor was right. Shutting off Moby's signaling prompted them to come. She pushed aside the curtain over the door's sidelight. There was only one man. Actually, a giant. She tipped-toed to the parlor's front window and viewed him from the side. His yellow-gray hair spiked in all directions. Dressed in a black suit, he wore a white shirt unbuttoned at the collar and his tie askew, as if he'd dressed in a hurry. He was one of the guys at the morgue the day they found Barton's body. She jumped when he pounded on the door with his open palm.

"Mrs. Darnley, open up," he urged. "It's important that we talk before it's too late," he went on, "Please. Let me in." Then, whispering to himself, she heard him say, "It's cold as my mother-in-law's looks out here."

She watched as he turned to face the street. On a second glance, the man appeared quite harmless and genuinely concerned. She couldn't take the anxiety any longer, the not knowing who these guys were and if they could help her. She went to the door, bent down to the mail slot in the middle of the door, pushed it open, and asked. "Who are you and what do you want?"

Through the slot, she watched as his legs turned to face the door. "Let me in. I'll explain," he commanded.

"Are you kidding me? It's Christmas morning. Don't you have a family to be with?"

The man squatted in front of the mail slot, revealing a face with wide thin lips and a mouth full of craggy teeth. He said, "My name is Earl T. Byrd, Byrd with a 'y'. I'm with the federal government, ma'am. You're in a lot of danger and I'm here to help."

"Ha." Her rebuke gave her courage. "My father used to say whenever someone uses the words 'federal government' and 'here to help' in the same sentence, they're after your money or your freedom. I don't have any money so it must be my freedom you're after. Am I correct, Mr. Byrd?"

After a minute and no answer, she dared to ask, "Which agency comes bearing gifts on Christmas morning?"

A mumbled "I'm with the bureau" filtered through the door.

"The bureau? You'll have to explain, Mr. Byrd," she said. Now she was taunting him.

"FBI. Now, can I come in?"

"Put your badge in front of the peephole," she said. When he did, she followed up with, "Are you armed?"

"What sort of question is that to ask an FBI agent? Of course, I'm armed," he said.

She, for reasons she had no idea why, was getting to this guy. "Put the gun in the flowerpot. To your left."

"Ma'am, an agent of the FBI never relinquishes his firearm."

The answer gave her confidence that he was who he said he was. She double-checked the chain then turned the deadbolt and cracked the door. "What do you want?"

The guy's lips were blue. "Ma'am, can I come inside? It's cold out here."

"Yeah? Cold as your mother-in-law's looks? Ah, no. You can't come inside."

He rubbed his arms. "I'm here because you're in possession of a valuable asset which the federal government considers vital to our national security. They need you to hand it over."

"Moby gave you the slip, did he?" She smiled.

"Look, all I'm askin' is you give it back and we'll not press charges for stealing classified information." He appeared nervous. This guy didn't act like any FBI agent she'd ever seen on TV or the one who came to their house that time John was arrested for spitting on a Boston police officer while at one of his "Natural Life" rallies.

"Give him back? He's not mine to give back. If he wants to go with you, that's his choice. I don't make choices for others, Mr. Byrd."

"Mrs. Darnley, my boss, he can get anxious about these situations and—"

"Is that a threat?" Surprising herself, she was actually enjoying her boldness.

"I know it's in there," Byrd's whispered voice strained. He turned his head at the sound of someone coming up the stairs. The agent's broad stature blocked Amara's view.

"Hello?" John Darnley was at her doorstep.

Panicked, she slammed the door. As she fumbled with the chain, she prayed to the God she had abandoned, "Oh, God, oh,

God. Please, please, don't let that man call me Mrs. Darnley in front of John." She swung open the door and said to John, "What a nice surprise!" Presenting Byrd with an outstretched arm, she added, "This is Mr. Byrd. He seems to have lost a friend and is looking for him. He was just leaving." She motioned for John to come inside, then faced Byrd, "I'll keep an eye out for him. Merry Christmas!" She quietly closed the door. Placing an ear to the door panel, she listened for his departure. Finding John staring at her, she jabbed her thumb at the door and said, "That was strange. Right?"

John, seeming confused, asked, "Why is it every time I see you, you're surrounded by strange looking men asking the whereabouts of others?"

"What can I say? Persistent men are drawn to me," she said. She motioned for him to follow her into the front room, where she could see which way Byrd went.

As she turned her attention away from the window, John offered her a gift. "I couldn't wait to give this to you. Consider it a Christmas apology for leaving you alone at my place the other night. Had to help a client get bail." Glancing around at the remains of Trevor and Moby's Christmas hoedown, he said, "Took a chance that you were home."

The sound of a car door slamming drew her attention back to the window. Earl T. Byrd was getting comfortable behind the wheel of the all-too-familiar black sedan across the street.

"Alice?" John was holding the gift out to her. "Hope you like it."

The present felt warm, warm from being inside his coat and next to him.

"Open it," he urged. "It's a first edition."

She tore the green and red striped paper and stared in wonder at one of the most popular stories of the late twentieth-century— *Harry Potter and the Philosopher's Stone.*

"You mentioned it was on your reading list."

"I did?"

He tugged at the collar of her tatty secondhand sweater. "At the restaurant the other night." He paused and then added, "My friends, they all like you by the way. "

She swallowed to soothe her dry throat. "I liked them, too" was all she could manage.

"I asked my cousin Stu to express ship a UK version over. It came late last night." He took the book from her and turned to the title page. "His bookshop is one of the author's favorite hangouts so he was able to ask her to sign it for you. See?"

She took the book from him and read the author's note: "Alice, Stuart says you're a future fan. Enjoy. J.K. Rowling."

"It's lovely," she said.

AI bots coming to her rescue, FBI agents stalking her, surly roommates out of control, being fifty years away from home, none of it mattered. She hugged the book to her chest and bowed her head.

He wrapped his arms around her waist. "I can't stop thinking about you." He pulled back. "Are you crying?"

Gripping the book tighter, she sniffled and said, "Noooo. I'm just having a day."

"Look at me," he urged. He cupped her chin and tilted it up. "What's the matter? You don't like the book?"

"No!" she protested. "The book is beautiful. It's the nicest gift you've . . . I mean . . . it's the sweetest thing anyone's ever done for me." She caught herself before saying the gesture was the nicest thing he had ever done for her.

This moment felt like all the tender moments they shared as they had grown older together. When he'd returned from his two-year "journey into the wilderness," as he'd called their separation, John seemed a changed man. She'd written it off as his atonement for his physical outburst toward her, thinking his sour moods would eventually return. But they never did. He had become a man with a different view of the world. Something in him had changed. Up until the last day of his life, John Darnley celebrated their reconciliation by doing something kind for her every single day. Something like giving her a first edition of one of her favorite books.

The young man before her now was not the ambitious progressive she married in 2002. The man before her was the confident romantic with whom she'd spent a month in Tuscany for their twenty-fifth wedding anniversary.

He squeezed her around the middle and leaned in to kiss her on the lips.

She placed her fingers over her mouth and mumbled, "Morning breath."

Gently pushing her hand aside, he said, "What does it matter? I want to kiss those perfect lips every morning for the rest of my life. If you'll let me." He pecked her lips. "But now," he said, "I have to drive the folks to Christmas service. Want to come?"

She crinkled her nose. "I'm a little underdressed."

Releasing her from his embrace, he took her hands and asked, "Can I see you again?"

She nodded, unable to control a grin as it spread across her face.

"The folks are leaving tomorrow morning. I'll swing by and pick you up for lunch?"

As he dropped her hands, she remembered the African violet she'd carried home from the shop, hoping it would boost her spirits. "Wait. I've got something for you." She retrieved the plant from the kitchen table and brought it to him. "Remember this?"

"I forgot all about it," he said. "Thanks. I know Mom will love it."

She stood at the door, watching as he drove away. Agent Byrd saluted her from across the street. She stuck her tongue out at him.

As the short day waned, Trevor and Moby still hadn't returned. Amara had spent the entire day alone, rereading her favorite book while curled up in blankets. From time to time she daydreamed about John wrapping his arms around her waist. And now, as the room filled with shadows, she touched her lips. What was it he said to her? He wanted to kiss her lips for the rest of his life? She bolted up out of her cocoon. He had fallen in love with her. "Oh, no. How is this happening?" she groaned. He'd fallen in love with the wrong version of her. He'd fallen in love with Alice Epps.

Chapter Twenty-Eight

AT FARLEY'S HOUSE
CHRISTMAS NIGHT, 1999

At five o'clock, Amara turned on the table lamp. Reading the book had calmed her, allowing her to view her situation more clearly. How could she have been so obtuse? Brenda and Farley had tried to warn her. Perhaps it wasn't too late. The next time she saw him, she'd tell him she was leaving town. Alice Epps would disappear. And, by New Year's Day, John would have forgotten all about her and taken one glance at Amara Vivian Graves and fall in love with her, instantly. Right, if this was a fairy tale, she scolded herself.

At half-past, the doorbell rang. She called out to the empty house, "Dinner's ready!" and jumped up from her chair. Over the phone, she'd begged Nadar, Ramesh's replacement at Bombay's, to bring her some curried rice.

Agent Earl T. Byrd stood at the door holding up two white paper bags.

"Dinner's on me," he said as he invited himself in.

"Where's Nadar?" she asked.

"Don't worry. I tipped him," he said.

A bit shaky, she struggled to keep from thinking about what

may have happened to the clueless private first class. She led Byrd through the parlor and into the adjoining dining room. Pulling the pocket doors together, she left him at the table choking down a bowl of rasam. On the back porch, she quickly tied a red bandanna around the bannister, signaling Trevor to stay away from the house. Back in the kitchen, she picked up a paring knife for a defense and then tossed it back into the sink. If the G-man wanted to take her, he would have done so at the front door. He was here for Moby.

"This stuff is fantastic," Byrd said. "What's it called?"

"Ah . . . . soup?" She sat and served herself.

"It's warming me up! All day in an unheated automobile is not my cup of tea."

Amara put down her spoon and asked, "You're not with the FBI, are you? And Earl T. Byrd sounds like a clown's name, a made-up name."

"I'm a scientist, an AI behavioral predictor. I've been attached to the bureau for a temporary assignment. The boys in the basement call me E.T." Embarrassed, he lowered his head as he said, "The gun was my idea." He wiped his mouth with a paper napkin and said, "Must say, I never thought I'd like Indian food."

"Drop the best friend act," she said. "What did you mean by needing to talk to me before it's too late?"

"What do you want to know?" he asked.

"Everything," she said.

Placing his refolded napkin on the table, he said, "Please believe me when I tell you I'm on your side, Mrs. Darnley. I don't have all the answers but I'll tell you what I know." He cleared his throat and went on, "Just like you, I'm from 2049. I was sent to retrieve the AI server you call Moby. You can imagine how people here would react if they knew about its existence and what it's capable of."

"Are there others like Moby here?" she asked.

He shook his head, "No. That's why I'm here. We don't know how or why it came here."

Holding up her hands to embrace the room, she asked, "So this is all real? I'm not hallucinating?"

"That is correct, ma'am. What does Farley call y'all? Way Backers?"

"What did you do with Farley?"

"Ma'am, I can't answer that one."

"Can't or won't? Where are the others? Brenda? Ramesh? Barton?"

"Barton Hobbs, according to the newspaper, died while running from the local narcotics squad. I believe you attended his memorial service. His live-in girlfriend is a doper, too. My associates tell me you might want to rethink letting Sondra, a.k.a. Sissy, Eubanks stay here. She'll steal anything that's not nailed down."

"What about Brenda and Ramesh? What did you do with them?"

"Can't answer that," he said.

"Why are we here?"

"Are you looking for an existential answer?" he asked the question with open hands.

"Don't play around with me," she said.

"Sorry, I've always wanted to say that."

Pressing her index finger on the table, she asked, "How did I get here? This space. This time."

He cleared his throat. "You're living in 1999 because you wanted to be here or because you thought about it a lot. At least, that's what we suspect is happening."

"You mean they haven't figured it out? Is it happening everywhere? Can we go back?"

"Whoa, whoa, whoa. One question at a time," he said.

Amara took a deep breath and then asked, "What's happening to us? And don't give me any mystic bull about us wanting to be here."

"Farley and Brenda had some creative ideas on what's happening," he said. "But we're still trying to figure it all out."

She wasn't getting any straight answers from this guy. "What's happened to them?" she demanded.

"Ma'am, I can't say."

"What is going on?"

"We think there's a glitch in the software."

"Ha. Ha. Want to try again?"

"I'm serious," he said as he picked at his leftover naan. "We think the system software on the medical nanochips all of us have been ingesting over the past two decades is somehow reacting with the new contacts and locators in, some would say, a negative way, more or less. But we still haven't been able to determine how it's happening."

"But, I haven't worn my contacts for days. And you know the locators don't work here. There's no quantum network or a single public data cloud for that matter for the locator to interconnect with," she said. "Besides, I turned it off."

"About that. You shouldn't have done that," he said.

"Why?"

He blew out a long breath. "Those clunky desktop computers everybody uses here? Remember how they became obsolete when everything got interconnected with storage drives and then along came the generic data clouds?"

"So, what's that got to do with anything?"

"And then the generic data clouds morphed into our national plexus of subnetworks like Nimbus and Galaxy."

"Will you get to the point?"

"Back in the day, to update that personal computer, you had to deliberately go out and buy a software upgrade on a disc, plug it into the computer and literally press an "enter" key to load it. If the upgrade was interrupted or never completed, the PC never quite acted the same afterwards. Remember that? You'd try to reboot with the old software and if that didn't work, you'd try loading the new software, again. It'd get so even the geekiest guy you knew couldn't make it right. So you just chucked the computer in a landfill and bought a new one."

Amara bugged her eyes at him, "What does a history lesson in ancient computer maintenance have to do with me being dragged back to the twentieth century?"

"I'm gettin' there. We've found that *disrupting* that initial engagement, breaking the seal on a new firmware package, if you will, between the locator and certain restorative nanochip plasma, has made it tricky to reengage the chips and the subnetworks that support them. Somehow it's blocking your body's ability to get back to its present state. In a time, space, and matter kind of way."

Amara asked, "Is that what caused me to travel in time? To this place?"

"First off, you didn't exactly time travel. Not in the way Einstein explains it, anyway. You've not gone from point 'A' to point 'B' by traveling at the speed of light. You've gone from point 'A' to point 'A' but in a different time dimension.

"It's like this. Remember those old phonograph players our parents had? The plastic disc spun on a turntable and the needle floated over the grooves in the disc to produce the sound. Same principle as a program reading a sound or video file. The marker moves across the file data. You can replay the record or the sound or video file over and over, forward and backward. We believe we've stumbled onto the idea in which we can replay any event in our lives.

What was the last thing you remember about your 2049 existence?"

She massaged her forehead with her fingertips. "Someone putting me in the back of an ambulance. Maybe?"

"Before that," he pushed. "Why were you being put in the ambulance? Close your eyes and think."

Following his instructions, she closed her eyes and described the images. "Someone. Something had crashed into me," she said. Looking at him, she continued, "I was on a pedestrian walk. A kid's hoverboard rammed into my chest. Here." She pressed her hand to her sternum.

"Hmm," Byrd said. "It fits one of the profiles we've developed."

"Profiles?"

"From the other lane, the future, if you will, people are disappearing," Byrd explained. "No one could figure it out. Then a Dr. Lydia Coleman discovered a common denominator."

Feeling herself being pulled into his story, she asked, "How so?"

"She found that all of her patients using biochip plasma with universal elements—ah, do you know what that means, ma'am?"

She nodded. "Rosie explained it to me."

"Clever robot, Rosie," the agent responded. "Anyhow, we looked at all the people who were given the U.E.-based chips and found some of them had gone missing."

"You're thinking if there was some kind of disruptive activity, like my accident, the locators and contacts malfunctioned?"

"Something like that. In the profile you fit, our macro-forensics uncovered that the nanochips hadn't fully bonded with the new lenses when the disruption occurred. Then when Galaxy tried to bring you back online, the connection was lost, again. The locator was turned off in the middle of your reboot, so to speak."

Trying to grasp her situation, Amara dragged her fingers through her uncombed hair. "That explains why Dr. Coleman was so anxious about my outdated contacts." A second later, she added, "She knew! She knew about this and said nothing to me."

"Keep in mind, we're still wading around in the silicone ooze on this, ma'am. Testing millions of samples has become a daunting challenge."

"Go on."

"We're not totally sure our theory is, indeed, what's happening. You know, causing the brain to take the body to places it's been before." He sat back in his chair and asked, "Tell me. Were you thinking about this time or this place when the accident occurred?"

"I don't know. So much has been going on in my life. John, my husband, died. I'm having issues with my legacy work post. Turning seventy. The treatments. My children, they weren't coming home for the holidays. This was my first Christmas without my family. But you know all this."

His voice went soft. "Rosie's downloads gave us most of the details."

"Rosie?" Amara cried out. "Is she . . . "

Byrd shook his head. "Goochland Recycle."

She wrapped her arms across her middle, feeling as if she'd been punched in the stomach. "Rosie's gone?" she whispered. "What's happening to me?"

"Here's my theory. When you were struck by the board, in that zepto-second in which your new locator lost a critical virtual link between your optic nerve cells and the billions of nanochips flying around inside you, Galaxy Network somehow mistook that as a signal to delete your existence."

"What do you mean 'delete my existence'?"

"There's the glitch. For a second or two, Amara Vivian Graves-Darnley didn't exist in our world. We haven't figured out why, but when the chips in your brain reconnected to Galaxy, via the locator, the plexus couldn't find you in some of the subnetworks. As your thoughts of this time were transmitted into the mix, Galaxy started relearning who you were. Then, somehow, your lifeline markers were loaded out of sequence. We're still trying to re-create the events so we can test them in our labs."

The spicy soup churned in her belly. "Are people in 2049 looking for me?"

"Rosie sent out a distress beacon when you didn't come home. Moby somehow caught it. CEL sent the server around to have an old timey ethernet connection transmission with her. Then, wham-oh! Moby disappeared."

"Does Megs know? What about my children?" she asked.

"As far as they're concerned, you're a missing person." His eyes showed no pity. He reasoned, "Think about it. If this little snafu is ever uncovered, there would be mass hysteria. The crazies would want to travel back in time to see lost loved ones—and you've discovered for yourself that's impossible to do. Then you have the ones who'll want *all* the chip plasma siphoned out of their bodies. It would be a nightmare. Set the global trading systems back twenty years." He shuddered. "You'll have to agree that no one wants that to happen."

"So what you're saying is that I've got billions of malfunctioning nits floating around in my body and somehow they've transformed me to another dimension?"

He nodded. "Farley describes it better, calling them personal time channels. Your profile exists in all of them but if you physically try to be in more than one at a time, things go hinky. Hence, the collisions with cars, buildings, and whatnot."

"I'm getting a headache from all this," she said as she massaged her temples. Then, she recalled Desmond Kurts, the futurist on the theater marquee. "When can I go back?"

"It depends," he said, "I can measure your chip ratios to determine your chances of returning. Yours are good since you've only been off your proper channel for a few days."

"And if the tests say I can't go back?" she asked.

"The bureau has set up a temporary arm of the witness protection program to relocate people with that configuration."

"What if I don't want to go into your program?"

"Ma'am, that's dangerous." He looked at his oversized watch. "In six days, 1999 time, Moby won't be available to catch flying objects hurling at you."

A little too smugly, she said, "I didn't ask him to."

"I don't mean to alarm you, ma'am, but my job is to keep you alive. According to our latest data model, your personal time channels are for some reason bumping into each other at an accelerated rate. Without a reboot of your locator, come this time next week, it's going to be difficult for you to walk out your front door without falling off a building or kissing a trolley."

Hiding her fear, she said, "You're exaggerating."

He took her hand and offered, "I'm not, ma'am. I promise you. But let's not get ahead of ourselves. Let's find Moby before Sargent Harry, the Bot Fixer, screws up its operating system."

Amara suspected, jarring as his news was, that Agent Byrd wasn't telling her everything. She convinced a reluctant Agent Byrd that she needed time to process what he had revealed. She watched as his gangly body loped across the street and stuffed itself into the black sedan. An hour later he was still there.

Things he said made sense but she didn't trust herself to believe his scientific explanations; they were beyond her expertise of network technology. And, his gallant pledges of rescue contradicted Farley and Brenda's obsessive suspicions of government ineptness. She now understood why the Way Backers panicked, why they ran away. They didn't know whom to believe. And, now, neither did she.

By ten o'clock Trevor still had not returned. She'd worn a path from the parlor window, where she watched Byrd on his stakeout, through the dining room and to the kitchen door. Each time, she switched on the back porch light and hoped to see Ramesh's car. But a beam of frozen rain lit up empty concrete off the alleyway where they parked the car.

She crisscrossed her sweater over her chest. Standing in the hallway by the front door, the stillness brought attention to the radiators, which weren't bumping and hissing. She pulled down the flap of the thermostat cover and saw the temperature read sixty degrees. Spending an hour on hold with Virginia Gas, she eventually learned someone claiming to be the homeowner, one Larry Parrish, had canceled the service a year ago. The rep apologized for the company's delay in the disconnection. They quoted her the reconnection process, which required the current residents to visit the office and make a deposit. She grumbled at the phone receiver after hanging up, "Disconnecting heating services on Christmas Day? Really? In what universe is that okay to do?"

Upstairs, she searched among the clothes hanging in the small closet for her tap jacket. When she couldn't find it, she hissed, "Sissy." In a panic she ransacked her backpack and found that her earnings from the flower shop were missing. She stuffed her deactivated locator, which Trevor had placed atop the dresser, and John's Christmas card into the pack and slipped it under her pillow. Burrowed underneath every blanket in the house, she had never felt more alone. She dreamed of brandishing Farley's whisk broom in a snowy fight against a toothy FBI agent who was riding a screeching owl.

Chapter Twenty-Nine

The cold woke her at sunrise. Dressed and downstairs, she peered out the front window to discover Agent Byrd and the black sedan gone, along with the wintry rain. She left a cryptic message on the kitchen table for Trevor to bring Moby to the flower shop as soon as possible. Exiting the front door, she paused to gaze at the sad little parlor, somehow knowing she'd never see it again. She spied the book, John's gift, on the sofa, and scooped it up, stuffing it in her backpack.

Amara found Tandy and Evan in front of the closed Way Back Diner gazing anxiously at post-Christmas traffic on Broad Street. Private Nadar Handa had gone AWOL from 1999.

Evan bleated, "He didn't come back to the apartment after his night shift. Do you think they got him?"

"Hey," Amara said, trying to assuage his fears by rubbing his back. "Think about it this way, he's probably back on base, right now, making up some sick excuse about why he didn't make it back on time." To Tandy, she said, "Evan's going to have to do bus duty today. Trevor went out yesterday and I haven't seen him since."

"And Moby?" Tandy whispered.

She looked away.

"Aw." Tandy said, "tell me you didn't let that bacchanalian buffoon take Moby."

"We didn't have a choice. We had to get him out of the house." She relayed to him Agent Byrd's visit.

"So what you guys were speculating about the chips is true," Tandy said. He eased himself onto the icy bench. "What are we going to do now?"

"If you believe Byrd, the locators are misfiring on their initial installations. And the chips may or may not be faulty. Either way, I'm sure he's leaving something out," she said. "Let's talk to Moby."

"You think that rubber tub of transistors will know what to do?" Tandy asked.

"Twenty twenty-five Prague Resolution: No artificial intelligence code shall be used to intentionally harm a natural being," she quoted an iEEE standards passage written for the personal services robotics industry.

Tandy removed his stocking cap and scratched his head.

"Service bots can't lie," she clarified. "If Moby knows a way to help us, he'll tell us. But, we've got to make sure we ask him the right way. If our questions fall into security violation parameters, he could shut himself down and all we'll have is a creepy looking mannequin. Stand him in a corner with a silver tray for wine glasses and calling cards." She sat beside Tandy and asked, "Are you going to stay or go?"

"I've already said. I'm not leaving here."

She stood and brushed at her wet bottom. "Let's go find Moby."

At the flower shop, Tandy didn't bother flipping the "CLOSED" sign on the front door. The pair spent the morning in the back room working the phones. Tandy called all the Way Backers from

Brenda's list while Amara called Trevor's favorite haunts. Neither had success in locating Trevor.

Crossing off another name from the list, Tandy hung up the phone and said, "According to Goose Swanson's wife, he walked out on her two weeks ago."

"Who's left?"

Tandy fanned the air with the tattered page. "Not counting you and Evan, there's me, Trevor, and Larry Parrish over in Chester. And none of us want to go back."

"Did you say Larry Parrish?"

"He and Farley lived together on Mercer Street. First time the locals came snooping, Larry moved out," Tandy said.

"Call him and ask him to come over. Maybe by the time he gets here, we'll have located Trevor and Moby."

Someone was banging on the front door, causing the bell to jangle. Tandy picked up the phone receiver and said, "Find out who's wanting to buy flowers on Boxing Day."

Amara went to the front of the store and saw John, with his hands cupped on the glass, peering inside. He spied her and waved. She unlocked the door and invited him in.

"I stopped by your house and this strange bushy-headed guy told me you were here."

"You must have met my roommate, Trevor. You gotta love 'im," she said, relieved to know that Trevor had returned to the house but nervous that the two had met. John's crinkled forehead and steepled eyebrows told her all she needed to know about his impression of her male roommate. It wasn't a positive one. But in that instant, she affirmed to herself that she wasn't Amara, wife of John, she was Amara, woman of 2049 and she'd choose her own friends, thank you very much. She acquiesced, "He's in IT."

"Say no more." John held up his hands in surrender. He stepped aside to allow her to close the door. "You work on Sundays?"

"End-of-year inventory," she explained. She slid her hands into her jean's pockets to hide her uneasiness.

"Are you still available for lunch?" he asked. "There's a fascinating exhibit of Egyptian artifacts on display at the museum. Thought we'd catch some lunch and see it. What do you think?"

Looking down at her faded jeans, she said, "I'm not dressed for the museum." *And, too chicken to break it off with him*, she scolded herself.

Following her gaze, he countered, "Bowl of soup then? Garlick's Deli?"

"Alice?" Tandy called from the back.

"I don't think lunch is going to work for me today. Maybe we can meet at the museum later?"

"Three o'clock?"

"Four?" *Chicken.*

He responded to her negotiations with a playful smile, "Museum closes at five." He gently rubbed her arms. "Why are you fighting this? You know it. I know it. We're meant to be with each other."

"Alice?" This time the voice was closer. Tandy was standing in the doorway of the workroom, tying his apron around his narrow waist.

She pulled away from John and said, "Tandy, this is John Darnley. He's the gentleman who bought the African violet for his mother."

Tandy's eyes bulged at her. He extended his hand to John and said, "Always nice to meet a La Petite Fleur customer."

Turning back to John, she whispered, "I'll see you there at three-thirty," nudged him toward the door and waved at him as he reluctantly left.

"You still seeing that guy after everything that's happened?"

Tandy howled.

"Shhhh. He'll hear you."

He followed her back into the workroom. "Did any of the stuff Brenda preach sink in? You're risking not only your life but quite possibly his."

"I know that now. But he doesn't. Somehow he just finds me. It's like a giant magnet is pushing us together. He said Trevor is at the house, by the way."

Within the hour, Larry Parrish, Trevor, and Moby arrived. Amara briefed them on the FBI agent's description of the biggest software malfunction in computer history, faulty communication code embedded in locators and contacts worn by forty-two percent of the country's adult population. She shared with them the agent's predictions of her becoming roadkill within the next six days if she didn't go back to 2049 or follow him to an undisclosed location.

When asked if he'd seen Farley recently, Larry Parrish said, "Haven't seen him for a good while."

"Boys, let's go underground!" Trevor exclaimed. "I'm ready for some guerrilla action."

Ignoring the rebel, Larry asked Amara, "And you, are you going to take this agent's offer? Try and go back?" The melancholy in his eyes revealed to them all that he longed to return to his other life.

"I haven't decided," Amara said. She nodded at Moby, standing with his eyes closed. "I want to see what he has to say."

"She thinks the bot can verify what the agent told her," Tandy said. "I don't need a box of transistors and mirrors to confirm what I know is true."

"I can guarantee you Amara, if that agent's lips were moving, he was lyin'," Trevor added.

Picking up the significance of Amara's news, Larry said, "If what Agent Byrd says is true, we're *all* roadkill. One way or the other."

"That's the impression he gave me," Amara said.

"He's lyin' his fat mouth off," Trevor protested. "They're cleaning up their mess is what they're doin'. Getting rid of all of us. Either incarcerate us like lab rats or kill us. We know too much."

"And you know this how?"

"We've all been here for over three years and nothing's happened to us," Trevor said.

"What do you mean?" Amara asked.

"For one, I haven't had a run-in with anything for at least a year. How 'bout you, Tandy?"

Crossing himself, Tandy said, "Not since my '97 mash-up with a gravel truck on Broad Street."

Everyone looked at Larry Parrish.

He shook his head. "Can't remember the last time."

"Ramesh told me he created a Way Backer timetable of all the incident reports Brenda recorded," Trevor continued.

"Where is it?" Amara asked, recalling the report she saw at Brenda's.

"I don't know. Anyway, the table showed the frequency of the nasty occurrences diminishing for each person after the second or third week. Except one. He didn't tell me who."

They all looked at Amara.

"Me?"

Trevor counted on his fingers, "First day you drive, you almost go over a cliff into a quarry. Next, a dump truck almost flattens you. Your van gets stolen and Moby here finds it in another time channel twenty years away. The stereo speaker. The air conditioner." He leaned over the counter and said, "You're the only Way

Backer whose instances of personal time channel cross-overs are acceleratin'."

Oh, dear, she thought, she was having another day.

Chapter Thirty

AT THE MUSEUM
SUNDAY, DECEMBER 26, 1999

As everyone stood around Tandy's worktable, Amara approached Moby. She closed her eyes to envision how to extract information without the bot detecting unauthorized queries and shutting down. Then where would they be?

"Moby," she commanded, "is my name Amara Vivian Graves?"

"Yes."

"Are you employed by the Center for Excelling Life?"

"Yes."

"Do you have a second employer?" She held her breath.

"Yes."

"Ask him who," Trevor urged.

Amara waved him off. "How many administrators have access to your operating system?"

"Three."

Trevor raised his eyebrows.

"Is Harold Simmons Beauford an administrator?"

"Yes. Account activation at. Forty-five. Percent. Date. Not available."

Trevor beamed.

"Is Lydia Coleman an administrator?"

"Yes. Account activated. Day, one. Month, May. Year, two thousand. Forty-four."

"Is Earl T. Byrd an administrator?"

"Yes. Account activated. Day, twenty-three. Month, June. Year, two thousand, Forty-seven."

Raised eyebrows all around.

She changed tactics. "Moby, state the name of Employer One."

"Hello, Amara Vivian Graves," Moby said.

He didn't like that question. "Moby, state the name of Employer Two."

"Center for Excelling Life. District, Richmond. State, Virginia. Region, Northeast. Country, United States."

"So the agency took control of Moby," Trevor speculated.

"Not necessarily," Amara said. "Let's try this." She reached for her backpack slung over a chair and pulled out her locator.

Trevor grabbed her hand and said, "Are you nuts? The minute that thing's activated Byrd will be on us like a goose on moldy bread."

She jerked her hand away. "Give me some credit, will ya? I'm not activating it. Get the monitor and printer from the office." After the guys set up the equipment on the workbench, Trevor hooked them up to Moby. Amara placed the back of the locator in front of Moby's eyes and commanded, "Moby, read locator properties. State device model number and system version."

The bot's eyes scanned the device and stated the model and forty-character version number.

"Is this the latest production version?"

"Yes."

"Are there known bugs on this version?"

"Hello, Amara Vivian Graves." Another question he didn't like. She wondered how many she could ask before he shut his eyes for good.

Trevor took the locator from Amara and turned it on. "Send locator com code files," he restated the device model number, "to printer."

The humming printer seemed louder while they waited for a response from Moby. Would he obey or close his eyes and lock up for good? The humming stopped. A full minute later, the printer started up and spat out a single blank page.

"Damn!" Trevor exclaimed. "We're in," he said as he peeled off his Army jacket and pushed up the sleeves on his T-shirt. "He's sending but the printer can't handle it. Moby, display communication code files on monitor."

They all stared at Moby. Two minutes, then three minutes passed. The monitor beeped and blipped. Moby closed his eyes. They watched as the monitor's screen filled with dozens and dozens of file icons.

Trevor slapped Moby on the back and shouted, "Atta boy, Moby!" He shut down the locator then hovered a mouse over one of the files on the monitor and whistled. "There're at least a million lines of code here."

Amara glanced at the wall clock, one-fifteen. Now she was confident Trevor and Moby would get her back to where she knew she belonged. But there was still a lot of work to do.

She had to see John one more time, to tell him that she was going away. Hiking up her baggy jeans reminded her that she needed a change of clothes for the museum visit. She hoped the secondhand dress shop around the corner was open. No way could she show up in sloppy jeans and a paint-stained denim shirt for her last date with her man. She stuffed the locator back into her backpack and counted the bills in her pocket. They would have to be enough.

"What are we looking for?" Tandy asked.

"Anomalies," Amara said as she rolled Tandy's stool up to the worktable and patted the seat for Trevor.

"A-nom-a-whats?" Larry asked.

"How's your coding?" Trevor asked Amara.

"Rusty. Haven't done any, like, in forever." She sat on a stool beside Trevor and asked, "Didn't you say Evan was a robotics software engineer?"

"It wouldn't matter if he was a coding savant," Trevor said. "This'll take us at least a month to comb through all this."

"We don't have a month. You need to go buy a couple of monitors and keyboards. Larry and Tandy go find Evan. He's doing bus duty," Amara ordered. After they all left with their instructions, she popped around the corner to Village House of *re*Design. Luck was with her. Not only was it open but the store was hosting an end-of-year sale. She found a tartan wool dress with matching swing jacket. When the clerk heard Amara had a date for the museum, she threw in a pair of pumps.

Back at the shop, she changed into her new outfit. She sat in front of the monitor and clicked on the first file folder. There were multiple files inside it. "What a rabbit hole," she mumbled.

Trevor arrived with the extra monitors and placed them on the arrangers' worktable. In quick silence he and Amara set them up. Then, he said, "Coffee." While Trevor poured water into the coffee maker, Tandy and Larry came through the back door with Evan and a muscular woman with spiky hair wearing a hot pink tap jacket.

"We found him," Tandy said.

"This is Hunter. She was walking home from a party and

blacked out," Evan said. "Met her on the bus." Evan handed Amara the new Way Backer's locator.

"Did you turn it off?" Amara asked.

"At the bus stop," Evan said as he looked at the confused woman.

"We briefed her as best as we could on the ride over," Larry said as he removed his gloves and hat. "Got any coffee?"

Taking Larry aside, Amara asked, "Did you see anyone lurking around?"

Larry shook his head. "Not a soul."

Amara said to Hunter, "I apologize for being so abrupt, but we're under a sensitive timeline." She looked at the workroom clock, two-thirty. "What year are you from?" She compared the woman's locator to hers. The two were identical with the same firmware version printed on the back.

Hunter blinked like a child just up from a nap.

"Hunter? What year?"

"Ah, . . . '49? What the heck's going on? Did Amy put you guys up to this?"

"And what did you do in 2049?" Trevor asked.

Hunter blinked again.

"Do you have a coding background?" Evan asked in a quiet, polite voice.

"What?"

"Where. Do. You. Serve? For legacy credits?" Trevor commanded.

"I . . . I manage the Redwood Data Center off Caufield Road," she said. "Why?"

"Well, aren't we lucky?" Trevor said. He offered his chair to Hunter and said, "The communications code in your locator is wacked. We've got two days to find the error. Want to help?"

"My locator's com code? But that's impossible. It's brand new.

Besides, only the manufacturer has access to that level of code. How did you get access?"

Trevor pointed at Moby and said, "Meet Moby, AI assistant at Center for Excelling Life. And, an all-around nice guy."

"Hello, Hunter Grace Anderson," Moby said.

Hunter's face expanded. She pointed at the bot. "That's the installer who upgraded my contacts package. Am I dreaming? This is a dream, right?"

"When did this happen?" Amara asked.

Hunter eased onto the chair as she raked her fingers down her face. "Week before Thanksgiving. Maybe? I could use a kale-protein powder smoothie right about now."

Trevor motioned for Amara to follow him into the break room. He whispered, "Do you think she's a plant?"

"Meaning?"

"Meaning they sent her here!" Trevor seemed unsettled about Hunter showing up just in time to help with the debugging.

"Who would have sent her?" she challenged him.

"I reckon if she's a spy they'll be bustin' down the door before the day's out. We'll just have to be ready for them."

"I don't think she's a spy but keep an eye on her just in case," Amara said.

By the time they returned to the workroom, Hunter had taken a position in front of a monitor. Tandy was stringing cable. Evan was commanding Moby to turn off all his internet signaling applications and Larry was serving everyone coffee.

At 3:20 P.M., Amara stood and stretched. "I need a break," she said to no one in particular. Tandy was at the other end of the table, arranging a funeral spray. Larry was tucked away in the break room reading the Sunday paper. Their heads together, Hunter and Evan were intently confiding with each other at one of the monitor stations. Trevor mumbled at his, occasionally rubbing the sides of the monitor and cooing to it. Without detection, she put on her dress's matching jacket, wound a scarf around her neck, and left the shop.

The museum was a quick, three-block walk. She checked her reflection in the glass doors as she entered. Her hair was a tangled mess, but there wasn't anything she could do about it now as she puffed her bangs with her fingers. She spied John sitting on a bench in the center of the museum's grand hall.

As he stood, he reached to kiss her on the cheek. "You look stunning."

Embarrassed by his familiarity, she pulled away.

An events board nearby displayed a calendar of exhibits, including an oversized reminder of the millennial time capsule party to usher in the twenty-first century.

She froze. A flashback of the job interview with Arturo Santo caused her to teeter.

"Is something wrong?" John asked.

The tingling sensations rushed into her feet and hands. As she massaged her hand, dizziness overtook her. "What?"

"You're turning white," John said. His voice sounded far away, as if he was calling to her from the other end of the long hall.

The sensation of riding a carousel in the middle of the vast space overtook her. Translucent images of people and artifacts faded into other images, images from her future. Inside the whirlwind, she knew what was happening. She was being transported back, back to the day she walked this very hall with Megs and Arturo. As fast as they came, the images faded. Her vision sharpened. John's hands clasped one of hers.

"Alice, Alice," he prompted.

"What?" she feebly answered.

"What's the matter?"

"I'm . . . not sure. Better sit for a second." She sat on the bench.

"Let me get you a drink of water," he offered.

"Yes, would you?" she heard herself panting. She rested her head against the back of the bench. Fearing the time tunnel returning, she squeezed her eyes shut. And it came to her, their first date was to place boxes of mementos in the history center's Year 2000 time capsule to be opened in 2050. She had assumed they would make one together but he'd insisted they each have their own.

A wet bottle nudged her hand. "Here," he said. "Drink this."

Without opening her eyes, she unscrewed the cap and sipped cool water.

Someone said, "Sir, is she all right? Do we need to call for medical assistance?"

Amara popped her eyes open and exclaimed, "I'm fine!" She stood, spilling some of the water down her dress. "I'm fine, really. Something I had for lunch must be disagreeing with me." Straightening herself as the whirring images dissipated, she motioned with the bottle of water for John to lead the way to the exhibit.

And, finally, they were viewing a gold inlaid headdress, encased in glass, the last item of the collection. He ducked into a remote corner and pulled her in with him. Tightly embracing her, he kissed her full on her lips, then whispered close to her ear, "I've wanted to do that since we got here." She kissed him back. He took her hand and together they strolled out of the exhibit.

Thankfully, the floors and walls had stopped fluttering like a distant mirage. She managed to close her eyes or walk in the other direction whenever one of the banners promoting the Y2K time capsule party came into her field of vision. And they were everywhere.

They stepped outside as daylight was fading into winter's long night. The sharp air revitalized her. She needed to get back to the others. "This was lovely but I've got to get back to the shop. We're . . . debugging some software and I promised I'd help."

"How about later?" he asked as he took her in his arms.

"I can't," she said. She couldn't do it, she couldn't tell him she was leaving.

He leaned in and gently kissed her lips. "Until tomorrow, then."

She willed her lips not to tremble as she watched him walk away, leaving her for the last time.

Chapter Thirty-One

BACK AT LA PETITE FLEUR
SUNDAY, DECEMBER 26, 1999

As Amara walked briskly back to the shop, the faint echo of John's voice remained with her. "Until tomorrow." After experiencing the hallucinations in the museum, she realized there would be no tomorrow for them, ever again. Yet, she still yearned to be with him. She slowed her pace to catch her breath and brushed at her lips where he had kissed them. Their last kiss. She swallowed back the wailing that wanted to escape. This leaving him, knowing she'd seen him for the last time, felt worse, cut deeper, than seeing his shrouded body before the cremation.

To collect herself before facing Trevor and the others, she popped into the café next to the dress shop. She sat with her tea at a table by the window. Moisture from the warm air beaded on the cold glass, distorting her view of the street. As she dried tears with a sleeve, she felt someone looming over her.

"Go. Away," she said without looking up.

Byrd said, "Having contact with someone you know from your past is dangerous business. I'm sure Farley would've told you that."

Ignoring him, she drew circles on the foggy window.

"A reporter filed a grievance against your friend Mr. Johnson."

When she didn't reply, he continued. "Theodore, or Tandy, Johnson, proprietor of La Petite Fleur. His real name is Robert Canton. Did you know he has a criminal record? Using offensive vernacular."

"Let me guess. He called someone 'ma'am,'" she said.

Byrd flipped a bottle cap he'd found on the next table. "I can't say I blame him for wanting to stay here. But, either way, his options are slim."

This got her attention. "What are you saying?"

"There's no guarantee of a smooth transition over channel lines for Mr. Canton. With his low chip count, he might be ripped apart from the insides when we send him back." The lanky agent shook all over.

"He's not interested in going back. He wants to stay here and run his shop."

"I'm afraid that isn't an option."

"Explain."

"You know why. His awareness of things to come."

"But he's not interested in exploiting what he knows. He just wants to be left alone to arrange his flowers."

"We all know what becomes of good intentions, Mrs. Darnley. Take you, for example. You promised Farley you wouldn't see John Darnley, and yet there you were at the museum."

"I was saying goodbye."

"So you've decided to go back?"

"I didn't say that. But if I did, I'd have one condition," she said.

He hee-hawed. "There's no negotiating with the gods of physics." After biting his lower lip with his jagged teeth, he added, "They always win."

"I'll go if you'll agree to let Tandy and the others stay."

Byrd's voice took on an impatient edge. "You know I can't promise you that. Now, where's my AI robot?"

"You mean Moby?"

"Where is it, Mrs. Darnley?"

Amara sensed his anger escalating. Staring at him and not saying anything was her only defense.

"Tomorrow, then," he said. "I'll come by Mercer Street to get it. Make sure it's there."

She followed him out the door and watched him go east on Cary Street.

"Where have you been?" Tandy asked. "We thought you'd gone for good."

Amara massaged her temples. She was tired and hadn't eaten all day.

"Hunter found Moby's partnership license file," an excited Evan said.

Trevor pushed the boy aside and said, "It's the master access. We control Moby now. Plus, I turned off all of his auto-signaling applications."

"That explains why Byrd approached me just now at the tea house. He can't track him. How did you do it so quickly?"

"We asked him to help," Hunter offered. "I do it all the time when my team is running diagnostics."

"Piece of cake, apparently," Trevor said, rolling his eyes.

"And dumb luck," Hunter added.

"Does Agent Byrd know where we are now?" Larry asked, worried.

Speaking to the entire group, Amara said, "We must assume they know everything and are tracking all of us."

Tandy tugged at the gold cross around his neck. "What's our

next move? The Brenda plan?"

"What's the Brenda plan?" Hunter asked.

"Everybody scatters. Leaves town," Evan explained to her. Turning to the others, he added, "I found Brenda's exit kits with IDs and money. In the kitty litter box. But there's only three of them."

"I'll take one," Hunter said

"This time is like the Wild West. I wouldn't mind heading out to Vegas," Evan said.

Trevor playfully bopped him on the back of the head. "You idiot, that's the first place they'll look. Stick to small towns and you'll be okay."

Amara said to Hunter and Evan, "If you two have any doubt about staying, keep your locators. Don't destroy them. Apparently they're the key to this whole mess." She explained to them what Byrd said about the locator reconnecting with the chips.

"But what about the contacts?" Hunter asked. "They're needed to connect the locator's network access to our bodies."

"Yeah, about that," Amara said. "Do you suppose there's a work-around?"

"What do you mean?"

"I'm going back," Amara said.

They were all silent. Then, Trevor quietly asked, "You sure about this?"

To keep Trevor and Tandy from talking her out of it, she hurried on. "I've only got the one contact. My right one got lost in my fall." She reached into her backpack to retrieve the plastic contact case she bought when she first arrived. "Can I go back with just the one?"

Trevor shot up from his seat. "I got an idea."

Amara was relieved. Trevor had moved on. He wasn't going to

judge her for the decision she'd made. It was the right thing for her and for John. The trip to the museum had convinced her of that.

Trevor pounded on Tandy's ancient computer screen. "What if we signaled directly from the locator to the chips? Hell, the contacts are just dumb monitors. They allow us to see all the junk our brains are asking for."

"I don't know," Evan said.

"It's worth a try," Hunter offered.

"I didn't wear mine half the time. They messed with my ADHD," Trevor volunteered.

"Let's try reconnecting her by using the one contact first," Evan stated with caution. "The code's already written and Moby's programmed to run them. If it doesn't work, we'll alter the code and try your plan."

"There's a third option," Hunter said. "You can have mine."

"Kid, you've only been here, like, five minutes. Of all of us, you've got the best chance of goin' back," Trevor admitted.

"I'm not a kid, Trevor. I'm probably older in trips around the sun than you. I've lived for seventy-eight years and I've had more fun with you guys in the last day than I've had in decades. I say we wake up Moby and get this party started."

Trevor met Amara's eyes. "If you've made up your mind, no time like the present." He emitted a fake laugh at his own joke about time and its prisoners.

"What about Moby?" she asked. "Call it intuition, but I don't think Byrd is on official business. I think he's searching for Moby on his own. Either he's covering up a mistake or no one knows about Moby's special skill to surf channels."

"Well, he ain't getting him back," Trevor said. Then, as an afterthought, he said, "I'd like to keep him if nobody else wants him."

Tandy fluffed his fingers outward. "Just keep him away from me."

Larry waved Trevor off. "No interest. If y'all don't need me anymore, I'm going home to dig up my money and head on out." He took Amara's hand and said, "I hope you don't take what I'm about to say the wrong way, but, I hope we never see one another again."

She shook his hand. "Before you leave, call Virginia Gas and tell them to turn the heat back on at Mercer Street. For the Way Backers."

"I'm not leaving here," Tandy said. "I'm not going back to that awful place and I'm not running away. Someone needs to be here for the others that come."

"He's right. I'm stayin', too," Trevor said.

Amara said to Trevor and Tandy, "What happens when all this gets fixed and people stop coming? Besides, they don't want you here. Think about what happened to Funky Man and to Barton."

"Ha!" Trevor laughed. "Code as complicated as this, honey, Way Backers ain't gonna stop coming anytime soon."

Looking worried, Tandy slid his snips into his apron pocket. "I can't go back. Besides, I'm happy here."

Amara hugged him. "Thanks for all you've done for me." To Trevor, she said, "You're aware of the wrath that will rain down on you if you don't give Moby back?"

"Bring it." Trevor tapped his temple and said, "I changed the access sequence on Moby's system code."

"You aren't listening. They need us to disappear. And Moby's just more collateral. What's the cost of a single bot compared to what's happening to thousands of people?"

"Trevor, I advise you to listen to her," Larry added. "I get it that you want to play with the robot but keeping him increases the chances of them messin' with you."

"And getting killed like your friend Barton," Amara added.

Larry said, "She's right. Trevor, I advise you to leave this place."

Tears were streaming down Tandy's face. The rest were silent, perhaps thinking about their own journeys ahead of them.

Amara thought maybe they should pray but she'd forgotten how, so instead, she said, "I'm ready. What do we do now?"

Evan jumped in, "First we bring up your records in Moby's database and make sure they're complete."

"Wait, wait," Hunter interrupted. "Let's get everything on a white board and then ask Moby if the plan will work."

Larry shook his head and said, "Asking a robot to tell you what to do, I've seen it all now." He put on his coat and cap, waved goodbye, and left.

By the next morning, the Way Back Geeks, as they were now calling themselves, felt confident in their plan to thrust Amara back to where she now knew she belonged. While Trevor rigged up a Galaxy cloud in Moby's data storage drive, Evan and Hunter tweaked CEL's version of the locator's installation execution code and rebooted Amara's locator. Moby was smiling, exposing his *i*Hopes etchings.

Taking a break, Hunter stood in front of Moby, who was grinning back at her. "The master server at the place I work, or used to work, always smiled when corporate downloaded bug fixes or policy changes. It's like they're being fed."

"Brilliant, isn't it?" Trevor said. "In 2004, the M.I.T. kids inserted an applet on an AI dog they were developing for DOD. You see, in a lab, you spend a lot of time standing around drinkin' coffee and wonderin' if the firmware's done loading. So they created this short little program called "wagging the dog," or WTD. When code was done being loaded and tested, the dog bot automatically wagged its tail as a signal that it was done testing. It was the first emo-transference application. The first time developers thought about giving an AI device a soul. The idea from this app launched the personal service robotics industry."

"Wagging the dog? I always wondered what 'WTD' stood for," Hunter said.

Evan laughed and said, "Moby looks like someone just offered him a doughnut."

At 10:30 A.M., everyone watched as Amara popped in her one contact and switched on her locator. An initial connection was confirmed on the monitors which were connected to Moby. But Amara's locator and contact indicators flashed red.

"Moby, translate red signal indication," Amara commanded.

Thirty seconds passed. Moby responded, "Unable to link to Galaxy."

"We've got a mismatch in the Galaxy address code somewhere," Hunter said. "He's trying to link to the real Galaxy cloud network instead of the one Trevor built. Moby, list all Galaxy cloud addresses," she commanded.

An hour later, Hunter said, "I think they're all corrected. Let's reload and try to connect again." They got the same results.

"I need a break," Amara said. "I'm taking a walk."

"Keep the contact in," Hunter said. "We'll leave Moby up and running in case something changes." She hunched her sizable shoulders at the others. "You never know when the WTD might kick in."

Trevor sniffed an armpit. "Let's all take a break and meet back up at one o'clock."

Without realizing it, Amara found herself in front of the museum. The day felt just like the day she'd come to interview for the job working in the vaults. The chilly forty-two degree temperature had her missing her tap jacket. She wrapped her tartan jacket around her body. Banners snapped in the brisk breeze. As she read one, her toes tingled. The banner was a larger version of the flags she'd seen inside the day before, encouraging members to make history by placing something in the time capsule vault.

The signal on her contact now flashed yellow instead of red. In spite of the change in the warning, Amara went inside. Getting directions from the concierge, she followed a small crowd down a flight of stairs and through a long corridor to a dimly lit room. The museum had done a swell job of making the room feel like a time tunnel from a 1950s sci-fi movie.

"Large or small?" a girl, with a tartan headband matching Amara's dress, asked. She smiled at Amara. "What size box would you like for your artifact?" She pointed at Amara's backpack.

"I'm not . . ." Amara hesitated. She hadn't intended to leave anything. Changing course, she said, "The small one." She pulled the book John gave her two days ago and showed it to the girl. "For this."

"Oh, *Harry Potter*, that's a good one," she said.

After paying for the box, Amara was escorted by another volunteer to a table where patrons prepared their time treasure. "Inside your box is a template you can use to help you with your story," the guide said. "It's designed to make it easy for you to talk to yourself." He laughed. "Well, your future self, anyway."

Amara silently reviewed the template.

"Make sure you put your name on the first page," the guide chirped before leaving.

Squeals of happy kids on Christmas break echoed throughout the time tunnel.

Amara stared at all the white space on the paper.

She began to write.

Chapter Thirty-Two

HOME AGAIN
TUESDAY, DECEMBER 28, 2049

Each time Megs, or Kimberly, or that clever police detective asked about her ordeal, Amara told them she couldn't recall a thing, not one thing. This was untrue. She remembered it all but also remembered Farley's warning to tell no one. The tingling in her toes and hands that she'd learned to rely upon to alert her of possible danger had vanished. So she trusted no one with the truth.

Distracted by the flashing on her contact, turning from red to yellow then back to red, she left the museum's time capsule exhibit. As she turned onto the very side street where she'd found herself in 1999, the square in the corner of her optic screen changed from yellow to green, then blinked green. Images of a boy and a young man, both wearing tap jackets, flickered before her then disappeared behind an abrupt wash of light like film melting on a hot lit projector lens.

The roaring of a passing vehicle was replaced by screeching light. Either she'd just been creamed by a vehicle or she was on her way back. Not knowing how much time had passed, she was next aware of the single weighty thud to her sternum. This second time, the young boy, and not a police officer from 1999, helped her to her feet.

She breathed in clean, fresh air.

"What's today's date?" she asked the boy's father.

"The twenty-eighth? I think," he said.

The father insisted on seeing her home but Amara assured him that she was fine, more than fine. On the walk home she marveled at every person and every building she passed. Seeing both worlds at once, the old, sooty one lagged after the new one on a palette of trailing colors. She tried to blink away the double vision but the translucent images of old buildings loomed behind, around, and inside her current reality. Brilliant color everywhere energized her steps, making them lighter.

Rosie wasn't at home to welcome her. However, Kimberly was there with a person whom Amara had never met. After a frantic laying-on of hands to confirm that Amara was physically unharmed, Kimberly berated her for disappearing without letting them know where she was. All the while, Amara insisted on not remembering anything.

"I'd like to know where you got the glampy tweed outfit," Kimberly's friend Gus wanted to know. "If you ever remember, let me know."

The next day, Amara gathered her courage to go see Dr. Coleman, the memory specialist. She was prepared to be taken away, to where, she couldn't imagine. Convinced that Dr. Coleman would ask about her little three-week excursion, Amara practiced responses while in the waiting room.

Oh, that, I popped over to my past to visit my dead husband. Right, no. How about, I was practicing mindfulness and unplugged for twenty-one days. Not likely, Amara.

"Amara Vivian Graves." Someone gently tugged at her elbow. "This way, please." The medical assistant wasn't Moby. Following the new bot to the examination cubicle, she surveyed the area looking for the one who'd saved her life. As the new bot pulled out a chair for her, she asked, "Where's Moby? He helped me with my contacts last time." With a nervous laugh, she added, "Does he have the day off? Who are you?"

"My name is Neo," the bot said.

She tried again. "Is Moby here?"

Neo had nothing.

"Ms. Graves?" Dr. Coleman appeared on the cubicle's monitor. "Neo reports that he's having trouble connecting with your memory database. What's happening?"

Amara squinted her eyes and moved closer to the monitor. Somehow, Dr. Coleman looked different, her face askew. Amara tried to read the doctor's expression, to see if she seemed suspicious of Amara. But being without her locator and contacts for three weeks, she'd become rusty at reading faces on a one-dimensional monitor.

Alarmed, the doctor said, "We can't see your profile. Are you having trouble with your locator?"

"Yes," Amara said. She struggled to keep up. "I fell and lost my right contact."

"It shows here that your locator went offline on December eighth," Dr. Coleman said. "I don't see any record of interaction for approximately three weeks. Did someone contact you about this malfunction?"

Amara smelled whiffs of Farley's coffee and Ramesh's curry soup. She hoped they all were where they wanted to be on their own personal time channel.

"Ms. Graves?"

This time Amara felt Dr. Coleman's impatience. Readjustment to life in 2049 was harder than she'd thought it would be.

"Ms. Graves? Can you hear me?" the doctor commanded.

"Yes," Amara said calmly. However, her patience for impatient people was waning since her return.

The doctor continued, "At least three weeks of memory data is missing from your Galaxy account. I'll put in a report for a reload. Not wearing the contact must have caused the locator to spool the data into the holding basket."

"Holding basket?" Amara asked.

Dr. Coleman said, "A storage well for data without address tags. Don't worry, we'll find it."

Until she had a chance to figure it out on her own, she wasn't too keen on Dr. Coleman poking around in her data. Wherever it was. "Don't bother looking. I think I know where it is. My son gave me a brand-new bot for Christmas and when I went to sync it with my old one, I must have fat-fingered the data transfer option on the Galaxy account."

"That's dangerous," Dr. Coleman warned. "Since your body is connected to Galaxy via your new wellness program it puts the network's memory at risk. One bad virus from an unprotected contact could take the entire network down."

"I know, right. That's what my son said," Amara played along. Amara had lived, eaten, and slept network communications for forty years. Dr. Coleman didn't know what she was talking about; she should stick to medicine. To the doctor, Amara added, "I'll try to do better next time."

"We can see if we can retrieve it for you now," she offered.

"No, I'm fine. I'm sure it's all there on the old bot."

In a raised voice, like she was talking to Amara's hundred year-old neighbor, the doctor warned, "You'll have to sign a release saying I offered to restore it."

Neo appeared with an electronic pad and offered it to Amara.

"Sign at all the places marked with an 'X,'" she said.

Stalling, Amara said, "I'll need my contacts to read this." Then she asked, "Am I getting a new locator?"

"What's wrong with the one you have?"

"I seem to have misplaced it," Amara lied. Actually, she'd destroyed the device and buried it in the flower urn welded onto the columbarium niche holding John's aches at Hollywood Cemetery. She wasn't taking any chances of getting hurled back into her past again. She'd been there and done that, as her dad had been fond of saying.

"Neo, fetch Ms. Graves a full communication kit," Dr. Coleman ordered. "You should consider ordering our forgiveness package. It covers the replacement of locators and contacts. And your wellness insurance will pay for it."

"I'll just use my legacy credits. Do I have enough?" Amara had no idea what shape her account was in since returning from 1999. Kimberly had been home for over three weeks and there was no telling how many in-home services she'd abused.

"Looks like you've got more than enough," the doctor said.

Neo handed Amara her new communication kit and waited by her side as she put on the contacts and powered up the locator. As she'd done before, she gazed over the sea of customer cubicles and the bare trees outside. This time she accepted the bot's request to schedule a follow-up, which also allowed Neo to complete the locator's installation. "Thank you," she said softly to Neo.

"Make sure you fix your data content issue. And soon," were Dr. Coleman's parting words. If she was aware of Amara's little side trip, or the reason for it, Dr. Coleman wasn't showing it.

The doctor's insistence on retrieving the missing data sparked an idea for Amara. She would go home and activate the new bot Aiden had sent her for Christmas. On the steps of the clinic, she smiled to herself and thought never again would she complain about her children gifting household gadgets at Christmastime. From now on she was accepting all gifts with no judgment. Where had she heard that before, she asked herself.

That night over dinner, as Rosie's replacement stood in a corner humming and whirring, Kimberly's friend Gus talked about her mother's house bot, Wilhelmina.

"In case you were wondering," Gus said, "the name means 'willing to protect.'"

"How about I call him Mr. French?" Amara suggested. The sleek, masculine service helper, a Miracle Maid 2050, was dressed in a butler's vest and black tie.

"Mom," Kimberly protested. "Why are you always so literal? How about Iron Belly or Sir Sweeps-A-Lot." She laughed at her own joke.

Gus joined in. "Or, how about Dr. Data? Cyrus Circuits or Laser Head?"

Raising her glass of water, Amara said, "I like René. For the philosopher René Descartes."

"Seriously, Mom?" Kimberly accused.

"It's my bot, so I get to name him," Amara said firmly. "After dinner, let's activate the settings and get René to do the dishes."

"An ancient patriarchal philosopher who said, 'I think, therefore I am,'" Gus said. "That's something I can get behind."

After breakfast on New Year's Eve, Amara watched as Kimberly and Gus smeared red paint all over her new linen tablecloth. It read: My body! My choice! They planned to attend a rally to protest the state ordering seventy-year-old Jane Bledsoe to abort a fetus. An incensed Kimberly tossed her hands in the air and shouted,

"Whatever" when Amara declined an invitation to join them.

Amara had other plans. Watching Kimberly and her new sidekick walk toward the HT station, Amara summoned René. They waited in the apartment lobby as John's autopod emerged from the underground garage. Putting her faith in her new friend René, she left her new locator and contacts in her nightstand drawer.

The night before, with René's help, Amara had located Rosie's beacon signal. René reported that the signal was originating from the Goochland recycle facility. The signal gave Amara hope that her old friend had yet to tangle with the wrecking ball.

A neon sign proclaiming to "Help You For Less" hung over a low building sprawling over what was once a cow pasture. At reception, a stout man pointed at René and asked, "You turning that in?"

"No," replied Amara. "We're here about an inquiry I sent earlier. I'm looking for a Don Key 484, named Rosie. Someone sent her here a few weeks ago." She added, fiercely, "Without my permission. I'm here to reclaim her."

The man tapped his right earbud and stared past Amara at the white wall. "Kimberly Graves-Darnley?" he asked.

"That's my daughter. While I was away, she had Rosie recycled." Then she repeated, "I did *not* give her permission to do such a thing."

"Says here she's been reprogrammed as a lab assistant."

"What's that mean?" Amara asked.

"Anything. We probably got her disassembling and sorting circuit cards and transistors. Wait right here." He disappeared through a door behind his counter.

Amara turned to René and said, "Go to Rosie."

René brushed passed her, opened the door behind the counter and entered a cloud of noise.

Amara followed.

"Hey! Y'all are not supposed to be back here," someone yelled.

Ignoring the warning, she spied a sign swinging from an exposed steel rafter and read, "Sargent Harry's Repurpose Lab." She followed René to the glass-walled room standing amid the indoor junkyard. Behind the glass walls, bots of all shapes and sizes rested on long metal tables. A swarthy man, seeming familiar to Amara, was talking to the receptionist.

Standing at the glass door of the room, René reported to Amara, "Access key code not found in my database."

Amara pounded on the door to get the men's attention. When they looked her way, she called out and waved. "Ramesh!"

The man did not appear to know who she was, a friend from way back. However, he was happy to show her around the lab and explain the valuable contributions the repurposed Don Key 484 was making.

"This bot has increased our capacity for disassembling printed circuit boards and sorting the components," Ramesh said. They were standing in front of a metal box with arms busily plucking miniature components and placing them in various sized bins lined up on the table.

"What happened to Rosie?" Amara asked. "You know, her outer body, her face?"

"Oh, you mean her casing? The outer skin we sell to an AI manufacturer. They melt it down and reuse it. We send the metal to our SMD department for flattening. It gets shipped out to a partner plant that makes flower boxes."

"SMD?" Amara asked. She reached for René's hand and squeezed.

"Oh. Scrap metal department," Ramesh said.

They'd come too late to say goodbye. Rosie had transitioned up into The Cloud.

"We saved all Rosie's data. State requirement for instances such as this one. Would you like me to upload it to a network cloud? Which one do you use? Galaxy?"

"Can you transmit it to René?"

"Don't see why not," Ramesh said, his eyes still devoid of recognition.

Stunned by finding Rosie and her friend Ramesh in their altered states, Amara pointed at the sign above the lab and asked tentatively, "Is Trevor here?"

Ramesh paused from his task of transferring data from Rosie to René. "Who?"

"Never mind. I knew a guy from way back who worked with Sargent Harry."

A bead of sweat trickled down the side of Ramesh's face. This worrier was her Ramesh, she was sure of it.

"The WTD alarm will let us know when the download is complete," he politely said.

"How long will it—"

Her question was interrupted by René. "Transfer complete. I like these doughnuts. May I have some more, please?"

"Bots," Ramesh said, as he rubbed his hands along the side of his khakis. "They say the craziest things these days."

On the ride home, René announced through the autopod's speakers that Amara had an audio message from Moby, which was recovered from Rosie's data content files. The time stamp on the message flashed Thursday, January 6, 2000, on the dashboard's monitor. She asked René to play the audio file. It was Moby's mechanized voice but Amara knew it was Trevor speaking.

"Hey, let's rock 'n' roll! You didn't make it back from your walk and all systems confirmed a successful installation, so we're all here assumin'—hoping—you made it back. Evan and Hunter decided to stick around and play with Moby. That reporter fella? Moby was right. He got himself flattened like a pancake in a pile-up on I-95 around Fredericksburg. And Earl T. Byrd-brain still hasn't caught us yet. After Tandy confirmed the van wasn't in the apartment complex, we assumed it was on Brewery Street, like Moby said. So we decided to send Moby over to fetch it. Moby came back but we're still waiting to see if the van shows up. Ha. Ha.

"Oh, and another thing. Tandy says that moon-faced fella keeps comin' by askin' for you. He said the guy seems to have a real bad case of lovesick blues. He told him you went to India to visit Ramesh. Sorry about the lie but you know why we had to do it. Anyway, hope that makes sense to you. See ya in the stars."

She had her proof. She'd experienced the bending of time as Dr. Desmond Kurts had described. Yet, she doubted anyone, outside of Byrd's FBI basement lab, would ever believe her.

Chapter Thirty-Three

Back in the city limits, Amara asked René to tag Megs for a Juicy Vibes meetup. She found her friend sitting at the counter with two large honey-banana smoothies, although she'd have much preferred a 1999 chocolate milk shake and a side of salty, hot fries.

"This is René," Amara said as the friends hugged.

"I see. So, not only have you decided to upgrade your household assistant, you've programmed the new one to follow you around. Interesting."

Amara knew that tone. Megs was fishing for an explanation on her mysterious disappearance. Well, she wasn't getting one. Amara loved her friend too much to expose her to the darker side of their fountain of eternal beauty treatments. Instead, she thanked Megs for the smoothie and took a sip.

"Oh! I almost forgot," Megs said. She dug inside her bag and pulled out a wrapped gift. "Merry Christmas!"

"You shouldn't have. I didn't—"

"It's just a little something. Open it."

Nestled in the gift box was a transparent tablet framed in oak.

"Go ahead, turn it on," Megs encouraged.

Their heads together, they watched the one-minute clip from a Christmas party at Amara and John's house. Megs jabbered on about how people never made photos or video clips anymore since Galaxy recorded everything in real time for them. Amara watched without saying a word. There they all were, her family, at Grace Street. The video ended with a close-up of the hosts standing in the keeping room off the kitchen. Amara, in the video frame, displayed a tight-lipped smile. John appeared transfixed at something behind her.

"I believe this was the Christmas right after John sued everybody," Megs said in a solemn tone.

"Yes, it was the Christmas I sat for a studio portrait. The one he kept bugging me to do." The video board glowed with the last frame and she pointed at the portrait, "See, it's sitting in the chair, behind me." Then she added, "He left me after New Year's." The hair on the back of her neck tingled.

"That's right. He moved in with Beck's friend. What was her name?"

"Keekee Biddle," Amara said as she stared at the grainy pixels which made up her husband's face.

"Did they have—you know—and affair?" Megs asked softly.

"What do you think?" Amara said, her way of letting her friend know she didn't want to talk about it.

"I'm sorry, I didn't mean to—"

"No, I'm sorry." She held up the frame and pressed the play button and watched the scene play out again. Then she set the player to photograph mode and selected the last frame, the one of John and her. Looking up from the picture, she said, "I didn't mean to sound so ungrateful. This is lovely. Thank you."

Changing the subject, Amara asked, "What are you and Barry

doing for New Year's?"

"He's wrapped up in the Bledsoe case, you know the one I told you about that day you came to the museum for the interview?"

Amara nodded. "Kimberly's still in town." She left it at that, not caring to elaborate on her daughter's latest cause.

"Tammy and I are going to the time capsule opening gala tonight. Dr. Kurts will be there. I can't wait to meet him. You should come." Her locator whistled out the first few notes of *i*Hopes' latest holiday jingle. "Hey, sweetheart," pause, "How fab!" Megs took a hurried sip of her drink, then said, "Gotta go. Tams got us a mother-daughter appointment at Che Betty's for a style. The opening ceremony starts at nine. Meet us there!"

Amara motioned for René to take Megs's stool. Before powering down the tablet, she tapped on the area of the portrait sitting on the chair, a Christmas bow draped across the top. When it came into focus, she took in a sharp breath.

The portrait made it all clear. It explained everything.

Keekee Biddle's libertine ways weren't what had lured John away from their marriage. That blame went to the woman in the portrait, the woman John fell in love with in 1999. That woman was Alice Epps.

Not wanting to return to her apartment to endure Kimberly and her pal commiserating over all the world's injustices, Amara asked René to scroll through the day's events and happenings. First on the list was a reminder of the evening's gala at the museum.

"Follow me," she said. "Let's see if we can get our time capsules without all the late night pomp and glamour."

In the museum's banquet hall, Amara recognized one of the guides. Sandy Fraser, one of John's closest friends, must have opted to age naturally, like John. The man looked as old as the mummy in the Egyptian exhibit—sunken cheeks and papery skin.

He asked, "Creating a new capsule or retrieving one from 2000?"

"Retrieving," she said.

Waving his thin arm, he presented the room on his left, which was filled with kiosks. He smiled at her. "It's good to see you, Amara. You're looking as glowing as ever."

"Sandy," she replied, blushing at her guilty thoughts of Sandy as an Egyptian potentate. "As I recall, we each got our own capsule. Will they let me have John's?"

"I don't see why not. They let me have my Talia's." Sandy escorted her to the first kiosk. "Just key in your member number or name and the system will retrieve them for you."

In the spirit of the celebration's theme of time travel, a conveyor belt, similar to those used in old fashioned airport baggage claims, rolled out the time capsules—shoe boxes wrapped in newspaper. An electronic notification was transmitted to the patron when the capsule arrived. René blinked then announced, "Proceed to the carousel for your journey into the past to begin."

Sandy said, "I'll leave you to it."

At a table, she peeled back the seal on her box and opened it. There wasn't anything inside that she wasn't expecting. With a quick read from a naively, youthful note she'd written to herself, she discovered all of her predictions had come to pass. She'd gotten married, had kids. She'd led a successful life, albeit so normal that it bordered on miserably average, not counting the past month. She folded the letter and tossed it back in the box. She had no regrets, she assured herself. She opened her once favorite brand of lip balm to discover it cracked and dried. She placed her Y2K paper tiara souvenir on René's head, then tossed it back in the box. Rattling around in the bottom of the box was her company pager. She'd gotten into trouble at work for that one. She'd joked with John, saying, "Wish I could put *this* in the box."

He'd laughed and said, "Go for it." Joking, he'd pretended to put his own in the box, saying, "Here, put mine in there too!"

Setting her box aside, her unsteady hands reached for John's. It was lighter than hers. She shook the box. Her voice cracked when she whispered to René, "Secrets of a young lawyer." His absence still stung. Inside she found a single sheet of notepaper with La Petite Fleur letterhead and a promotional giveaway pen with a silk flower taped on its cap. One of the petals crumbled when she touched it. She read aloud the words on the barrel of the pen, "Hope you enjoy your flowers as much as we enjoy delivering them."

The yellowed paper was brittle from residing inside a cardboard box for fifty years, the ink of John's eloquent cursive handwriting faded and pale.

The connection between the three of them: John, Alice Epps, and herself flowed from the paper to her hands. The note read:

A., they say you've gone. You've left me behind.
I'll store my yearning inside this box and think of you when stars
shine bright on cold wintry nights.
All my heart's love, J.

She read it again. "Oh, no. What has she done to our lives, John?" She looked toward the ceiling to delay the tears from pouring over her cheeks.

The connections flooded through her.

In her misplaced resentment, Amara had blamed his mistresses—his causes and Katherina Biddle—for his emotional detachment during their early years. Farley had warned her, but she'd failed to listen. As a Way Backer, she'd twarted their love at first sight moment; she was the one who had set their lives onto its uneven path.

In the video clip, John stared at Amara's portrait as if he'd seen something unbelievable, an aberration. Because of it, he left his wife of eighteen years. Before he left, he'd accused Amara of being an impostor. Only now, with the hindsight of time-travel memories, did she understand his words' meaning.

In the years after their reconciliation, their lives were filled with devotion and love, love of passion, love of kindness. Love he'd wanted with the other "her."

"Alice Epps, you husband-stealing hussy."

She walked to the kiosk and asked for Alice Epps' memory capsule, half expecting the machine to tell her it wasn't available or didn't exist. Back at the table, she gathered the items and placed them in her box.

René announced, "Proceed to carousel for your journey into the past to begin."

"Really?" she asked, surprised.

Alice's box was heavier than the other two. Inside was John's gift to her; the book with his Christmas-Valentines card bookmarking the page she was on when Agent Earl T. Byrd showed up at Farley's on Christmas Day, 1999. Underneath the book was Alice's letter to Amara.

She unfolded the crinkled papers. Her handwriting was the opposite of John's baroque flourish. She was the left-handed engineer who printed in blocked letters. Atop the two-page accounting of her experience, she'd written a note.

Christmas, 1999
Amara, here is your proof. All that you experienced did happen.
Alice.
P.S. Leave John in the past, just as I am doing as I write this.

Love isn't something you order on demand, how you want it. Love is a gift. Don't try to bend it to your will. Accept love as it is given. And be grateful it chose you.

Amara rubbed the thin scar along her hairline. She didn't recall writing the postscript but took the message to heart. As she was leaving, Amara took Alice's advice and tossed John's capsule along with his letter to Alice into one of the oversized trash bins near the exit. She stowed the book and Alice's accounting of events inside her own capsule.

"Tomorrow," she told René, "we're selling John's autopod. Make it happen."

Chapter Thirty-Four

René followed Amara out of the time capsule exhibit, up the stairs, and into the grand hallway. Among the sparse crowd, she spied a slender woman with a bun at the nape of her neck. The woman was following a small man with bright red hair, neatly trimmed. Her mind flashed to the snapshot of Desi Kurts and his dirty yellow bandanna. Amara followed them into the small library beside the gift shop.

"It's you," Amara interrupted the pair's conversation.

To the young woman, the man said, "Tell him we'll do the interview in here." He faced Amara and asked, "I'm afraid I've not had the pleasure. You are?"

Amara extended her hand and said, "My manners. Where are they? My name is Amara Vivian Graves. I believe we have mutual acquaintances."

Taking her hand into both of his, he said, "Dr. Desmond Kurts."

"Dr. Kurts, forgive my being so forward but may we talk? About the Way Backers? I know you're probably very busy preparing for your program tonight but I just need a minute." She noticed the shift in the light in his eyes when she dropped the Way Backers expression on him.

Casually, he surveyed the area, then asked, "Did he send you?"

"Who? Did who send me?" Amara asked.

Kurts waved her off and walked toward a closed door at the back of the library.

"Wait," Amara said, following him, René at her heels. "No one sent me, Dr. Kurts. I just need to talk to you about your, you know, your personal experience. You know, living in 1999 with Funky Man and Farley Dickenson and the rest of the Way Backers."

He turned to face her. "How do you know those names?"

"Because I was there. I showed up the day after the men kidnapped you off the street. In front of the Way Back Diner."

Dr. Kurts' eyes widened, revealing the same surprised expression as the one in Farley's photo of Desi Kurts. "This way," he said. He led her into a small conference room and invited her and René to sit under a painting of an eighteenth-century English countryside. "You have five minutes." Pointing at René, he added, "And turn that thing off."

She instructed René to turn off his audio and video inputs and said to Kurts, "At the advice of my wellness counselor, I entered into the CEL program to deal with my depression. You see my husband, John Darnley, died and I was having difficulty—"

"John Darnley? As in John Darnley of the Natural Life movement?"

"The same," she admitted.

Kurts laughed, "Ha! That's rich. The wife of the man who wants to send us back to the Stone Age is using biochip plasma therapy."

"I'm not here to have a philosophical debate with you, Dr. Kurts," she said. "I'll leave that for your audience tonight."

"I apologize. But you must see the irony of this?"

"As my baby sister used to say whenever our parents expressed their unhappiness with her life choices, 'Whatever.'"

He motioned for her to continue.

For the next few minutes, she conveyed to Kurts her own Way Back experience, omitting her special relationship with Moby. She ended with her question. "How did you get back?"

As he stared at the painting over her head, Kurts told her his story. "I was a professor and on a downward spiral in my life. Poor lifestyle choices, addiction. I was told using biochip plasma would save me. So I did. After a year or so, I fell back into my old habits and one morning I found myself in a dumpster. And I eventually learned that I had somehow been zapped to 1997. Through a series of flashbacks I begin to recall what had happened. A gang of thugs had attacked me. Anyway, I was so confused. You know what it was like. My whole life had disappeared, literally, overnight. So I drifted. I found myself here in Richmond and this kind Englishman took me in."

"Farley?"

"Yes, you know him?"

"I lived with him for a couple of weeks. Then he disappeared. Have you heard from him since you made it back?" she asked.

"No. I suppose you're here for answers about what happened to you," he said.

"I know the mechanics of what happened. About the software glitch. Do you know a guy named Earl Byrd?"

"E.T. Byrd? Yes."

"He approached me and explained what's happening with the biochip plasma and the connection issues."

"What he's told you isn't common knowledge. I'm surprised he told you *anything*. Did you have a unique circumstance?"

"If you mean, am I someone special or of great importance, no," she smiled and relaxed for the first time since returning from 1999. Telling her story to another human being released the anguish of grief she'd carried around inside her since John's death. She felt the light spreading in her chest and flowing into her arms.

"Lucky for me, I made it back to my rightful place in time. I'm interested in hearing about your return experience," she said.

"I'm afraid I can't tell you that. I've an agreement with Dr. Byrd and others to not talk about personal experiences."

"But your claims of traveling in time seem very personal to me."

"What I meant is that I can't talk about how I made it back to my sanity." He looked away, seeming embarrassed by the proclamation.

"Are you saying your experience occurred only in your mind?"

He didn't answer her question.

"It really happened to me," she refuted. She felt Brenda's pinch on her arm from that first day at the Way Back Diner, smelled Ramesh's curry and Farley's coffee, and she felt John's embrace. "I have physical proof." She set her time capsule shoebox on the table. "In here I have artifacts and hand-written letters that prove that I lived through the month of December 1999 for a second time."

Kurts shifted in his chair. He appeared uncomfortable with her disclosure.

"Mind you, this proof will never see the light of day," she assured him. "It's too personal."

No one spoke for a time.

"All right. I'll tell you. But if this gets back to me, I'll deny I ever said it."

"Who am I going to tell, Dr. Kurts?"

"Byrd, he took me to a place. Don't ask me where because I don't remember. He rebooted my locator with some new software, had me reset the passwords, and gave me something to help me sleep. When I woke up, I was back in 2040. At my house, as if nothing had ever happened." In measured breaths, he said, "Just like that, as if I was awakened from a hypnotic trance." Tears rolled down his face. "The experience gave me a second chance at life." Kurts wiped away his tears with the back of his hand. "Forgive me. I don't like talking about it."

"Me neither," she agreed.

Thinking of Tandy, Amara held back her suspicions about Byrd wanting nothing other than the best for the Way Backers. She asked, "Did you trust Byrd?"

"How do you mean?"

"When he approached you, you obviously trusted him with your life. To help you get back. Do you think he had your best interests in mind?"

"Mrs. Darnley, E.T. Byrd is the *only* person I trust in all of this," he said.

"You say that as if you're still in touch with him," she said.

A soft knock on the door preceded Kurt's assistant entering. She whispered something in his ear. He nodded and thanked her. She left as quietly as she'd entered.

"For those of us who have succumbed to this new way of life, Byrd and his team are vital to our survival. It's their work in research and testing *and* influencing the policies of politicians and governments that will guide us, ergo our species, to the next level of our evolution. Now, if you'll excuse me, I have an interview with the local news streamers."

Amara thanked him and left with René.

Her conversation with the nervous little man helped her see what John and his Natural Life movement colleagues were attempting to expose. People like Byrd and Kurts, and herself if she was honest, were trying to cheat death. Man's attempt at changing nature's way always ended badly, John used to say. What have we done, John?

Outside the museum, the shadows had grown long. A tall, willowy man, his black string tie flapping in the wind, approached her. His face, his entire body for that matter, seemed crooked, off-center, like a walking Picasso.

The pair picked up their conversation where they had left off, fifty years ago.

"Mrs. Darnley," he said as he slowed to her stride.

"Agent Byrd," she replied.

"You've had an opportunity to speak with our nation's leading expert on bending time," he said.

Unsure of Byrd's meaning, sarcasm or stating a fact, Amara said, "The man's mind is mush."

"Crazier than the Mad Hatter. Did he cry? He does that a lot. Beware of the man. He'll find some way to use whatever you've confided in him."

Quoting Kurts, she said, "I'll deny I ever said it."

"Can we go for some Indian cuisine? All of the sudden I'm craving a bowl of rasam."

"What did you do to Ramesh? He's a zombie." she accused.

"I'm told he's developed MDD?"

"English, please."

"Memory Displacement Dementia. Memories of past lives, fried. Buzzed. We think it's caused by the shock of reinstatement."

"Duh! You think?" Hugging her time capsule, she gazed past him at the bare trees illuminated by the museum's grounds lighting. So, friendship was fleeting in this new world of hers. "And Farley and Brenda? Do they have this MDD?"

"Brenda's working with me," he said.

"Well, well, she learned that going back could be done." Amara felt vindicated.

"Oh, and has she ever. Because of her, we've moved up in the world. We're fully funded and have a lab at Quantico. An entire floor." Pulling his ski cap over his ears, he stressed, "And I can assure you nothing has been displaced from *her* brain." He laughed. "She's always right. I mean, not just most of the time but *always,* like a gall dern machine. This treatment affects us all differently and she, somehow, won the memory lottery."

"And Farley?"

"We're still looking for him. The wily rascal gave us the slip. Has he contacted you?"

She stopped abruptly and, in a fit of ire, said, "What does this look on my wrinkle-free face say to you? Huh? Let me translate. It says, 'If I did know where he was, I wouldn't tell you.'" John and Kimberly were right. She had to get off this freakshow ride. At her next rejuvenation appointment, she'd ask to have the biochip plasma flushed from her system. That was if they'd allow it, something else for her to worry over. She called out to René, "Let's go."

Byrd filed in beside her again.

"What happened to your face?" she asked.

He cleared his throat. "Too many time channel changes. Doctors say I have to give it up. I'm looking for my replacement. You interested?"

"No," she said. "Goodbye, Agent Byrd."

She walked away with René following close behind.

On her way back to her apartment, Amara thought about Alice's postscript, about accepting gifts as they were given and with humble gratitude. Alice was right, Amara had to accept the gift of love as it was given. She couldn't bend it to fit her own wishes. This truth, she realized, applied to the gift of time as well. ❧

Author's Letter

Before I started writing *Talking to Herself,* I followed the example of author Lee Child and spent time in a thinking pose—horizontal on the sofa. There, I pondered:

What would an ordinary day be like in 2050?

By 2050, is it conceivable that robotic technology will give us pervasive, affordable "manpower" like the book's characters Rosie, Moby, and René? I hope so. Today, the military and manufacturers rely on robotic entities to do their heavy lifting. This year Toyota introduced "human support robots" to assist attendees at sporting events. Imagine Moby shouting, "Cold beer. Peanuts!" Early versions of Rosie are among us today.

As artificial intelligence (AI) evolves, how will it impact the human experience of recalling memories? Like the story's fictional organic nanochip plasma and communication locators, can technologies with communication components (think Wi-Fi, Bluetooth, Radio Frequency Identification, and Near Field Communication) be embedded in our bodies for the convenience of interacting with thousands of devices, data clouds, and systems on a universal machine-to-machine grid? It's possible. The technology exists today.

For the time travel element, I wanted the story to capture the possibility that traveling to one's past could happen in the near future. To do this, how could the story sustain a state of suspended disbelief when Amara travels from 2050 to 1999? Aside from the "blink of an eye" magic, like *Outlander's* Claire Fraser's passing through a stone, what could be a plausible cause behind the characters hurtling over past decades?

Currently, nanochip technology is being injected into the human body for medical applications such as disease diagnosis and drug delivery. Other more commercial applications are bound to follow. What if, in our newly configured bodies, a missing set of software code, not unlike that reported by the annoying 404 Not Found error we've all encountered on our laptops, causes a malfunction in a common application used by a large portion of the population? It could happen. It's only a matter of time.

Thank you for reading *Talking to Herself*. I hope Amara's story has inspired you to think about your own future and how it is shaped by the past.

Sincerely,

Melissa Powell Gay

2020

A bit of reading went into preparing the story's plot outline. I brushed up on the layman's version of Einstein's theory of relativity and reread Stephen Hawking's popular books.

On the advancement of machine-to-machine computer technology, I reviewed books and periodicals on the fourth industrial revolution, Internet of Things (IoT), artificial intelligence (AI) and robotics. Check out Kevin Kelly's *The Inevitable* and Yuval Noah Harari's *21 Lessons for the 21st Century*.

For the creative side of the story development, I read a few novels with varying plots of time travel. Two books that had an impact on *Talking to Herself* were *Time and Again* by Jack Finney and *Goodbye for Now* by Laurie Frankel. Other novels of the time travel genre that I have enjoyed were *A Christmas Carol* by Charles Dickens, *Outlander* by Diana Gabaldon, *11/22/63* by Stephen King, and *The House on the Strand* by Daphne du Maurier.

AUTHOR'S ACKNOWLEDGMENTS

tip my iMac nib to Deborah Miller and Marilyn Shaw for their invaluable and honest editorial advice. I gratefully thank beta reader Fran Nielsen for her feedback on the story's technical jargon and readability. And, to Inkwell Book Co., I offer my applause for another beautiful design.

I am grateful for my husband, Glenn, who endures my daily out loud readings and one-sided conversations with characters, often behind the closed door of my home office.

MELISSA POWELL GAY

Made in the USA
Middletown, DE
18 December 2020